FLIP-FLOPS, FIESTA AND FLAMENCO

The Mediterranean Dream - Book 1

DONNA HEPBURN

Donna Hepburn/Junction Publishing

United Kingdom and New Zealand

www.junction-publishing.com

junctionpublishing@outlool.com

Publisher's Note: This is a work of fiction. Names, characters, places, and incidents are a product of the author's imagination. Locales and public names are sometimes used for atmospheric purposes. Any resemblance to actual people, living or dead, or to businesses, companies, events, institutions, or locales is completely coincidental.

Ordering Information:

Quantity sales. Special discounts are available on quantity purchases by corporations, associations, and others. For details, contact the "Special Sales Department" at the email address above.

Flip-flops, Fiesta and Flamenco/Donna Hepburn. -- 1st ed

For my best friend Roxy; who unfortunately is no longer with us. She drooled a lot, stank more than a bit and covered my best clothes in dog hair, but she was always there for me, loved a wee drunken dance on a Friday night and her unique personality inspired more than a few of the animal characters in this book.

I would sooner be a foreigner in Spain than in most countries. How easy it is to make friends in Spain!
    – George Orwell

❧   I   ❧

Just another ten minutes. Abby Sinclair pulled the duvet over her head trying to ignore the insane, yappy barking from Ethel, next-door's manic Poodle. Strains of Noel Gallagher's *If I had a Gun* nudged at her mind. She *should* shut the window at night, but since the hot flushes of middle age had arrived, the bedroom had to be cool. Another side effect of ensuing old age was her bladder, arguing that no way was she having those extra ten minutes' snooze time. Resigned, she opened her eyes, taking in soft grey damask wallpaper. She'd chosen the décor a week after Mark, her husband of 16 years, had left the marital home. The first time since before they'd married, she'd chosen anything herself.

Before flouncing off, Mark had made decorating decisions in the home. Shuddering, Abby remembered the sterile bedroom. Neutral carpet, white walls, white bed. She'd hidden every bottle of lotion, perfume, and moisturiser, and God help her if he came home from work and there was a speck of dust, or heaven forbid an item of clothing flung haphazardly onto the bed or floor.

She had been a different woman in those days. Thin to the point of gaunt (Mark wouldn't allow her to gain weight). Sharp, stylish bob, cut and straightened every week (Mark liked precision). Nothing less than tailored clothes, designer brands, high heels.

Rising at six every morning, she would shower, dress, style her hair, and put on a full face of make-up before taking up residence in the compulsory stark kitchen to become dutiful little wifey, preparing breakfast for her husband who would enter – suited and booted –at seven on the dot.

After kissing the top of her head, he'd settle at the table in his favourite chair, munch his way through a healthy bowl of muesli then enjoy perfect eggs Benedict. After drinking the obligatory small glass of freshly squeezed orange juice, he'd read *The Guardian* whilst indulging in two teeny cups of Italy's finest espresso. As he performed his morning ritual, Abby prepared breakfast for her sons, fruitlessly trying to keep the peace between the boisterous pair before their father left for his job in a large bank in the city.

Once she'd dropped the boys at school, she would spend an hour in the gym, swim thirty lengths, and, time permitting, do a spinning or Pilates class. Then, back home to spend the rest of the day cleaning, or preparing food for one of the numerous dinner parties Mark insisted on giving. Evenings surrounded by stuffy bankers and their pompous wives, sprinkling their boastful chatter about villas in Tuscany, palatial homes, or stocks and shares, with monotonous guff about Miranda, Penelope, or Jeremy's gap year, while disdainfully picking at their food and unsuccessfully attempting to feign enjoyment.

If only they knew that she, Abby, had been born to a single mum on a council estate in Newcastle, yet here she was mingling with the upper crust. She'd become a real life Stepford wife.

There was routine to every aspect of her life. Sex on Sunday morning, predictable and boring, eyes closed, while Mark's pale, white arse pumped rhythmically until, with a burst of uncharacteristic groaning, face the spitting image of a startled wildebeest, he would collapse on top of her. The days of him bothering to find out if she'd enjoyed it no longer existed. Just as well, as she definitely hadn't in a long time.

Bridge Club on Wednesday evening was equally tedious – Marks's friends competing at both cards ... and life. Sunday dinner with Lord and Lady Snooty (Mark's Mum and Dad) was not only tiresome, but also incredibly stressful as Abby tried to control two unruly boys in their mausoleum of a house. Two hours of, "Daniel, please don't touch that. Andrew, for God's sake, be careful. Don't run boys. Stop fidgeting. Don't play with your sprouts. Get that frog outside. Now!"

So when Mark's Friday night with the boys, or Saturday morning golf became longer than usual – often resulting in him failing to come home – Abby immediately knew something was amiss. Two months later, she confronted him and after an evening of tearful excuses and pathetic whining, he packed his bags and shacked up with his secretary in her penthouse apartment down at the docks. Janice, with her pale, fragile hair, love of all things pink, massive boobs, and limited intellect. Twenty years old going on five. Sugar Tits. His trophy girlfriend. She was welcome to him!

That was ten years ago and boy, had things changed since. Abby still lived in the former matrimonial home; after all, it was an impressive Georgian townhouse and was convenient for the boys' schools. She'd paid off the remaining mortgage with the divorce settlement and now it oozed character from every pore. Gone were the thick shag pile carpets and in their place, lovingly sanded floorboards. Rooms bright and full of colour told a different story. *One of real life.* Struggles to make ends meet, while bringing up two boys alone. Tears, anger, laughter, and loneliness all lurked in every corner of this house.

Also gone was the perfect Stepford wife, and in her place, the real Abby Sinclair – slightly overweight, middle-aged, long, brown tangled hair stretched out over numerous purple pillows, yesterday's tracksuit slung over a chair, hungover, and bursting for a pee. The final straw propelling her from the comfort of her bed and warm duvet was the booming fart exuding from the current man in her life. The stench, on top of two bottles of wine she'd guzzled last night was too much.

Pushing herself up from the bed, Abby held her nose and headed for the bathroom. As she lurched from the bedroom, she groaned as the door at the far end of the narrow hallway slammed shut.

Damn it. She must do something about an en suite.

H opping about in a faded, tattered *Muttley* onesie outside the bathroom, Abby considered her plans for the day.

The deadline for the article she was writing, on the mating habits of the Peruvian guinea pig was due today, but it was nearly finished and wouldn't take long to complete. She was meeting Lou for lunch and was looking forward to seeing her best friend. The proverbial chalk and cheese gelled like the proverbial house on fire. They had met years ago at university, when Abby was studying journalism and Lou, English Language and Literature, and had remained friends despite Abby's ten years of marriage to Mark.

Since the divorce, Lou usually stayed for a few days when she visited, but this time she was being all mysterious and said she had 'something' to sort out. It was probably another bloke. Lou had never married, but was addicted to internet dating, and wasn't short of hilarious tales about her experiences when meeting potential suitors, or the motley crew, as they were often referred to.

She'd met several, none of whom ended favourably, but some of her stories were enough to split Abby's sides. There was 45-year-old barrister, Neville who told Lou he'd attended Cambridge where he'd achieved a Master's in law. He lived in a pimped up rectory and drove a top-notch shiny red *Porsche*, and a *Harley Davidson*. Not at the same time, of course he'd pointed out. His online photo had actually been an early picture of Enrique Iglesias, although that had escaped Lou. Turned out he was sixty-two, worked in *Specsavers*, looked like *Mr Bean*, and was just as nerdy.

Three weeks later, Lou arranged a meet with Brian, the owner of a recycling business who described himself as more than open-minded. In fact, he was a fat, bald Glaswegian binman who had a 'thing' for women dressed in black rubber. He was gagging for Lou to don a rubber catsuit while he sucked on her toes as she called him a maggot. Apparently, when he'd revealed his fantasy, the look on her face was priceless. Needless to say, Lou binned the binman.

The icing on the cake was Gary. How Abby cried with laughter when she heard the tale of the good-looking guy whom Lou had befriended online. They chatted via instant messages, then texts, and eventually spoke on the telephone to arrange a meeting in town.

Arriving slightly earlier than agreed, Lou kept her eyes peeled awaiting Gary in the bustling mall. Pacing up and down, the minutes ticked by until her watch read 10:15, thirty minutes later than the time agreed for the meet. There had been no word from him to confirm his whereabouts or reason for the delay, and Lou, being a reliable creature, was in no mood to text, call, or chase a bloke who couldn't comprehend the meaning of punctuality.

Eventually, assuming he was a no-show, and feeling more than pissed off at being mucked around, Lou was ready to leave, but not before picking a bone with the tall girl who'd been gawking at her all the while. She hated being stared at by complete strangers and her hacked off mood was such that she was ready to put lanky firmly in her place.

In her unashamedly bold way Lou approached the girl, taking in the fashionable threads, cascading blonde hair, and perilous stilettos perched on the end of fabulous, long enough to be continued tanned legs. As she drew near, Lou had the oddest feeling she'd seen the girl before. *She could be Gary's sister they looked so alike.* It was then Lou's eyes locked on the woman's throat, instantly spotting the bulging Adam's apple, and realised she'd been had. Again! *Yikes! This was* he. Gary was a tranny.

Lou roasted Gary for leaving her hanging around for almost an hour and conveniently forgetting to mention his cross-dressing, but agreed to have coffee with the kinkster as his zany sense of humour and scathing tongue appealed. She learned he had numerous outfits, adored the sensation of being feminine, was a self-confessed rebel, and loved to shock.

When he declared he had an appetite for dressing as mature women and often, especially during sex, kitted himself in garb à la Mrs Doubtfire, she almost choked on her latte. Despite his assurance he was all man where it mattered, Lou respectfully declined the offer of a fun-filled, not-so-vanilla relationship. The image of sitting astride a tranny queen sporting grey wig, girdle, and *Bridget Jones* big knickers, with hairy pins swathed in wrinkled surgical stockings was more rot than hot and for her, definitely not!

She ended the two-hour chat with a parting comment. "Gary, darlink, I couldn't date a man who'd constantly hog the mirror, swipe my nylons and lipstick, or whose legs are better than mine. You take care now, biatch! Ta-ta."

At least Lou was wined and dined occasionally, that is if, when she saw who was walking towards her, she didn't pretend to go to the loo and leg it through a window or down a fire escape. Once she got her knickers caught on a window latch and a security guard had to rescue her, the same guard she dated for three months after he'd caught her in the uncompromising position. The relationship fizzled out, when tired of playing the superhero to Lou, he moved on to another damsel in distress.

Abby couldn't remember the last time she'd been on a date ...and sex? Forget it! Apart from a fumble with an eager young insurance salesman a couple of years ago, the nearest she got was a night in with a *Love Honey* catalogue and a bumper pack of *Duracell*.

Keening her ears, Abby could hear whispering coming from the bathroom.

"Yes, we're back together. I think it's really serious this time. He says he loves me and I think he might ask me to move in."

More giggles and muted conversation. Abby couldn't believe the girl was discussing her love life and preparing to move into *her* home while she stood on her own landing maybe thirty seconds away from peeing herself. She tapped on the door and sat down trying to stem the imminent flow.

A large thump from her bedroom announced the arrival of her one true love. Chester may not have been everyone's cup of tea as a bedmate. He was a bit on the weighty side, farted like a trooper, snored, was a tad smelly, and his face looked as if a bus had hit him head on, but for the last seven years she'd adored him. He had her wrapped around his paw. Plodding slowly along the hall, he stopped about a foot away for maximum impact, sat down, and proceeded to lick his balls. The six-stone British bulldog knew who was boss of the Sinclair household, and it certainly wasn't Abby!

The toilet flushed and the bathroom door opened. "*Ugh, gross.*"

It was as if Chester's intention had been to offend the girl.

"Sorry, Mrs Sinclair. Didn't know you were there."

Abby, sitting on the top stair, gazed up at what could've been an Amazon warrior princess. Long, slender coffee-coloured legs went on forever. A *Pink Floyd* T-shirt she recognised and was quite sure wasn't meant to stretch that much, barely hid the girl's modesty and certainly accentuated her blatantly visible assets. A pretty face and short spiky pink hair completed the ensemble and identified her as Paisley – not Nicki Minaj on stilts – Andrew's on-off girlfriend.

Abby smiled. "Good morning. Is Andrew not working today?"

"He's not in 'til eleven. We came in late last night with a takeaway, and some friends. Sorry if we woke you."

It wasn't quite an apology and Abby felt her blood begin to simmer. However, her bladder won out and muttering, "Don't worry about it," she slid past the six-foot goddess.

Scowling, she firmly closed the bathroom door.

Once downstairs, Abby entered the war zone that only last night had been her tidy living room. Cans and bottles littered the floor and coffee table, and one of her best crystal drinking glasses lay forlornly on its side, the contents pooled on her beautiful Turkish rug.

Chester was sniffing the sticky mess, but obviously preferred Chinese food to vodka as he'd filched a large tray of leftover spare ribs and arranged them across the floor in an abstract artwork of barbeque. The ashtray was overflowing, and the room stank to high heaven. She ignored the long-haired chubby guy sprawled on her sofa, wearing a T-shirt proclaiming he loved big butts, and a pair of grubby jogging pants barely containing his shameless morning glory.

Abby quickly opened windows, even though the cold February air made her shiver. Determined to have a coffee before she tackled the mess, she shooed Chester into the kitchen and making as much noise as possible, to hopefully embarrass the intruder into pissing off before she returned, switched on the kettle.

Standing at the back door five minutes later, with a large steaming cup of *Kenco's* finest, and cigarette in hand, Abby let out a huge sigh of relief as she heard the front door open and bang shut. Chubby had gone.

She gazed at the ominous black clouds. She hated winter, even more so these last few years. The constant greyness, the ever-present feeling of damp seeping into her aging bones, biting cold winds, and, more recently, the threat of the river bursting its banks and flooding. Last year, water had reached several houses a couple of streets away resulting in many people losing all their possessions, their distress heightened when it had taken an age to dry out their homes. The government had promised millions to build flood defences but they were next to useless – both the government, and so-called defenses.

She finished her cigarette and warmed her hands around the mug watching Chester who finishing his morning patrol of the garden for any intruders, including squirrels, birds, frogs, and especially cats, was now having a conversation with Ethel through the fence. Chester snorted and snuffled in his own special way while Ethel yapped hysterically fit to burst.

Head hurting, she turned back into the house to begin the mammoth clean-up operation.

There was no way she would finish her written article before leaving to meet Lou. It had taken almost an hour to remove the hideous stains from her rug. Not long after, Andrew had launched himself down the stairs arguing with a distraught Paisley. Apparently, it seemed the romance was off again and her with it, as she marched to the front door slamming it behind her. Andrew was going to be late for work and Abby was to blame for not ironing the one shirt he wanted to wear.

Her youngest son had been a bonny baby, but his blue eyes now lacked their sparkle. He wore his hair scraped back into a greasy ponytail and had grown a beard, which added at least five years to his twenty-one. His constant frown gave him a sullen air as if he had the world's worries and debts on his young shoulders, lack of exercise and a penchant for pepperoni pizza had piled on the pounds over the last couple of years. His job in a call centre, sitting on his arse striving to convince people to switch broadband, electricity, telephone – Abby couldn't remember which – hadn't done him any favours either.

"Perhaps *you* should have ironed it, instead of coming in pissed with your mates at four in the morning and wrecking the place." The dressing down was firm.

"Oh, Jesus, Mum. Don't be a nag." Uninvited, he took a cigarette from her packet. "I'm out with the lads tonight so don't make me any food."

Giving her a peck on the cheek, he bolted out of the house, which descended into silence for five minutes until the postman arrived, prompting Ethel to start her incessant barking again. Oh, fuck.

Knowing she was going to be late for her meet with Lou, Abby fired off a quick email to her editor explaining that something had come up and she would get the article to him before close of business.

Flying around like a ferret on crack, she took a quick shower. Thank the Lord winter was here and she didn't need to shave her legs. Chester watched suspiciously, while she sat on the edge of her bed trying to arrest some control over the mass of curls billowing from her head and pondering what to wear. He hated it when she left him in the house and no doubt would be thinking how to exact his revenge.

Lou, of course, would be stylish as ever. Slim and athletic, she preferred classic, tailored clothes and could look a million dollars in a LBD. Abby didn't have much call for smart togs. Most of her work she did from home, and she rarely had a night out. Deciding on thick black tights, cowboy boots, and a long green cable knit jumper synced with a wide belt, she actually looked passable apart from a few dog hairs and an odd-looking stain on the hem. A quick swipe of blusher and coat of mascara and she was good to go.

"I won't be long, baby" she cooed at a decidedly unimpressed Chester before a loud beep announced the arrival of the taxi.

Strains of *Pulp Fiction's* theme tune filled the cab, as Abby received a text confirming her destination. *Bloody hell.* Lou was pushing the boat out today right enough.

Frantically, she scrabbled in her handbag to ensure she had her credit card. The £47.50 she had in her purse seemed insignificant now that she knew they were dining at the expensive eatery of Lou's favourite celebrity chef.

"He isn't going to be there" she mouthed at the screen, feeling her face reddening as she looked up to see the taxi driver staring at her in his rear-view mirror.

"Alright back there, love?"

"Yes, thanks."

Nosy git. All she needed was for him to start on about the government and the immigration situation, which had dominated the papers the last few days.

Adjusting the jumper to show less cleavage and staring out the window, she hoped to avoid further conversation. The streets were quiet given it was Monday lunchtime. Nameless figures shuffled along buried in heavy coats, heads bent low against the almost horizontal rain promised in the weather report the night before. The dark, wet, cold buildings looked uninviting and she couldn't imagine why anyone who didn't absolutely have to, would be out in this climate.

"Don't you think?" The voice interrupted her thoughts.

"What, sorry?"

"The government letting in all these bloody foreigners."

"Err, I don't know much about it," she said hurriedly. Her assumption was correct then. He had started wittering on about the government and immigration. She hoped it wouldn't go on, she really couldn't be bothered.

The driver leered at her. "Hot date is it?" He was beginning to grate on her nerves.

"Actually, I'm meeting my surgeon to discuss my sex change." She wished she had the balls to take a snap of him on her camera phone. The look on his face was hilarious.

Muttering something she couldn't make out, he fiddled with his sat nav, thankfully remaining silent until they arrived at the entrance to the restaurant.

"Posh place this, need a bloody fortune to eat here. Anyway, enjoy yer food," he mumbled, avoiding Abby's gaze as she handed over a tenner to pay the fare. "Oh ... and err ... hope the err ... you know what goes well," he stuttered, thrusting a fiver change into her open palm.

"That's too much change, isn't it?" She was sure she shouldn't have been given that much.

"It's fine," he said hurriedly. "Must dash, got a few fares to pick up."

It was obvious the guy couldn't wait to get away after she'd mentioned a sex change.

Bending down, Abby gave him a peck on the cheek, nearly peeing herself laughing at the look of horror on his face.

She wanted to say goodbye but didn't get the chance as tyres screeching, he took off faster than Lewis Hamilton burning rubber.

Entering the modern, stylish waiting area, Abby immediately realised she was underdressed for the occasion. Stomach in knots and silently cursing Lou, she stared as a tall, immaculately suited man walked towards her.

"May I help, madam?"

"Erm ... yes ... reservation for Louise Walker," she stammered, nearly taking the man's eye out as he moved in to help remove her ancient denim jacket.

"Miss Walker is already here. You must be the friend she is waiting for. Would you like a drink, madam?" Warily, he stood out of flailing arms reach, ready to escort Abby to her seat.

Abby smiled at the man who she now knew to be the Maître d'. "Large G and ... gin and tonic please." *Sod it.* At these prices, she may only have enough cash to order a small side salad to eat but what the hell. She needed a drink.

Tristan, the man's badge proclaimed, led the way through the throng of movers and shakers, eating such delicacies as tuna carpaccio and confit duck legs. *Yes, she watched Masterchef.* Despite its blatant quality, the restaurant was poncy and sparse. Expensive cutlery, and wine, and water drinking glasses sat on pristine white tablecloths, while fancy white napkins were fashioned into more positions than the Kama Sutra.

Finally, Abby caught sight of Lou who was talking animatedly into her mobile phone and waving her over. Smiling, she forgot about

Tristan who had come to an abrupt halt, causing her to smash her nose into his poker-straight back.

"I'll bring your drink, madam," Tristan growled disappearing towards the bar, no doubt to swap tables with some poor, unsuspecting underling who'd end up waiting on her and Lou.

"Geronimo! Girl knows how to make an entrance." Lou laughed.

"Oh, you saw, hawkeye."

"Never mind that. I've been dying to try this place and well, I've had a bit of luck, which I'll get to later. I know it's full of posh twats but the food's supposed to be awesome."

"I just hope they do cheesy chips," Abby joked.

"It's my treat ... order what you want." Lou picked up the elegant menu and looked over the impressive selection, a mischievous smile on her face.

"Jeez. Have you won the lottery, Lou?"

As Abby suspected, a tall redhead approached with a tray containing her much-needed drink. Tristan, having absconded to the far corner, was removing the coats of and fawning over an elderly couple who had just arrived, stinking of money. The woman, complete with parma violet shampoo and set, showed off bingo wings and a visible panty line, while the man, surely related to an elephant judging by the size of his nose and ears, busted out of Saville Row duds.

"So, Abby, how are the boys?" Lou asked, sipping at a glass of South African Shiraz.

Abby took a swig of her drink. "*You're interested in the boys?*" She was becoming increasingly suspicious by the minute. Lou obviously had news, but was dragging her heels. "They're fine ... driving me mad, as usual. Come on, Lou. Spill."

"All in good time, my dear," Lou replied, eyes twinkling.

Louise Walker was the epitome of elegance. Short, blonde hair softly framed her heart shaped face. Large, sapphire eyes sitting above high cheekbones sparkled with confidence and amusement. The generous mouth loved to giggle and talk, at times uttering cutting, acerbic comments that made people frown or hoot with laughter, depending on their present mood or degree of intelligence. Lou was the kind of woman who demanded attention. When she walked into a room people couldn't help but stare, and not in the 'look who's just fallen over' Abby style entrance.

The waitress returned with their starters. A steaming bowl of French onion soup topped with croutons and gruyère for Abby. Lou had chosen Caesar salad. The aroma of the soup was mouth-wateringly good and Abby, so busy concentrating on the gastronomic delight, missed Lou's next sentence as she tucked in.

"Sorry, Lou, what was that?"

"I said ... I've won a pile on Wingo Bingo."

"That's brilliant, and so lovely of you to treat me with your winnings. I take back everything I said about this place. This soup is delicious."

Abby finally looked up from the bowl of rich onion paradise when Lou didn't reply. "What?"

Lou couldn't stop grinning "I won four hundred grand. I've bought a house in Spain and want you to come with me."

Abby's squeal of pain caused several diners to look over in disgust as she dropped her spoon into the hot broth, spraying her cleavage with molten liquid and melted cheese. Stunned, yet excited, she fought off the helpful waitress, ineffectually dabbing her with expensive napkins. Eyes watering, she could barely speak.

"Spain?" She gasped. "On holiday?"

"No."

Lou waited patiently while Abby gained control. Finally, the waitress removed the offending liquid and sidled off.

Casually, Lou said, "Not on holiday, Abby. To live."

Abby took a large glug of gin and tonic. "I can't move to Spain. What about the boys? What about Chester? The House? It's impossible!"

"Why? The boys are men now and can look after themselves. Chester can come with us."

"What about Sylvester and Tweetie Pie?" Abby persisted. "He hates cats."

Sylvester, aka Mr Mischief, a four-year-old, nimble, long-haired black and white tuxedo, and Tweetie Pie, the sedate − although she did have her moments − seven-year-old tortoiseshell were Lou's adored feline four-legged friends.

She waved her hand in the air, dismissing Abby's previous comment. "Relax. I'm sure they'll learn to get along."

"I don't think so. You underestimate Chester at your peril. Andrew found that out last week when he locked him out of the living room and Chester shit in his best trainers."

"Yikes! Good old Chester. You know what they say, Abby. Shit for luck. Maybe he thought his doings would improve the pong of Andrew's sweaty feet." She grinned. "We'll introduce them slowly ... it won't be a problem."

Lou delved into her bag to retrieve her mobile and scrolled through a dozen or so pictures showing Abby, a stunning whitewashed farmhouse with a balcony running around the first floor. French windows opened onto incredible views of mountains and the Mediterranean. Gardens surrounded the lower floor, where patio doors opened to paved seating areas and terraces. Grapevines hung overhead, and jasmine, hibiscus, and bougainvillea were in abundance. The scenery was a feast for the eyes.

"There's three acres of land, a kennel area so we could rescue a few dogs ... oh, and just look at the pool." The glittering water looked so inviting, even on Lou's iPhone.

Abby was speechless and near to tears. Living in Spain had been her dream for as long as she could remember. "It looks amazing, Lou. I'm so happy for you," she whispered.

"You could be happy for *us*. C'mon, Abby, stop making excuses." Lou's firm, but kind voice had a sing-song lilt. "Didn't it used to be your dream to live in Spain?"

"Well ... yeah ... but I can't just up and leave. It's a nice thought, but I can't."

"OK. Look, I'll get the bill. I'm sick of everyone looking down their bloody noses. I'm flying to Malaga this evening to sort the final legal stuff and need to grab a few bits before I go.

"Let's hit the shops and have a few drinks to celebrate. Take a few days to think about what I've said, please, and let me know."

After paying more than Abby spent on shopping for a week, for the abandoned meal and exorbitantly priced drinks, the rest of the afternoon was a blur, alternating between expensive shops, wine bars, and pubs. Giggling and joking, they staggered into changing rooms trying on outrageous outfits and generally having the best time Abby could remember in a long time. Lou bought Abby a pair of *Havaianas* flip-flops and a beautiful multi-coloured silk maxi dress, making her promise she would at least come on holiday soon.

In return, Abby bought Lou a *Bagpuss* T-shirt. "I know you won't wear it, but it'll remind you of me."

Lou grinned, knowing Abby had drawers full of cartoon T-shirts as well as hoodies proclaiming she'd studied at every university in the western hemisphere. It was the perfect gift and, as she said goodbye, it was hard to stop the tears flowing.

"Promise me you'll consider it." Lou pleaded, hugging her friend so hard she squealed.

"I promise," Abby whispered, pulling away and waving a tearful goodbye.

Buying the T-shirt had taken the last of Abby's cash, so she jumped on a bus crammed to the hilt. She'd just stepped off the number 12 when the heavens opened and sent rain lashing down as she walked the half-mile home – a soggy carton of greasy chips making up for the earlier forgotten lunch – and wishing she'd asked Lou for a sub to take a taxi.

Wrinkling her nose appreciatively, Abby inhaled the aroma of warm vinegar, wondering with a heavy sigh what it would be like to live in constant
warmth and sunshine.

❧ 6 ❧

Arriving at her gate, bedraggled, soaked, and more than a little sozzled, Abby was surprised, and annoyed to find Mark's swanky silver *BMW* parked outside. *What the bloody hell did he want?*

He had only been to the house twice in the last three years – once to pick the boys up for their Grandad's funeral and more recently, Andrew's 21st birthday party, where Abby had begrudgingly put aside her own feelings and invited Janice too. She spent the whole evening avoiding the couple, sitting in the kitchen overdosing on vol-au-vents, drinking gin, and feeling sorry for herself.

Closing the front door with too much force, she stood in the hallway clutching the carrier bag containing her precious gifts to her chest. Lou would be at the airport now she thought, miserably. The rain had given her panda eyes and her hair stuck to her head in ringlets. She knew she looked a mess, smelt of the chippy, and was tempted to go straight upstairs.

"Is that you, Mum?"

Damn. Too late. There was no escape now.

Gritting her teeth, she gingerly opened the living room door. Mark was leaning against the fireplace as if he'd never left. His raven hair had definitely seen more than a splash of Grecian 2000 of late and his solid taut physique had developed a slight paunch. His head thrown back, laughing at something Daniel, their eldest son had said, he stopped abruptly, a look of irritation passing across his face as Abby entered the room.

"Bloody hell, Mum, are you drunk? You stink of drink. Look at the state of you."

Andrew, subtle as a sledgehammer, came into the room from the kitchen, tailed surprisingly after their tiff this morning by Paisley, carrying a tray filled with china mugs and a plate of chocolate biscuits. Her luxury chocolate biscuits she was saving for the marathon *Grey's Anatomy* pyjama day she intended having sometime soon. *Bitch.*

Paisley set the tray down on the table and went back to close the kitchen door, preventing the arrival of the canine bulk.

"Thought you were going out with your mates."

"Yeah, I was but didn't bother as you can see. That's if you *can* see, the state you're in. Anyway, never mind about me going out. I asked if you were drunk?"

"I have had a couple, yes."

Abby, bristling at his tone, hiccupped and slightly swayed. She was furious.

Paisley had never made her a cup of tea in the two years she'd been screwing her son.

Traitor. And how dare Andrew question her sobriety in front of the enemy?

As if knowing she was on Abby's mind, a barelegged Janice, dressed in fluffy pink angora jumper, impossibly tight pencil skirt, and stupidly high designer stilettos, rose from the sofa and teetered over to stand by her man. Possessively taking his arm, she looked straight at Mark's ex-wife.

"Are you alright, Abby?" she enquired softly, completely oblivious to the undercurrent in the room.

Piss off, Sugar Tits. She looked like bloody candyfloss and just as sickly sweet. The urge to spew her spiteful thoughts was overwhelming but Abby kept her mouth firmly shut, afraid of what she might say. She could hear scrabbling at the kitchen door and desperately wanted to let Chester in. Mark was allergic to dogs. After his confinement, Chester would punish someone. With any luck, he'd piss all over Janice's *Jimmy Choos*.

Abby wanted to disappear into the floor as the stares became darker, Janice became sweeter, and she found it more difficult to hold her tongue. *Who in the hell did she think she was,* this constipated Marilyn Monroe reject firing questions at her in her home?

"Dad's got an announcement." Daniel piped up.

At least he had some comprehension that you could cut the thorny atmosphere with a knife.

"Really?" Abby raised an eyebrow wishing he would get on with it. She was feeling decidedly queasy. The room felt like a merry-go-round that she wanted to get off. Maybe Mark and Sugar Tits were emigrating. *Hallelujah!*

"Yes." Even Mark looked uncomfortable.

Janice, sensitive as ever, continued to stroke his sleeve. "Go on, babe, tell them."

"Janice and I are having a baby."

Silence.

His words took a few minutes to sink in, especially to Abby's already befuddled brain.

Then everyone began talking at once. Words of congratulations filled the air and up piped the traitorous bitch Paisley, "Oh, we should get champagne."

The boys jumped up heartily slapping the absent cheating bastard they called Father on his back.

Abby felt the room spinning. She wanted the floor to open up and swallow her down. She was 46, with absolutely nothing going for her, two grown sons who treated her like shit, an editor who treated her worse than shit, and an ex-husband, and his trollop who'd just rubbed her face in shit.

"I've got an announcement, too." Abby gulped loudly above the delighted din. Mashed up, fatty chips were frantically clawing their way up her oesophagus and she guessed she only had minutes before they popped up to say hello.

"That's petty, Abby ... even for you." Mark in his element now, lapping up being the centre of attention.

"I'm going to live in Spain," she stated matter-of-factly, ignoring her ex's comment.

As proof, she produced the flip-flops with a flourish.

Silence again, only this time not in a good way.

"Fuck's sake, Mum, who do you think you are? Shirley bloody Valentine!" Andrew spurted tea down his shirt. "It's bloody nonsense."

"What about us and the house? You're not selling up are you?" Daniel whined, fiddling with his glasses.

At twenty-five, he was uncannily like his father, in personality as well as looks. Good looking, yes. Paisley was always comparing him to Tom Hardy – much to Andrew's disgust – and yes, Abby could see the resemblance if Tom Hardy had a poker shoved up his arse, thick-rimmed spectacles, perfectly coiffed hair, and worked in the scintillating world of company accounts. *Daniel.* No emotion. Just practicalities.

"You're more than able to look after yourselves, and the house is paid for. All you'll need to do is pay the bills; even you pair can manage that, surely."

"Don't be ridiculous, Abby, you're not going to live in Spain." Janice forgotten, Mark's face had turned an apoplectic shade of crimson.

"I am ... with Lou ... she's bought a house." Like that explained everything.

"It's bloody disgusting, that's what it is." Andrew, now in full flow his chins and belly wobbling in synchronisation, almost frothed at the mouth. "Two slappers in Salou."

Paisley sensibly had retreated and stood by the door wringing her hands.

"That's enough, Andrew! Don't speak to your mother like that." Mark puffed out his chest.

"Well, it's true. She's abandoning us to go drink sangria and shag Spanish waiters."

Purposefully, Abby walked unsteadily across the still sticky, damp rug she'd scrubbed that morning and harshly slapped Andrew's livid face. Turning, she faced them all, speaking in quiet, but firm tones.

"I *am* going to live in Spain. Maybe I *will* drink sangria and shag a hundred Spanish waiters ... maybe not. But, whatever I do, it's none of your damn business. Any of you. Got that?"

She could feel eyes burning into her and the murmur of voices fading as she purposefully strode into the kitchen to let Chester out into the garden. Pulling a cigarette from the packet, she lit up, and inhaled, the deep drag bringing on an urgency to spew. Leaning over, she vomited into a large plant pot, wiped her mouth, and ground the cigarette on the soaked paving.

Fishing for her phone in her wet pocket, she tapped out a text message. Why had she said she was moving to Spain when she knew that wasn't possible? *Or was it?*

Looking up into the wilderness of a dismal grey sky, grotesquely brimming with a heavy mass of black cloud threatening another ugly downpour, Abby's head was all over the place as her right index finger hovered over the send button.

Think, Abby. Think.

But it wasn't Mark and his young dolly bird's baby announcement, nor treacherous Paisley or her sons' demeaning, mindless comments, nor even Lou's unbridled enthusiasm that made up her mind. Granted, that little list was more than enough to make her up sticks. What sealed it was Chester. As he mooched aimlessly round the garden in the sodden grass, eyes sunken, ears almost disappearing into a squashed face that looked as miserable as she felt, Abby felt a lone teardrop trickle down her cheek. As if willing her to make a decision, Chester let out an unusually long, sorrowful whine prompting Abby to burst into sobs, and her finger to come down heavily on the send button.

The message to Lou was short and simple.

Count me in x

By the time she reached Terminal 2, Lou was also feeling the effects of a red wine overload.

After a thorough search at the hands of Barry, a sweaty jobsworth in security who was a dead ringer for an orangutan, she bought a sandwich and a large bottle of water and settled down in the departure lounge on an uncomfortable blue plastic chair. She made sure to sit as far away as possible from the tantrum-fuelled toddler throwing a wobbler outside *McDonald's*. His parents appeared to be struggling to placate him and getting nowhere fast. *Yikes! She hoped the little horror* wasn't on her flight.

Munching her way through the cheese and ham baguette, which might as well have been pink plastic between two sheets of orange cardboard, Lou switched on her phone. Despite feeling like shit, her heart leapt with joy at Abby's message. She wondered what had changed her mind, but her battery was nearly dead so she couldn't phone. She'd message later on Facebook when she arrived at the hotel.

Switching off her mobile, Lou looked around. The lounge was busy for a 21:30 flight, filled mostly with businessmen and retirees looking for a drop of winter sun. The couple opposite were having a row about him flirting with one of the check-in girls and some suited pot-bellied geriatric, with sparse grey hair and a noticeable twitch, was giving her the glad eye. She was beginning to wish she'd paid extra for first class. A large TV screen soundlessly transmitted *News 24/7*, occasionally interrupted by adverts for various duty-free shops. Floor to ceiling windows enveloped the harshly lit space in the thick blackness of a cold February night, flashes of aircraft lights intermittently breaking the darkness.

Lou couldn't wait until she arrived in the hotel in Malaga. Her head ached and her mouth felt drier than Gandhi's flip-flop. She knew she was in for a hectic few days finalising everything. True, the house had been an impulse buy, but she knew purchasing a property abroad was fraught with difficulties and was determined to ensure the i's were all dotted and the t's all crossed. She thought back to when she had won the money. It had been difficult keeping the secret from Abby. They usually had no secrets and that had been the way for the past twenty-six years.

Glugging almost half the bottle of cool water, in an attempt to relieve her parched mouth and throat, Lou's mind shot back to the time when she and Abby met.

Freshers' day. A gang of giggling girls had gone to the pub and Lou had been unusually fascinated with the firebrand of a girl from the North East, her polar opposite in both looks and manner. Wild-haired and gesticulating rampantly, Abby was in full flow, passionately discussing foxhunting,

Abby was a lover of causes back then. Lou knew her childhood hadn't been good. Her father had left when she was young. Her mother, a weak, bitter woman had a drink problem and there had been a succession of stepfathers and uncles, some worse than others. Yes, Abby always fought for the underdog. They had become inseparable and ended up sharing a flat. What fun they had. Parties lasted days, nights spent curled up on the sofa with a glass or six of wine, talking about their past and spouting dreams for the future.

On one such cold November evening, she and Abby were having a few drinks and one of their cosy pow wows. It was cold out, and the forecast predicted snow. That's when Abby had first mentioned Spain.

"Wouldn't it be lovely to live in the sun?"

"Hmm." Sleepily, Lou curled her toes in front of the two bar electric fire hoping there was enough on the meter to last the rest of the week.

"One day, I'm gonna live in Spain." Abby had uttered the little snippet with such determination in her voice. Such passion.

"Of course you are, and I'm gonna live in Timbuktu." Lou grinned.

Abby didn't say anything further on the subject, but over the next couple of years she collected anything Spanish. Pottery, art, a superb range of cookbooks. She was a good cook and most meals she made for friends were Mediterranean inspired in those days.

Then, she met Mark.

"Flight TCX5478 now boarding at gate 5B," the nasal voice announced over the Tannoy.

Jolted back to the here and now, Lou opened her eyes, and stifled a yawn. Dumping the empty plastic bottle in the bin, she heaved herself from the uncomfortable chair. Clutching her boarding pass, she reached for her cabin case before following the herd.

Once settled in her seat, thankfully well away from the screaming brat, who having been silent for all of five minutes had taken umbrage to the idea of flying and began creating again, Lou, in an attempt to blot out the din, closed her eyes and let her head fall back against the headrest.

Her mind drifted back to earlier thoughts. *Ah, yes. Mark.*

She had hated him from the beginning and thought he was a sanctimonious weasel. She couldn't understand what Abby saw in him. Looking back, it was probably security. Yes, he had money, and money was the reason to indulge in all manner of madness, but he was tighter than a mouse's waistcoat. When it was his round at the bar, he would have easily given Usain Bolt a run for his money, scarpering to the gents like hot shit off a stick.

Their wedding was extravagant, although heavily one-sided. Abby, having no family to speak of, and no money, had barely any say in the elaborate society event planned by Lydia, Mark's uber-controlling, matriarch of a mother.

Unimpressed by her beloved son's choice of bride, which she harped on about to anyone who would listen, she arranged a family get-together that would have rivalled Charles and Diana's do.

The only two decisions Abby insisted on making were Lou as Maid of Honour, and her choice of wedding dress, which the two friends had selected at a vintage fair, much to Lydia's disgust. The elegant 1920s ivory gown was the epitome of the opulent *Gatsby* era. Layers of chiffon draped over Abby's curves in flapper style, intricate iridescent beadwork shimmered like a rainbow when catching the light, and tiers of beaded fringe fell gracefully to the floor. Keeping in with the flapper style, she'd opted for nude, T-strap, kitten-heeled shoes. A beautiful, authentic beaded headband, with chains of pearls, complemented the whole outfit and with crystals weaving through her long, dark hair, Abby looked divine.

Regarding it as the last bastion of being able to make her own choices, the fabulous wedding gown now hung in a dark corner of Abby's wardrobe.

Lou's dress was a shorter version of a similar style. In sapphire blue, to match her eyes, the gown enhanced her fair complexion and blonde locks. She'd chosen the same style and colour of shoes as the bride and completed the look with a gorgeous beaded, bejewelled, feathered headband.

The groom, best man, and ushers wore cravats the same shade as Lou's dress, which perfectly complimented their dapper top hat and tails.

To be fair to Lydia, she had stuck with the Art Deco theme. The glossy black wedding invitations and wedding breakfast menus embellished with gold *Rennie Mackintosh* columns had cost a fortune. She'd bought a navy blue outfit for the nuptials, as near to black as possible. Lou pulled a face as she recalled the exact words Lydia frequently grumbled throughout the day in her harsh, grating voice.

"It's almost a funeral losing my baby boy. I always thought he would end up with Amelia."

Amelia Forbes-Smythe was the only child of Lydia's close friend, Vanessa. Her father was an MP and she fit in perfectly with Lydia's delusions of grandeur, although as Mark had whispered to Abby, she had a face similar to a horse, a rhino's arse, and a laugh like a chimpanzee who'd just seen the bill for this bleeding wedding.

Of course, Abby being three months gone on the big day didn't sit too well with her in-laws either. The whole event from start to finish was a disaster of epic proportions. Lydia's sobbing started the second she arrived at the front pew and continued more or less throughout the day, even during her grumbling and moaning about Mark's choice of bride as she sniffled annoyingly, carefully dabbing at her eyes and nose to avoid smudging her make-up.

"How many fucking hankies has she gone through?" Lou recalled whispering, while standing next to a pale shadow of her friend.

Abby smiled, nodding in all the right places, but the passion had gone from her eyes. They looked dull, vacant; the eyes of a dead fish on a cold slab.

Lou shifted in her seat trying to make herself comfortable and wishing again she'd opted for first class. Yesteryear's memories still fresh in her mind she relived more of Abby's nuptials, shuddering slightly at the recollection of Lydia's booming voice, subtle as a steamroller, as Abby walked down the aisle with Lou by her side.

"Oh, dear, that second-hand dress makes her look rather fat. Don't you think, Hugh?"

Although henpecked and meek, Hugh was just as snotty as his overbearing wife and grunted in agreement. The ill-timed, malicious insult and subsequent grunt had echoed around the church accompanied by the titters of snobs and tossers.

The vicar, of indeterminable age had a bad case of eczema. He also had a lisp and liberally sprayed both bride and groom with spit throughout the ceremony. A dark cloud hovered over the guests as the photographer snapped pictures outside, Lydia manoeuvering herself in front of Abby in most of them. Then there was best man Tim, one of the few friends of Mark Abby could actually bear, who having swigged *Glenfiddich* all morning, slipped, lost his balance, and almost toppled head first into an open grave.

After the Church of England ceremony, which totally ignored Abby's Catholic faith, came the disastrous reception held at a stately home, which totally went against Abby's preference for something less formal. Sitting at the top table between her new husband and Lou, Abby felt so out of place. Lydia's grating foghorn of a voice could still be heard rabbiting on about bloody Amelia Forbes-Smythe, who thankfully had buggered off on a gap year to Nepal so wasn't invited to the shindig. Abby wished for a large gag to silence Lydia as she watched guests she barely knew, and cared even less about, tucking into duck à l'orange or Dover sole, barely touching her own limp looking flatfish smothered in creamy clam sauce.

As she played with her food, she heard a commotion at one of the tables off to her left. She turned her head to see Mark's great uncle Monty turning a vivid shade of plum.

"Bloody hell, Lou. Look, the poor old bugger's choking," Abby whispered.

Lou, who'd just finished a first aid course the previous week rushed to the old man's side.

It was like watching a cross between Linford Christie and Florence Nightingale as she charged across to perform the Heimlich manoeuvre on the gasping pensioner. Eventually, he coughed up the offending fish bone bang in the face of the vicar who, hovering ominously, was probably ready to give the toffee-nosed old coot his last rites.

Instead of a live band or disco, Lydia had arranged a string quartet. Stuffed shirts shuffled around with trays of champagne cocktails, which had Abby not been three months gone would have made the day bearable, if she'd slugged enough of them. At least fifteen would do the trick she guessed, as another blast of Handel's *Water Music* punctured the air. Oh, for some Madonna!

The few friends of Abby who'd received an invite soon buggered off, most likely to the local pub. Lou remembered fervently wishing she could join them. She'd been to more enjoyable wakes.

Lydia interrupted their first dance by insisting Mark take her for a twirl, making some comment that he had the rest of his life to dance with Abby. Lou remembered cringing at the audacity of the woman just before one of the flower girls, who took Mark's place as Abby's dance partner while he waltzed the foghorn around the floor, had the nosebleed to end all nosebleeds all down the front of Abby's dress.

From the day they were hitched, Lou hated the way Abby began to allow Mark to control her. The master puppeteer held the strings and the cute little doll danced. Slowly, painfully, the firebrand disappeared.

Gone was the wild hair, Bohemian, kaleidoscopic garb, comfy boots and shoes. Instead, she began straightening her hair, wore expensive, stuffy clothing, and heels that were totally out of character and neither looked, nor felt good. She lost that flamboyant, devil-may-care stance, stopped waving her arms around in synchronized swimmer style as if giving directions to a blind man when she talked.

In no time, Mark had succeeded in chipping away his wife's individuality, robbing her of that free spirit, which had fascinated Lou when they'd first met. There was no more dancing on the pool table, shouting about government cuts, the state of the nation, and animal testing. Gone was the large vibrant poster of the beautiful flamenco dancer she had above her bed and sadly, there was no further mention of Spain.

From Lou's lips escaped a half spoken curse, her face taking on a mean look as she reflected on how that arsewipe had controlled her friend's life. Then she smiled, a victorious smile, feeling proud that over the years, since splitting with the jumped-up prick, Abby had stood her ground. More than that, she'd bitten the bullet and decided to join her in Spain. Finally, shedding the old skin and embracing the new, leaving behind unpleasant memories, and breaking free from her boys.

Oh, Lou knew Abby adored her sons, but man, were they ruined. She only hoped Abby wouldn't change her mind at the eleventh hour, or be made to take a guilt trip courtesy of Andrew and Daniel, who in Lou's opinion had had too much of their own way, and still did. They had zero respect for their mother and needed taking down a few pegs. Friends and acquaintances often said they couldn't understand how a wonderful woman such as Abby could have given birth to two arrogant ingrates. With any luck, Abby's departure would make them grow up and see sense.

Lou slowly opened her eyes to check the time then lowered them shut again. Mercifully, the wild child had quit his crazy ranting. More than likely sleep had taken hold and transported him into a land of sweet dreams. Geronimo! Thanks, Mr Sandman. I love you.

Excited tingles rushed through her body. Yikes. Not long to go now before touch down.

Have yourself a nap, girl. You'll need a fresh head when you arrive.

9

Walking through the exit of Malaga airport approximately two hours later, Lou felt a frisson of excitement. This would be an adventure for both her and Abby, a new start. The clear sky above shone with thousands of twinkling stars and a soft breeze caressed her, whispering promises of happiness and new experiences.

The taxi driver spoke excellent English making the ten-minute drive to the hotel pleasant and stress free. Lou was travelling to Estepona the following morning to meet the estate agent who'd promised to accompany her to the solicitors dealing with the sale of the property. The same law firm were also helping her obtain a Numero Identificado Extranjero (NIE), a tax identification number required for almost any financial transaction – opening a bank account, arranging utility bills and, of course, buying a house.

Although it was almost midnight when she arrived at the small hotel, the restaurant was still open. Feeling peckish, she ordered a lovely meal of fillet steak with patatas bravas – roast potatoes in a fiery tomato sauce. A bottle of Rioja sat on the table and although she found it difficult, Lou didn't give into temptation to sink the lot. Instead, she poured half a large glass and happily, sipped, thinking of the adventures she and Abby had in store as she remembered her friend's text message. *Count me in.*

Consider yourself counted, Abby. I'm delighted you changed your mind.

The vibrant poster above Abby's bed, the one close to her heart, was soon to become a reality. How wonderful for her ... for them. Lou had to pinch herself as she drained the remainder of her wine, smiled broadly, and retired to her room.

In her dreams that night, she danced flamenco wearing a stunning black dress adorned with tiers of lace, which she flicked from side to side in time to the passionate beat. Shouts of olé filled the smoky air as she fiercely stomped her feet and clapped her hands in time to the sensual rhythm. She peered over an intricately carved fan at a slim-hipped guitarist, his eyes filled with desire locking with her own, the music building to an intoxicating crescendo as she tumbled out of bed and found herself on the floor in a tangle of sheets.

Olé!

Tuesday morning dawned bright and sunny.
      After donning a pair of cream Capri pants with matching lightweight jacket, magenta sleeveless blouse, and sensible pumps, Lou pulled on a mammoth floppy straw sunhat and grabbed her sunglasses. Slinging her bag over her shoulder, she went to grab a coffee from the hotel's buffet breakfast. Happy and smiling, she sipped the warm drink looking through numerous photos of the wonderful house she now owned. After draining her coffee, she strolled to the front desk requesting the receptionist to kindly phone a taxi to take her to Estepona.

The journey took around an hour. Lou spent most of the time on her mobile describing the scenery to Abby who ooohed and aaahed in between coughing and sneezing. Lou was delighted Abby had stood up for herself in the ensuing argument that had gone on for an hour after Mark and Janice had left the previous evening. Lou wasn't surprised at the goings on and once again thought those spoiled rotten boys needed a bloody good kick up the jacksy.

"Send me loads of photos," Abby croaked. "Chester, stop that."

"I will, and don't let those boys change your mind. *What is that dog doing?*"

"He's dropped a bit of bacon I gave him, and is digging his way through the pillow to get it." She put the speaker on so Lou could hear the noise that matched a pig snuffling for truffles.

"Bacon sandwiches in bed. How devilishly decadent," Lou giggled.

"Yes. Isn't it though? D'you know the only person being civil to me is that floozy, Paisley? I'm starting how I mean to go on, Lou. Thinking about myself for a change."

"That's the spirit, girl. Look, I'm gonna have to go. I'll call this evening." Lou tapped the phone off as the sign for Estepona came into view.

Palm trees lined the road and the taxi driver gave her a potted history of the town as she gazed entranced at the picturesque white-washed buildings.

Unlike other Costa del Sol resorts, Estepona had retained much of its charm. A white-walled centre with narrow, cobbled streets led down to the promenade and modern marina, where she was meeting Jesús, the estate agent. Choosing to walk the last few metres, she paid the taxi fare and strolled through the numerous small, pedestrianised plazas full of tapas bars and restaurants. Finally, she located the *Plaza de las Flores* and the small café bar where they had arranged to meet. As she was early, she ordered hot chocolate and churros then sat people watching at a small table on the terrace.

Even this early in the year, there were a few bods enjoying the morning sun. Mainly pensioners interspersed with groups of friends nursing hangovers from either birthday, or stag, and hen celebrations. Five girls sat to her left, each wearing a T-shirt declaring they were on *Stacey's Hen Party*. Lou spent a good thirty seconds trying to guess whom Stacey might be, eventually settling on a sallow-faced redhead. Her make-up looked heavy, as if she'd applied it with a trowel, and she looked desperately miserable. Yes, that was definitely an, 'I'm getting wed soon' visage.

A large, blowsy woman sat opposite digging into a plate of pastries, crumbs flying as she lambasted her small, terrified looking husband who glanced around nervously to see who was witness to his abject humiliation.

"Buenos días, Miss Walker. Sí?"

Lou looked up into a pleasant smiling face. Light brown, wavy hair flopped forward while striking green eyes crinkled, smiling at the corners. A slightly hooked nose and wide generous mouth were not at all the Antonio Banderas features she was expecting. Gulping down the last of the sweet, sticky doughnut and taken aback as he bent to hug her, she eyed him as he proceeded to take the seat opposite.

After a leisurely chat in Jesús's good albeit broken English, he escorted her to a nearby bank where a pretty girl named Penelope ushered them into the manager's office. It was here, for a small fee, Lou procured a certificate of non-residence. This enabled her to open an account and receive a pin number. The card would be waiting when she returned to the UK she was assured.

Next stop was an innocuous looking building where she picked up an application form to obtain the NIE. After photocopying her passport, and an interminably long wait in a moderately short queue, she received confirmation that the NIE would be ready in six weeks.

"Phew!" she breathed, "that was like an operation. What a palaver."

Jesús laughed at Lou's pained expression, explaining that Spanish bureaucracy was renowned for being extremely trying and something as simple as paying a bill or a trip to the post office could be a day's outing. His sound advice would be to take a drink and a book with her next time.

Blimey! Abby would love that with her bladder.

✺ 11 ✺

At three in the afternoon after almost a day spent completing a mountain of paperwork, and forms, the hour Lou had been waiting for arrived.

As she and Jesús drove out of Estepona towards the hills, Lou pulled off the sunhat and laid it across her lap. Filled with an animated sense of anticipation, she brushed a lock of hair from her brow and drank in the stunning panorama. Sapphire eyes shining, mesmerised by the breathtaking scenery, impossibly blue sky, and sun that shone on and on and on, she had to keep telling herself this was real. She was here. In Spain. Now! In no time at all this beautiful place would be where she called home. Lou had seen photo after photo of the house she'd bought, but this was the first time she'd be seeing it nose to brick so to speak.

The Sierra Bermeja Mountains loomed in the distance as they flashed past olive groves between luxury villas and urbanisations. Dogs lay panting under the shade of orange trees, while cats sprawled happily in the sun. Small, whitewashed villages or pueblos interrupted the magnificent landscape. Lou's thoughts fleeted to her two precious furbabies she'd left back in the UK, in the pricey animal hotel they'd become accustomed to when she took trips, which wasn't often. No doubt, they'd be living it up. *The Aristocats ... eat your heart out.*

Likewise, her cats would have a ball here too, lounging in the sunshine as she peeled them both a prawn. Chester would find his feet bless him. He'd have to build an understanding with her moggies, and vice versa. She would keep a sharp eye on her brood to make sure they didn't run rings round him. Chester wasn't built to run. Mind you, neither was Tweetie, Lou's own furry beach ball. She could run when she had to, which was infrequently. She preferred the lazy life, queening it with attitude. Sylvester was the one to watch. That bundle of fluff could get up to all manner of mischief.

Her thoughts then turned to Abby. She would love it! Lou just knew.

Within thirty minutes, they passed through a small square dominated by an ornate fountain and equally ornate village church.

"This will be your local village," Jesús explained as Lou looked at the pretty, cobbled streets.

Wrought iron grids known as rejas covered the windows of traditional town houses, colourful pots of cascading geraniums overflowing in vibrant shades of pink, red, and orange.

"It's beautiful," Lou breathed, spotting three women dressed in black holding a heated conversation outside one of the small shops surrounding the plaza. There were also a few restaurants and cafés, with small terraces housing a scattering of checkered clothed tables, although most seemed empty.

"There's a market every Wednesday and a fish van Monday afternoon, but you won't be far from the main shopping areas on the ring road outside Estepona where there are English supermarkets."

Lou breathed a sigh of relief. She didn't mind the odd paella, but seafood wasn't really her thing and food was one issue that mattered. Whilst doing her research, she'd discovered the Spanish ate many things that would never pass her lips. Bull's testicles and pig's ears were two of the delicacies that stuck in her mind. Seemed not much of the animal went to waste over here. Well bollocks – bull's or otherwise – to that! You can keep your nuts and lugs, señor, this lady ain't buying. She would definitely be checking her tapas before taking a bite.

The road became narrower and steeper as they left the village and her finca came into view ten minutes later, which she guessed was probably a thirty minute walk. Jesús said he had a few phone calls to make and dropped her in the drive to look round the place on her own.

"Adiós," she beamed, puffing out her chest at her use of the Spanish word for goodbye.

As he drove away with a wave and a grin, the inflated chest soon became deflated when she realised she'd have to learn a shitload more Spanish than the handful of words she knew presently.

As well as saying goodbye, she'd wished to thank him for his assistance, but held back from trying to be too clever as she knew she would make a complete tit of herself. She had learned the Spanish word, but the pronunciation was a tad iffy. *Gracias* invariably would have come across as *gratchiass, graceiass, grassyass, or greasyass.* Better keep schtum until her command of the language was slightly more fluent. Of course, she could have spoken in her native tongue. His English was solid enough and he would have had no problem understanding.

You are a tit after all, Lou. Next time she saw him; she would be sure to thank him – in either language – for his help.

❧ 12 ❧

Settling the straw hat back on her head, Lou hoisted her bag on her shoulder, and clutched the keys tightly in her fist.

The photos she'd seen didn't do the place justice. Even though the house was on a hill, the surrounding land was flat with a magnificent variety of trees: avocado, fig, olive, orange, lemon, apple, pear, cherimoya, pomegranate, plum, and almond. *No shortage of fruit salads and smoothies then.* What they would use the remainder for, God only knew. There was a kennel area along one side of the house and a large vegetable/herb garden, which the previous owners had started and tended. She knew that from the brochure. Aubergines, peppers, chillies, and tomatoes grew in abundance and Lou knew Abby would likely keep the garden and nurture it.

Opposite the kennel was a chicken run. Steps led down to no less than three outside seating and eating areas, a built-in barbeque dominating the dining area adjacent to the pool. She could imagine evenings spent there, balmy and relaxed with new friends, dipping in and out of the cool water, while smoky scents of cooked meat drifted enticingly and glasses of sangria poured and sipped.

Looking out to the cobalt blue horizon, pots filled with flowers were everywhere. As she followed the path farther around, she came to a lawned area and another shady terrace with patio doors devouring the whole wall from one of the bedrooms. As she peered through the window, she immediately decided this bedroom would be hers. It was perfect. She'd bought the property fully furnished, and a large four-poster bed monopolised the room complete with mosquito net and a massive old trunk at the foot, more Caribbean Colonial in style. The furniture looked antique and the terracotta tiles, draped with haphazardly strewn colourful rugs created a cosy feel.

Lou was desperate to look inside now. Thrilled to the point of bursting, she rushed through a small rockery and cactus garden. Hands trembling with excitement, she unlocked the door leading into the kitchen. High beamed ceilings made it seem cool. There were no units in the large space. Exposed white stone compartments under the worktops were empty now but she knew they would look wonderful filled with kitchen paraphernalia and pottery, as would the many shelves around the walls, also seemingly made of stone.

A large range commanded one side of the room. In a small room, off to one side, Lou was thrilled to see a desirable selection of modern appliances. She stood for a moment next to the Belfast sink, looking through the window out over the mountains. She had a nice home back in the UK, but nothing like this. Through an archway, she entered the living room. The windows were higher here, which gave the room a cooler feel. A large leather corner unit and a wood burner were the only items in the room, yet it had a sensational snug ambience.

As she went out into the hall, she knew from recollection of the plans there was a small study and shower room off to one side. She ignored that for now, and walked up the traditional stairway, each tread faced with attractive Spanish blue and white picture tiles. The upstairs needed some work. Lou wanted to make a living area up here for Abby, as there would be times they would need their own space. The largest bedroom would do just fine and, as all rooms up here had doors leading out to the wraparound balcony, she knew Abby would revel in it.

The property had the benefit of a private well and water supply. At the rear was a sloped grassy bank with a bridle path. She clicked away on her phone, taking oodles of pictures, trying to capture the atmosphere of her beautiful house. The property had eaten up almost three quarters of her winnings.

Standing here, looking out over the Mediterranean, she knew it was worth every penny and more importantly, it felt like home.

✖ 1 3 ✖

The ensuing weeks saw both women in a frenzy of activity. Lou had a large three-bedroom flat and had collected mountains of junk over the years.

Evenings were spent head deep in boxes discovering treasures from years gone by that she definitely couldn't part with. She finished all the work she was doing for current clients and was ready to take a break from proofreading and editing for a while, though she guessed she could return to it if required once she moved.

The weather that February was the worst in years. Snow, rain, hail, and the constant bite of a north wind fought to penetrate the many layers required every time she left home.

Abby was on the phone constantly, asking pointless questions and generally panicking about anything and everything. Apparently, Chester had been up to no good, getting jiggy with Ethel, next door's Poodle, and causing no end of neighbourhood tension. Lou couldn't imagine the chubby lump having the energy to do much on that front, telling Abby as much while trying hard not to laugh. She hoped Abby wouldn't change her mind before the time came to leave, especially over a Poodle pregnancy.

Lou's next-door neighbour Callum had agreed to drive the friends to their new home after she'd gone round to see him, initially to complain about the loud music. However, after a couple of *Aldi* beers, a few puffs on his 'herbal' cigarette, and a handshake on negotiating transport, she'd returned home feeling slightly sick and more than a little attracted to the gangling young man.

Abby had lost most of her friends during her marriage cum prison sentence to Mark, but still kept in touch with a couple of old mates from university – Lou obviously, and Jenny. Jenny was ever so posh, and it had been a tremendous shock to everyone when she left her physiotherapist husband of twelve years to move in with Clare, her daughter's tennis coach. She'd now been living with Clare for six years and they were tying the knot in May.

Abby invited them for dinner to give them an early wedding present, an exquisite china coffee set she'd been given for her own wedding but never used. *Two birds, one stone*. It was beautiful, if a little ostentatious, and hadn't cost her a penny. Serving up a spatchcock chicken with new potatoes and veg, she listened intently to their wedding plans.

"You must come visit us in Spain," Abby offered, waving her fifth glass of Chardonnay haphazardly, totally forgetting about the home-made rice pudding in the oven.

"Sure we will, thanks," Jenny replied, wrinkling her nose and tentatively pointing at the oven. "Pooh! Is that something burning?"

"Oh, shit! The bloody pudding." Abby staggered towards the large stainless steel *Smeg* ineffectively wafting a tea towel before opening the oven door. She pulled out the ruined blackened mess, raised her eyebrows, and dumped the scorching dish onto a steel trivet before opening the back door to release the smoke.

A disgruntled, sleepy Chester shuffled outside and cocked his leg on a plant pot. Perilously wobbling on three legs, he gave Abby evils, no doubt for daring to interrupt his snooze. Clare was guffawing at something Jenny had said and Abby thought what a lovely couple they made. Thinking on her feet, she pulled a tub of *Haagen Daaz* from the freezer.

Disaster averted.

Apart from the boys, Abby had no family to bid goodbye so was spared emotional farewells.

Lou, however, came from a large tribe, and wasn't so lucky. The only girl in a family of five, she underwent the whole shebang. Sister-in-laws clutching at her, wishing her well, and exclaiming, "But how will you manage in a foreign country?" as if she were going up in a sodding rocket doing a solo trek to the moon.

Amanda, her youngest brother Rick's wife was pregnant with their second child and looked as if her craving for *Greggs* sausage rolls was getting the better of her. She clung like a limpet and snivelled like a child when saying goodbye, which had a domino effect on the middle two sisters-in-law, Diane, and Helen who followed the leader. After the three in-laws had practically squeezed Lou to a pulp, she received another onslaught in the arms of her two remaining brothers, George, and Stephen. They hugged, hugged again, kissed, and wished her luck. They hoped she would be happy. It would be lovely, they said, if they could visit occasionally, and would she please promise to keep in touch as much as possible once settled, although they realised she was a busy lady.

Then, it was the turn of Ian, the eldest, and his dour other half, Brenda, who seemed somewhat disgruntled that Lou hadn't shared her good fortune among her many nieces and nephews. Well, they could bog off. The last two Christmases she'd received a pack of tea towels and a thousand-piece jigsaw of two cats sitting in a pot of flowers, which she still hadn't attempted to piece together. There had been no cards or gifts for her birthday in the past three years, and even well wishes over the phone had been late ... and hurried. They were getting bugger all. There were no embraces from Ian or his wife, just a nod of the head, a weak smile, and a half-hearted comment telling her to look after herself.

The two of them wouldn't be receiving an invite anytime soon.

Finally, Rick, the joker in the pack, who hadn't yet engaged in the touchy feely show, gathered Lou in his arms, cuddled her fervently, and whispered, "Give it hell, sis. Gawd help Spain. *The poor bastard.*"

He'd kissed her cheek, told her he hoped all worked out well, and said if she hated it she mustn't hang about with a face like a mashed up skunk, bringing misery to Spain and its lovely people. No, she should do the decent thing. When Lou asked what, his reply came back, snappy as ever.

"Shift ya arse, come back home, and buy a gaff in Florida like you should've done in the first place. That way, Ian, Brenda, and the kids could borrow the place for holidays," he grinned, giving her that saucy wink she knew so well.

Lou had tutted at him, laughed aloud, and then pushed him away telling him he was a cheeky devil. Rick was her favourite sibling by a long way and she loved the bones of him. Nothing like his three brothers, he phoned her regularly and as children, he always watched her back, making her laugh and protecting her from Ian's sly bullying.

He'd always been too soft for his own good, which was probably why he'd ended up with such a bloody wet blanket like Amanda. If worrying about sweet FA were an Olympic sport, she'd be Michael Phelps. She was always 'ill' and both her pregnancies had been stressful for Rick. He couldn't leave the house for more than five minutes without his phone ringing off the hook. Self-employed, he had to take his three-year-old daughter Jodie to work with him when she wasn't at nursery, while Amanda, greedy hog that she was sat at home with her feet up watching *The Jeremy Kyle Show*, gorging on chocolate, peanut butter, and bleating about her swollen ankles.

The emotion of bidding farewell, especially to her little brother took it out of her, and many evenings Lou crept into bed with her two moggies wondering if she was doing the right thing

15

Six weeks later. The day had dawned.

Abby had obtained Chester's pet passport and done a fine job of talking her editor round from sacking her for the late article. He'd also provisionally agreed to accept written articles about Spanish living.

Andrew was still barely speaking to her, but Abby had to concentrate on final arrangements and hoped he'd eventually come round. Everything had become a blur; so much to do, so little time. Seemed she was on track the day before until she started packing and realised she was in need of a few things. In a frenzied half hour dash, she'd picked up two swimsuits and fourteen pairs of knickers from *Marks & Spencer*, then hoofed it to *Superdrug* where she purchased a boatload of toiletries. Now, sitting alone in her kitchen, Abby nervously awaited Lou.

They were driving to Spain. Lou's friend Callum wanted to tour Europe in his refurbished *VW* campervan and apparently, Lou's offer of a few hundred quid had swung it. Abby looked round her kitchen and wondered if she would miss the place. Chester gave his opinion by blessing the air with one of his booming farts as the front door crashed open. Daniel, Andrew, and their other halves burst into the kitchen with flowers, wine, and chocolates.

"Thank God we haven't missed you," Paisley spluttered, giving Andrew a sharp dig in the back.

Cautiously, he moved towards Abby. "Sorry, Mum. Look, I'm not made up about you going, but if you think you're doing the right thing and you'll be happy, go for it."

Moving towards her, and hugging her awkwardly, Abby quickly brushed away tears.

Daniel opened the dishwasher and pulled out five clean glasses. "What time you leaving?"

"Around eleven." She chuckled, feeling relieved that she and Andrew were at least on speaking terms before her departure. "Time to have a glass of that Cava before I go, methinks."

Paisley was busy showing Daniel's girlfriend Chrissie photos of the house on Abby's phone, both girls gushing at how gorgeous and amazeballs it all was. Paisley had more or less moved in over the last couple of weeks. Abby had lost count of the number of times she'd nearly broken her neck tripping over the girl's Doc Martens at the foot of the stairs. Shocking pink hair dye, make-up, and *Tampax* boxes littered the bathroom.

Abby wished it had been Chrissie who'd moved in to look after her boys. She and Daniel had been together since school and were saving to get married. Mind you, the poor little bugger had been waiting ten years and Abby thought Daniel needed a bomb up his rear. He'd never been the impulsive type when he was a little boy. It used to take him an hour to decide what flavour of crisps he wanted. However, unlike Andrew, he was quite orderly.

Chrissie gazed at him adoringly.

She wasn't an unattractive girl, she just didn't make the most of her good points. She wore her thick, rich chestnut hair bluntly cut, at the chin of a pretty heart shaped face that fought for survival under a heavy fringe and large *NHS* glasses. Freckles, scattered across her cute upturned nose, stood out like ink spots on a blank page, but the tiny bespectacled, studious girl was intelligent and polite, not like—

Chrissie interrupted Abby's thoughts.

"What an adventure. You must be so excited." The girl smiled shyly.

"Yes, the world's your lobster." Paisley loudly proclaimed.

Lobster? Point made.

Intelligence and/or politeness were not high up on Paisley's list of qualities. In fact, Abby was having a hard job thinking what her qualities were, silently praying that cleanliness was one of them. Lobsters aside, Paisley would at least keep the place from developing into a squat, Abby hoped.

"I saw Mrs Wilson earlier," Andrew mumbled, mouth crammed full of pickled onion

Monster Munch.

Curiosity getting the better of him, he peered over the girls' shoulders as they gazed at photos of the new Spanish villa before continuing the latest news from 'er next door.

"She said she'd be round later. Chester's gonna be a daddy apparently. She didn't look best pleased about it either." He guffawed, bending down to pat the fat offender in a complimentary manner. "Well done, dirty dog."

Chester farted again, although not silent still violent, shot out his pink tongue to hoover up a stray snack then screwed up his already puckered face as the pickled onion flavour clobbered his senses. Struggling to imagine how the offspring of Mr Blobby, and the curly psychopath poodle next door would turn out, Abby shook her head.

Daniel poured each of them a glass of fizz, making a toast as he raised his glass. "To Spain! Free holidays, sun, sand, and sangria."

Strange, but Abby couldn't imagine Daniel in Spain. He didn't tan well and his preferred drink of choice was those annoying artisan craft beers with daft names like *Tom's Fart, Hog's Piss,* or *Brewer's Droop.*

The rest of the group raised their glasses and sipped, just as a loud klaxon sounded outside playing one of those crazy tunes. The blast of the horn set Ethel off on one of her barking fits.

"To Spain," Abby whispered.

16

Between hugs, goodbyes, and trying to cram an extremely reluctant Chester into his carrier, Lou finally hauled Abby's luggage to the front door.

"I told you we were travelling light." Lou scowled. "What the hell you got in this case? And please tell me those two boxes aren't coming too?"

Daniel struggled to lift the larger box and raised an eyebrow. "Bloody hell, Mum, it feels like a dead body."

"Stop fussin', the pair of you. It's only my sewing machine, laptop, and some ornaments."

"Only? What's only about? *Sewing machine?* What d'you need that bloody thing for?" Lou stood hand on hips, a shifty look on her face.

"Doh!" Abby twirled, managing to glare, at the same time as showing off the chiffon top
she sported. Lime green, and covered in pictures of lemons; an extreme Costa del fashion statement.

Paisley stood gawping, shoving her fist into her mouth to stifle a giggle.

Marching past them, carrying the smaller box, Abby stopped at the rear doors to the van.

"*Louise Walker.* What the hell's all this?"

Boxes of every shape and size crammed the van's small interior.

"Travelling light, you said."

Lou stood rooted, shuffling her feet on the path. "Yeah, I know, but it's stuff that means a lot to me."

Abby opened the nearest box. "DVDs? We are *not* moving to Spain to stay in watching *Pretty Woman*," she shouted, brandishing the plastic cover in Lou's face.

"What's in this one?" Abby asked curiously snatching another box from the multitude.

"*Hats*. Seriously, Lou, we're not off to bloody Ascot. Why you bringing these?"

"Didn't wanna get rid," Lou replied sheepishly.

"Well you can leave them here, and they can be sent over at a later date. There'll be no room for us with all this."

Lou pulled a face. "Yes, ma'am. Whatever you say."

Reluctantly she pulled out some of the boxes from the van. Callum came round from the driver's side to give her a hand. A bit of a hippy, good looking in a 'Jon Snow' kind of way, but lacking in personality, Callum had been Lou's neighbour for years. Approximately ten years younger, Abby had always thought Lou had a crush on him. Six boxes lighter, Abby was about to check the last one when Lou reached out to stop her.

"Leave that one," Lou demanded, grabbing at the box with both hands.

"What's in it ... something important like last year's OK magazines?"

"*No*. Abby, leave it will you!"

The two of them stood in the back of the van in a tug-of-war, each yanking at the box. Callum waited at the door, a blank expression on his handsome face.

When the bottom fell out, Lou's face turned scarlet. "Look what you've done now," she growled, turning her head to one side.

Abby glanced at the floor, bursting into giggles on seeing the box's contents piled at her feet. A small whip, a paddle, handcuffs, numerous saucy role-play outfits, two pairs of thigh high boots – one in patent red leather, the other in black PVC – both with pointed toes and thin, incredibly high stiletto heels, a selection of lace, PVC, and latex gloves, and two rather large vibrators in a satin-lined case complete with bumper pack of batteries.

Winking at Callum, Abby scooped half the kinky collection up in her arms. "On second thoughts, we'll be taking these after all." She grinned and still giggling, began refilling the box.

17

Lou's planned route, split over three to four days, would cover almost two thousand kilometres. Frequent stops for the animals and Abby's bladder was a must and, not wanting to arrive stressed and exhausted, Lou wanted to stop fairly early each evening so everyone could have a good night's rest.

She'd highlighted various campsites in red on the dog-eared map she clung to. Sitting in silence she listened to Abby and Callum discuss the merits of self-sufficiency, and jam and chutney making. Then Abby launched into her plan to petition the government and help with the rescue of the indeterminable number of Spanish greyhounds (Galgos), and Podengos, hunting dogs subjected to horribly cruel lives then usually abandoned or killed at the end of the hunting season.

It was a nice idea, and yes, they were going to rescue a few dogs, but, for reasons unfathomable, it irritated Lou how well her best friend and good-looking neighbour were getting on. Next, they would discover their mutual love of hoodies, tree hugging, and vegetarian recipes and there would be no stopping them. She looked over her seat to see how Sylvester and Tweetie Pie were faring. Tweetie, curled in a ball and Sylvester, sitting as still as a statue, both glared at the wheezing, snuffling brute opposite. Abby had thought it a good idea to place the carriers facing each other so the three amigos could become acquainted, but looking at Chester, and her beloved cats' faces, Lou was beginning to realise a canine/feline truce may not be as simple as she first anticipated.

The van chugged along at a comfortable speed. They'd spend their first evening at La Petit Foret, a campsite less than an hour from Calais. As the name suggested, the pretty site was in a small forest with only a few pitches under a canopy of trees, set in the grounds of not quite a chateau, but definitely a manor house. After pitching the tent Callum had brought, so the ladies could sleep in the van, Lou took them all for a meal in the local village. This was an opportunity for Chester to take a pleasant, long walk – something he could do with a helluva lot more of, judging by his size. While he was out, doing what dogs do, the cats could stay put and do what cats do, which would likely involve mooching in the camper, stretching their legs and either being up to no good, or sleeping.

It was quite mild for the end of March. The friends sat outside the restaurant eating crusty bread washed down with a generous carafe of red wine. Lou had ordered coq au vin, which the waiter had just brought to the table whilst Abby, trying to ingratiate herself to the *Game of Thrones* doppelganger, tucked into a rather greasy ratatouille.

Lou couldn't resist a gentle dig. "Should have brought some bacon for the morning eh, Abby?"

Abby glared at her. "It's OK. Callum has some of those instant porridge sachets."

"Can't beat a bacon sandwich though."

Chester looked to be the only one to agree, as Lou reached into her handbag to grab a cigarette.

Replenished and feeling sleepy, the friends and Chester made their way back to the campsite. Lou went inside to see to the cats, hoping she wouldn't find anything amiss, while Callum sat and rolled a joint. Abby plonked next to him gazing at the stars, Chester plonked next to her droopy eyes throwing Callum jealous looks.

It was turning chilly and Abby didn't object when Callum threw a blanket round both their shoulders, and placed his hand on her thigh. She could smell smoke and the sweet aroma of weed as he bent to kiss her, but she didn't mind. He pushed her back against the damp grass and she felt her nipples harden as his cold, calloused hand caressed her long since flat stomach under the hoodie. Her fingers fiddled with the button on his jeans and she felt a rush of moisture between her thighs *Oh, God. It had been so long.* She clawed at his back and pushed against his hardness, wanting him inside her.

"What the fuck!"

Just as Abby was about to lose control, Callum jumped up.

"What is it? What's wrong?" She pulled the hoodie down instinctively, sex all but forgotten as she imagined bears or even worse, spiders.

"Your dog just pissed on me."

Chester sat nonchalantly, eyes drooping, tongue lolling, as he puffed, panted, and grunted. Anyone would think the bloody mutt was laughing.

"Oh, God, I'm so sorry," Abby gibbered, mortified.

She scrambled to her feet, bundling Chester into the campervan as Callum ripped of his sweatshirt, the sleeve steaming slightly.

"Never mind ... forget it." He didn't even look at her as he disappeared into the small tent.

She closed the door quietly and fumbled for her sleeping bag, the only fumbling or warmth she'd get tonight.

18

L ou knew something was up the moment they all piled into the front of the van the following morning.

Yesterday, Abby sat in the middle as she and Callum chatted away like BFFs. This morning, Callum sat sullenly rolling a cigarette and Abby, squeezed up against the window with her hood up, was making a meal of biting her nails. The contrast was stark, the silence deafening.

Lou had her suspicions that something had happened last night when she'd gone to bed and she wasn't pleased. She dug out her iPhone and tapped the *Music* icon, stuffed her earphones in, and watched France flash by through the drizzle. They made good progress, even with the pet stops, and listening to her favourite tunes all day had softened Lou's mood. The campsite just outside Bordeaux was extensive; rolling fields leading down to a wide river, willow trees leaning over, flirting with the water, cows grazing lazily in the surrounding fields.

Abby jumped out of the van almost before it slowed to a stop. "I'm taking Chester for a walk."

Dragging him into the rain, she stomped off leaving Callum faffing about with the tent and Lou confused.

"Did you do something to upset her last night?" Lou asked, trying not to make the question sound accusing.

"Nope." He shrugged, noncommittally.

Lou decided to spend some quality time with Sylvester and Tweetie in the van. Fine trip this was turning out to be. She was starting to wish they'd jumped on a bloody plane. She must have dozed off because the next thing she knew, Callum had opened the rear door and Sylvester had shot out straight towards the ducks by the riverbank.

"Oh, Jesus!" Lou jumped up, cracked the top of her head on the shelf above, and pushing past Callum, set off after the mischief-maker.

Abby had been gone about an hour. On her travels she'd picked up an extra-long baguette, cold meats, a selection of cheese, and a couple of bottles of wine. She'd chosen red and white; a rich Bordeaux, and a dry Chablis.

Walking back from the supermarket she'd discovered a mile up the road, her mood had lifted and she chuckled as Chester rummaged in the hedgerows. She'd returned from a different direction, cutting down from the road to walk along the water's edge. As she drew nearer the campervan, she spotted the ducks and called out to Chester so she could put him on his lead. *Too late.* A ball of black and white dashed among the birds, sending them scattering in all directions and flapping into the water.

Clocking Sylvester, Chester wasted no time in thundering into the fray. Abby dropped her bags. Charging after her pooch, she screamed at the top of her voice while Lou arrived from the opposite direction hunting for her artful puss and wondering, with trepidation, why all the commotion.

It was too much for Sylvester. He shot up the nearest tree where he sat trembling on a branch. By now, Chester was almost at the water's edge and completely stuck in the mud. Lou tried to cajole Sylvester from the tree while Abby trudged up to her knees in a quagmire of murky sludge vowing to castrate Chester when she reached him.

As Lou struggled to clamber up the tree, Abby felt her feet leaving her shoes and, pitching forward, fell face first in the mud. Sick of her life, she raised her head knowing Lou would be pissing herself laughing. Lou probably *would* have been pissing herself if her situation wasn't as bad. Grabbing the runaway cat by the scruff in amongst her squealing and yelling, she lost her balance and crashed into the water below.

The two friends dragged themselves back to the blue *VW*, stinking and covered in silt, one clutching a bedraggled, jumpy moggy, the other collapsing under the weight of a decidedly muddied black

British bulldog, the eyes of one good looking hippy and everyone else on the campsite upon them.

Looking at each other, Lou caught a twinkle in Abby's eye. Before they knew it, they had both collapsed onto the grass giggling hysterically, while Chester growled at Sylvester, and Sylvester hissed at Chester.

Abby had the feeling war had been declared.

❧ 19 ❧

Even with the frequent stops along the way, Lou and Abby were tired and aching, but nothing could stop the ecstatic feelings inside when eventually they arrived at their new home.

No sooner had the van pulled onto the wide gravel driveway Abby was jumping out, her gleeful gurgles similar to a five-year-old kid at *Disneyworld*.

"Oh, my God, Lou, it's stunning," she gushed.

"But, of course. I'm a lady with impeccable taste." Lou smiled broadly, handing the keys to her friend's eager, waiting hands. "There you go. The small brass one. I'm sure you'll have no trouble unlocking the door. Knock yourself out!"

A fired up Abby grabbed the keys then rushed to the front door leaving Lou and Callum to unload the van. Breathing heavily with anticipation, hands quivering in excitement, she grappled with the lock until finally the door flew open. Taking a deep breath, she stepped inside.

OMG. Abby was in love. She floated in a bubble as her eyes soaked up the tiled floors, the whitewashed walls, the kitchen with large range and massive pine table. She adored the staircase with charming, traditional tiles, and, oh, my, her designated bedroom was an absolute dream. A generous bed took priority, fitted wardrobes ran along one wall, and alcoves filled with cubbyholes were perfect for photos, trinkets, and ornaments. The large, arched patio doors edged with wooden shutters were what Abby had always wanted. Opening onto a spacious balcony, they were a portal to the most spectacular views she'd ever seen.

On one side in the distance, the Mediterranean glistened in the spring sunshine as if the sparse, fluffy clouds drifting across the azure sky had scattered the surface with a million shimmering diamonds. Although still early spring, Abby knew there would be people on the long stretches of sand. She imagined children playing, their parents relaxing in the gentle warmth of the golden orb sitting like a fat Buddha miles above them.

As she walked around the corner of the balcony, palm trees swayed to a soundless melody before spiky olive groves overtook the vista, their rich green foliage in stark contrast to the dry dust at their base.

At the back of the villa stood the pièce de résistance. Above the beautiful pool area, the mountains stretched as far as the eye could see. Simulating the spine of an ancient beast, their majestic, breathtaking beauty astounded Abby, bringing a lump to her throat and a tear to her eye. Covered in a patchwork of green, they soared toward the heavens. An Egyptian vulture circled in the distance and from farther up she knew one could see the coast of Africa and over to Gibraltar.

She couldn't wait to explore, but Lou's shout interrupted her reverie and she practically skipped back downstairs to help bring their worldly goods inside.

Callum was awkward in his goodbyes. He declined an offer of a cool drink as he was meeting friends in Barcelona and wanted to get going. Lou privately thought he would also be grateful to escape the whiff of eau de fart, which had been making all their eyes water courtesy of Chester. Both women breathed a sigh of relief as the tatty blue camper drove back down the hill and out of their lives

"This is it then," Lou remarked. The friends looked at each other and hugged.

"I can't believe it." Abby was extremely emotional. "We're actually here."

A gecko sat watching them on a low wall through heavy lidded eyes, one claw raised as if waving a happy welcome.

"Yes, we are." Lou gave a small smile, silently hoping they'd made the right decision.

20

The first few days were hectic.

Jesús had sorted out the internet and phone line and thoughtfully provided a few provisions for their arrival. Potatoes, garlic, eggs, apples, and a box of cereal sat on the worktop. He'd also left milk, bacon, and cheese in the fridge, and had popped two bottles of wine in to chill, one white, the other rosé. Both slipped down a treat.

Despite Jesús's thoughtfulness, a shopping trip was still necessary. Although sold fully furnished, the villa lacked certain items. Crockery, cutlery, and cooking utensils were needed as well as cleaning materials, bedding, a few toiletries, and other essentials.

Abby had spent half an hour on the telephone to Sylvia – one of her Facebook friends – who ran a dog rescue just outside Estepona. She'd insisted on taking the couple shopping and showing them around the area in her clapped out transit.

Sylvia was a bundle of energy in a tiny frame. Short red hair surrounded a pixie face sporting a cute, little nose, full mouth, and twinkling blue eyes. Happily single, she'd lived in Spain for twenty years and was a fountain of knowledge on all things España. When first arriving in the country, she'd been shocked at the treatment of the hunting dogs left abandoned once the season had ended, and immediately began helping where she could. Expanded over the last eighteen years, the rescue effort boasted almost eighty kennels funded by the local ex-pat community, and wealthy locals.

It was the first time Lou had met her and the two hit it off immediately. Sylvia expressed deep gratitude when Abby and Lou volunteered to spend a day at the dog shelter the following week. She was hoping, with the kennel space they had, they could assist by taking some dogs too. Chester adored her on sight, plodding at her heels like a love-struck teenager.

Stocked up with provisions from the large supermarket in Estepona, the following morning Lou rose to a diverse mix of two odours – firstly, the delicious aroma of fried bacon, and second, a harsh, chemical smell. Abby was in the kitchen and the whole place stank of bleach. Lou hoped they would be eating breakfast outdoors.

"What's going on?" Lou enquired, staring at Abby and screwing up her face at the overpowering pong.

"There was a cockroach by the back door." As if that explained anything.

"Yeah … and?"

"So, I cleaned everywhere. Sylvia says you have to keep on top of it … floors swept and bleached every day and no crumbs anywhere … ever!"

To emphasise the point, she quickly wiped the breadcrumbs from the work surface, dropped them in the bin, and slammed the lid shut. "Bins emptied every day, and a shitload of this." She plonked a giant can of *Raid* onto the table. "I've been online and ordered a case," she proudly proclaimed.

"Uh-huh." Lou almost choked, eyes stinging and watering. "Whatever you say."

She strolled outside with her bacon butty, the smell of jasmine and orange blossom banishing bleach and insect repellent. Abby followed, carrying a tray with two mugs of coffee and a small bowl of fruit.

Abby slurped at her coffee. "By the way, I'm going to the village this morning. I'd like to see what the local shops have to offer and meet some of the neighbours."

Eyes still watering from the heavy stink inside, Lou quickly agreed to go with her.

"I think we should also enrol in Spanish lessons." Abby gabbled, taking another sip of coffee.

"Oh, Abby, I'm sure I'll manage for the time being. You're in such a rush to do everything. Let's just get settled first. Anyway, the way the Andalusians speak would make a Spanish teacher's hair stand on end."

She remembered her less than flattering attempts at the lingo, and was in no hurry to turn herself into Penelope Cruz, although she wouldn't sniff at the looks, the figure, or the money.

"But lessons are being held in the village hall. I saw the details on a flyer that came so there's no harm in asking while we're there."

"OK, you do that. Come on, let's get going. How about we try that quaint little restaurant in the square for lunch?"

"Sounds good to me," Abby beamed, gulping the dregs of her coffee.

21

An hour later, they were strolling down the hill, Chester bringing up the rear. As they approached their nearest neighbour's property, a small elegant man appeared at the gate.

"Hola. Cómo estáis?"

Abby waved madly and stopped to introduce herself and Lou.

He waved back.

Amazingly, Eduardo spoke perfect English with barely a trace of Andalusia's distinctive dialect, where letters and even whole words disappeared when reciting a tale, the words substituted with arms windmilling dramatically. He'd moved from Madrid where he worked as a teacher, when his young wife died in childbirth over twenty years ago. Felipe, his beloved son, now worked in the UK as an architect. The ladies absolutely must come for dinner this evening so they could get to know each other, he told them. He would invite some of the villagers along.

Around ten years older than Lou and Abby, Eduardo was handsome in an understated way. With tastefully tanned skin, grey peppered his dark hair at the temples and brown eyes twinkled below graceful brows, a small maze of lines crinkling at the corners when he smiled. His mouth fit his face perfectly, the nose and chin, well defined. The handshake Eduardo offered was strong, but hardened calluses told a different story in contrast with his elegant clothes. This was a man, who worked hard outdoors, although his voice was smooth and educated.

Abby thought he was lovely. She could tell he was going to be a good friend.

The walk to the village was pleasant, although Lou decided there and then that they would not be making many purchases. The walk back up would be taxing, especially for a hefty bulldog.

As they descended through the cobbled streets towards the elaborate fountain dominating the square, Lou was sure the three women garbed in black, whom she'd seen on her first visit, were still engrossed in the same heated conversation.

"Buenos dias." Abby offered a fetching, friendly smile.

As if struck by a snake, they stopped speaking, eyeing Lou and Abby up and down with undisguised curiosity. Abby pointed to the villa above them and explained she and Lou had recently moved in. Pointing to Lou, herself, and Chester, she made the necessary introductions. She may as well have been talking to aliens.

The trio curtly nodded and went back to their chat, gesticulating wildly as the conversation heated up.

Undeterred, Abby strode over to the little shop. Outside, there were beautifully patterned plant pots attached to the pristine white wall. A rail of colourful scarves and souvenirs, presumably for tourists enjoying a day away from the beach, added a wonderful vibrant splash to the starkness of render.

Inside, separated into many areas, the shop resembled a Tardis. On display were groceries, T-shirts with typical tourist slogans, hats, leather goods, and a huge array of alcohol. There was an area filled with small baskets of spices: pimento, paprika, cloves, the aroma heady and pungent. Sacks of dried goods including rice, flour, and pulses were in abundance.

Behind the counter, which displayed an impressive selection of cheeses, stood an elderly, plump woman. Hanging from the ceiling and framing her head, a choice range of cured meats and spicy sausages looked tempting. Maybe her generous girth had developed as she shuffled a couple of inches to take bites from the delicious suspended meats bobbing in the air. Lou dismissed that notion when the woman smiled invitingly, revealing several gaps in a sea of fleshy gums. The woman spoke carefully to avoid any saliva escaping from her puckered mouth.

"You are the ladies who move next door to Eduardo, sí?"

Abby was impressed with the woman's English before realising she must have to deal with holidaymakers on a daily basis. "Yes we are. What a lovely shop."

At times, Abby's over-the-top pleasantries grated on Lou's nerves. She wasn't just a glass half-full person. She was a glass half-full of the best champagne, sparklers, and a cherry on top person. She had a habit of saying what she thought people wanted to hear and that wasn't always the case.

Lou mooched around the store, scrutinising the surprisingly impressive selection of wine, leaving Abby babbling to the woman behind the counter. When in Spain, choose Spanish, which is exactly what she did, choosing three bottles of red. Two Rioja and a bottle of Torres Sangre de Toro, all of which Lou knew were far less pricy than their counterparts back in the UK. *Result.*

Yikes! Grabbing the last bottle from the shelf, she was spooked when she clocked an ancient old man lolling in a semi-dark corner, a large ginger cat at his weatherworn feet. He watched her from pale hooded eyes, barely visible in a sea of wrinkles and furrows. His gnarled, veiny hand curled around the top of an old walking stick and crooked, scraggy legs, resembling dark leathery twiglets, shot out across the floor.

"Ah, that is my father-in-law." The woman behind the counter advised.

The old man grunted before uttering a stream of Spanish, which Lou doubted was complimentary. As he spoke, spittle rained down onto the cat's head and his teeth had long since abandoned his gums. Obviously, there wasn't a dentist in this village judging from the oral hygiene of the scrawny fangless fossil, or that of his in-law who was heading the same way.

Lou hurriedly paid for the wine before practically dragging her friend away from the shop mid-conversation. Abby could talk some, even when she didn't speak the lingo. At least the Spanish woman's English was a damn sight better than the English woman's Spanish.

"Hey, where's the fire?" Abby pouted, jokingly. "And what type of wine did you buy?"

"You'll talk for bloody England, you will. Here, I'll show you."

"Spain, Lou. We're in Spain, not England."

"Yeah, OK, smartarse. Europe then. You'll talk for Europe. Here, have a peek."

"Pot kettle, I'd say. You can't half witter on when you get going. I've often thought of—"

Lou cut her short. "Are you gonna look at this vino, or not?"

"Alright. Keep your wig on." Abby pulled the bottles from the carrier one at a time, looked at the label, and then replaced each one. "Mmm, lovely. So you went for tinto, not blanco or rosado."

"Eh? What you on about?"

"You went for red, not white or rosé. My Spanish is coming along, sí?"

Had she thought about it long enough, Lou would have probably worked it out, but she didn't and she hadn't and that was that. She gave Abby a semi-sarcastic smirk and nodding her head replied, "Sí. Now what's Spanish for stop wittering on and shift your arse?"

Abby pulled a face and followed Lou. As they were heading to Eduardo's later, they took a rain check on the pretty restaurant, even though the waiter cleaning the tables outside had the pertest backside Lou had ever seen. There were two other shops in the village: a small bakery that had Abby licking her lips, and a small building which appeared to be an art gallery of sorts, displaying a closed sign

Peering through the window, Lou thought some of the work was worth a better look. She dabbled a little herself and thought it would be interesting to meet the owners. Maybe they would be at Eduardo's that evening.

Dressed in cool clothing and wearing shades, the girls had a pleasant day soaking up the sun as they strolled, with Abby insisting on chatting to as many people as she could in an effort to prove how well she was grasping a new language.

Arriving back at the villa late afternoon, they had a long, cold drink, rested their feet for half an hour then time to get glammed up for the get-together at Eduardo's.

Abby took forever to get ready. She wore the expensive multicoloured silk maxidress Lou had bought for her. It was a touch revealing in the cleavage department, but hey ho, you only live once. She painted her nails a neutral colour then spent an age trying to gain a Cleopatra effect around her eyes. Finally satisfied, she piled her hair on top of her head, pulled out curls to surround her face and slipped her feet into her beloved flip-flops.

"You look beautiful." Lou grinned, as she watched Abby in true Hollywood glamour glide down the stairs as if she were about to sashay across the red carpet at the *Oscars* looking not unlike a plump parrot.

Lou looked lovely. She'd brushed her golden hair until it shone, face bare of make-up or, as Abby suspected, artfully made to look that way. Showing off her tan to perfection in a short, dark blue shift dress, she complemented the outfit with a chunky silver necklace, bracelet, and earrings, and painted her finger and toenails with glittered silver polish to match her jewellery. Easing her size fives into incredibly high-heeled silver sandals, Lou completed the ensemble with a tiny silver clutch bag and was good to go.

"Yeah, so do you." Abby returned the compliment.

Grabbing the bottles of wine purchased earlier, Lou precariously teetered down the hill, with Abby, in sensible footwear, striding ahead.

23

E duardo's house faced the road and was older than Lou's place. Most of his land was at the rear of the property where pigs and chickens wandered about pecking and snuffling in the dry pasture.

As she and Abby walked around the side of the building, they were surprised to come face to face with an enormous terraced area. Eduardo didn't have a pool, but there was plenty of room for one. Roman statues, water features, and huge urns overflowing with a riot of vivid flowers made an impressive statement.

In one corner burned a massive stone barbeque where Eduardo, happy as any man in charge of controlled pyromania, stood brandishing a pair of tongs. Bi-fold doors opened from his living room allowing the sound of Miles Davies to drift on the soft evening breeze. The room, designed in the style of a gentleman's club, housed dark green leather sofas and richly coloured wood furnishings. A grand piano and floor to ceiling bookcases gave an intimate, yet elegant feel. Abby could imagine him comfortably lounging, engrossed in a newspaper.

"Ah, ladies." Admiring their outfits, a smiling Eduardo approached the two women and performed the compulsory air kissing. "How lovely you both look. Let me get you a drink before I introduce you to some friends." Abby noticed he kept glancing at Lou. His eyes drank her in, but she seemed oblivious. She recognised about a dozen people there, particularly the three crows she'd spied that afternoon in the village. Two seemed to have husbands, the third was alone.

Eduardo carried out the introductions. "Carmen ... Isabella,

Bernadette ... meet Abby and Lou." There was a round of hand shaking, smiles, and greetings.

Carmen was the only one who could speak English well so Abby, despite her earlier showing-off antics in the village, had to struggle with her basic Spanish to be polite. The crows' husbands sat together at a table drinking, playing a card game that involved a glut of shouting, arm waving, and strange body language. Seeing they were dressed in shirt sleeves and grubby trousers, Abby was on the verge of telling Lou that she felt a bit overdressed when she noticed her friend staring at a man who'd just arrived.

"Ah!" Eduardo gestured. "You must meet Juan. Like you he is new to the area and will soon be teaching flamenco in the village."

He steered Abby and Lou over to a tall, slim, dark-haired man. Classically Latino, with brooding features, Abby thought he looked smarmy, but Lou seemed entranced, declaring how much she would *love* to learn the traditional Spanish dance, much to Eduardo's disappointment and Abby's astonishment, as she knew Lou had two left feet.

Juan leaned over grazing both their hands with his dry lips. Abby felt her skin crawl. His hooded eyes reminded her of the geckos in their garden, and pound to a penny he'd slopped a whole tub of *Brylcreem* on that slicked-back hairdo.

"Enchanted to meet such beautiful ladies." With an arrogant air, the man looked them both over, his almost black eyes lingering excessively on Lou.

Oh, please don't let him be her next mistake, Abby silently prayed.

Feeling decidedly unwelcome, much like a third nipple, she reluctantly left the two of them to get to know each other. She believed Juan's seductive voice to be a smokescreen for his dubious sincerity. She doubted Lou would learn much about the slimeball. He didn't look the sort to let the truth get in the way of his fantasies and was already wittering on about his bloody Porsche.

She helped Eduardo with the barbeque and met a few other locals, including Father Tomás, the priest who ran Spanish lessons in the village hall, which Abby said she would attend on Wednesday evenings.

Eduardo told her about Christine, the lovely lady who ran the art gallery who was away presently, visiting family in Holland. He also mentioned the English couple, Elaine and Ken who ran the British bar in the village. He hadn't invited them this evening. He mumbled something about the couple not really mixing with the locals, preferring the ex-pat community in Estepona.

Overall, the evening was a success. There was plenty of food and drink. The jazz changed to Spanish guitar as the evening wore on, and surprisingly, one of the crow's husbands stood up and gave everyone a rendition of a beautiful Spanish love song in a deep baritone, which everyone applauded enthusiastically. Abby told Eduardo about her plans to buy chickens and grow vegetables, listening intently as he gave her a few helpful tips and promised to assist as much as he could.

About one in the morning, Lou was still deep in conversation with the Latino Abby had named Juan-ker. That's all I need, she thought. They'd just arrived in Spain and Lou was going nuts over some sleazy bloke. Well, not if she could help it. There was no doubt he was good looking, but there was something about him she didn't like. Something she couldn't quite put her finger on. *Shifty.*

Lou was oblivious to everyone as she gazed up into Juan's eyes. Like infinity pools, they sucked her in and she was in danger of drowning. She was usually sharp when it came to men, and could tell a tosser a mile away, but even though she knew this dark god was talking shit, she couldn't help but cling on to his every word. Her whole body tingled with lust for the man she'd just met. *Yikes. What in hell's name was wrong with her?* He stroked her arm gently as they spoke, about what she couldn't remember, her skin burning where he touched and she wanted his touch all over.

When Juan invited her back to his home, which conveniently was the house above hers on the hill, Lou accepted without a second thought. If he'd asked her to, she would have ripped her clothes off there and then.

❧ 24 ☙

Juan Romerez had been surprised to receive an invitation to Eduardo's get together. He'd only recently moved to the village, and largely kept himself to himself. The spacious, minimalistic villa perching on the hillside like a giant sugar cube was perfect for his purposes.

Unashamedly modern, stark white walls interrupted only by vast windows and steel beams featured on the upper floor. The lower floor housed a treble garage and four bedrooms, each with fashionable shades of white walls and polished concrete floors. In all but one of the rooms, a double bed stood alone beneath a diaphanous mosquito net covered in a sterile white sheet.

The upper floor was a huge open plan space, again a blank canvas. White and stainless steel fought for dominance in the kitchen's ready-for-use expensive cutting-edge appliances. Cupboards stood empty behind high gloss doors. The living room was devoid of clutter. No shoes, magazines, or abandoned coffee cups. A huge plasma TV was the only decoration to adorn the walls. Two white leather sofas faced each other, a glass coffee table in-between and a bottle of scotch and full ashtray the only evidence someone actually lived there.

The villa was poles apart from his permanent residence in one of the worst slums in Seville Las Tres Mil Viviendas, a huge housing project notorious for violence, drugs, and crime. Home to gypsies and thieves, with some of the best flamenco dancers in the world thrown in for good measure his apartment there had no hot water, intermittent electricity, and was overcrowded. The perpetual smog of hashish hung heavy in the dense, humid air.

His gitano (gypsy) heritage was not only apparent in his swarthy good looks, but also his dancing. Flamenco was a way of life into which he'd been born, not just the soundtrack to two weeks on the beach, as most tourists saw it. His father died when he was a baby, and his mother had done whatever she could to bring up six children. She spent her days outside the city's main train station trying to persuade tourists to have their palms read or picking the odd pocket.

Their small ground floor flat housed two families but was spotlessly clean. There was little food. His mother could work wonders with a weekly shop of potatoes, chickpeas, peppers, and eggs. Evenings spent outdoors with friends and family were always a celebration with much smoking, drinking, and the inevitable flamenco telling stories of love and loss. Juan had been dancing for as long as he could remember and made a decent living from it. The dancing also enabled him to meet rich foreign women, which was how he made his real money.

He had seen Abby and Lou in their garden from his front facing bedroom window, immediately dismissing the dark-haired woman. She looked too much like one of his own. The slim blonde, now that was a different story. His preference was definitely for golden-haired maidens where work was concerned.

As he watched and plotted, the smile never reached his eyes.

Loud banging wrenched Abby from deep sleep.

After a pleasant evening with an excellent host, she'd left Eduardo's villa around 3:00am to walk home. Lou had disappeared with Casanova long before she'd decided to leave. She couldn't believe she'd been ditched for a fella only days after arriving, but Lou wasn't into serious relationships, not after Simon, so Abby wasn't all that concerned.

The banging continued. *Bloody hell, Lou must have forgotten her keys.* Abby grabbed a T-shirt off the top of her suitcase – which she still hadn't unpacked – and what appeared to be a pair of Daniel's jogging pants. How they'd snuck in there, God only knew. Chester, curled like a tubby orange and white beanbag at the foot of her bed, opened one sleepy eye, shut it, and immediately went back to his dreams. Holding on to the pants around her ample boobs – Daniel was 6ft 4 and around 17 stone – she descended the stairs, forgetting that last night before bed, she'd tied her hair back with a leopard skin thong. If Lou had the greaseball with her, Abby knew she'd be mortified at the state she was in. Intending to give Lou a piece of her mind, Abby swung open the front door.

Oh, my! Gulping hard, she stood staring, gob-smacked at the vision.

Wearing a vest top that did nothing to hide his toned, taut muscles under golden skin, the most beautiful man Abby had ever seen loomed in front of her. She practically fainted looking up into the piercing à la Paul Newman blue eyes. Small lines appeared briefly at the corners as he smiled. Hair, the colour of honey, curled into the nape of his neck and she imagined her lips there on his pulse. She guessed he was in his mid-thirties. *Jesus, what was the matter with her.* Remembering her ridiculous outfit, she blushed, clutching the faded pants tighter and raising them higher up her midriff.

"Louise Walker?" he enquired, the soft Devon burr a surprise.

"Er, no ... I'm her friend."

He raised an eyebrow quizzically looking her up and down. "Oh, I see."

"No you don't ... I mean not in that way." She had an absurd desperation to let him know she and Lou weren't a couple of rug munchers.

"We just share the house that's all. That's why we need the work done on the bathroom down here so we can have one each."

She was babbling and flustered as she stood aside to let him in. Only now remembering the thong holding her hair, she gasped and reached up to remove it forgetting the joggers – six sizes too big – that were sliding rapidly towards her ankles, and desperately hoping the T-shirt she was wearing covered her modesty. Beetroot red she stepped out of the pool of grey jersey at her feet.

"What's the matter? Haven't you ever seen an extremely embarrassed woman before?" she snapped. "The bathroom's through there."

She could tell he was dying to laugh as she felt her blood rising. How dare he stand there gawping insolently, all glorious and sexy?

He bent toward her, his warm breath caressing her ear, "Not as sexy as you, no."

Bloody hell, she hadn't expected that! Trying to retain what little dignity she had left she bolted up the stairs, no doubt giving him a perfect view of her plump arse.

25

A bby was sitting on the terrace writing a list of vegetables she wanted to plant when Lou arrived home. Totally immersed in her complicated diagrams and piles of post-its, she hadn't heard her come in.

"Sorry about last night." Lou flopped onto the sun lounger, kicked off her sandals, and reached for the bottle of cold water on the table.

"It's OK." Abby didn't want the gory details so faked concentration on the reams of paper.

"The builders are here," she mumbled nonchalantly, her heart beating faster at the thought of the Adonis fiddling about with the plumbing inside.

"Yeah, I know. He's a bit of all right that Paul, isn't he?" Sylvia recommended him. "Apparently, he does a lot of work for the Brits around here."

"I hadn't noticed," Abby lied, sensing her face beginning to flush and redden.

"Hmm, of course you hadn't." Lou smiled. "Make them a cuppa will you while I get out of these clothes." She picked up her sandals and stood up. "Sylvia's taking me to buy a van later and I thought we could go get some chickens when I get back."

The blatant bribery of purchasing chickens worked. Abby not only made the two labourers a cup of tea, but also threw in a generous plate of sandwiches and a selection of biscuits. She was rather relieved, yet disappointed in equal measure, that Paul had to grab a part needed for the job when she entered the shower room with refreshments. The men had made good progress and Paul's mate, the small dour-faced Geordie, had no problem polishing off the mountain of ham, cheese, and pickle butties she'd prepared.

"Alreet these like," he mumbled, a desert storm of crumbs spraying from his bulbous lips.

A porky, deft hand shot out to grab another roll, which he began chomping on before he'd even swallowed down the half-chewed bite in his mouth. "Aye, cannit whack a crackin' sarnie like."

"Glad you like," Abby smiled, chuckling to herself at the man's broader than broad Geordie twang. "I must get on."

Excusing herself, she cleaned the house from top to bottom and was outside checking the chicken run for holes and making sure it was habitable for the new arrivals, when she heard a beep-beep.

Turning her head, she beamed as Lou emerged from the newly purchased vehicle and strolled over to check it out.

Abby knew if they'd still been in the UK, Lou would have bought a flashy car.

A stylish *Audi* perhaps, but this was the compromise. An old *Citroën* that had once been bright red, it now resembled something from a bygone age. The windows were grimy, and there was a funny smell coming from the interior, but Sylvia knew the old man who'd sold it, and he swore it was reliable.

Sylvia had also given them directions to the chicken shop approximately twenty miles away. Standing back from the main road, the place had once been two large barns, subsequently converted and now selling everything agricultural. The first stocked with tractors, tools, various farm implements, and feed, the other filled with cages.

A putrid stench nearly knocked Lou out as the large sweaty owner opened the door. She couldn't tell if the stink was his BO, manky breath, the inside of the dark shed, or a combination of the three. The noise inside also battered her senses. All she could hear was a riotous medley of non-stop squawking, quacking, and even squealing from pot-bellied piglets in a filthy pen.

Yikes. Abby would want to take them all home.

Abby stood behind her peering into the gloom as the human version of King Kong retreated to a bench to roll a cigarette and leave them to it, confident there would be no shoplifting.

Lou – as usual – wished she'd worn more sensible shoes, as mud, or maybe something worse, oozed into the flat pumps she wore. She also wished she'd brought a pair of ear muffs and a peg for her nose. Abby was no better prepared, but she didn't seem bothered, ploughing forward to look in the small cages.

"I hope you know what you're looking for." Lou grimaced, fishing for a tissue to cover her nose and mouth. The smell was rank.

"I know we need some Andalusian reds," Abby pronounced expertly "They're really good layers and ..."

Lou had switched to selective hearing. With respect, she couldn't have cared less. She didn't know the difference between an Andalusian Red, Chicken Little, or Foghorn Leghorn. The odour in here was the worst ever and that included the incident years ago, when a disgruntled ex-boyfriend sneakily stuffed a mackerel down the back of her sofa. Three weeks passed before she found the source of the offending whiff. *What a mess.* Following months of bleaching, professional cleaning, and innumerable bottles of *Febreze*, the strong fishy niff finally became a light aroma that finally disappeared

"I'm gonna wait in the van, if you don't mind," Lou announced, backing towards the large barn doors.

"No, don't mind at all, you go ahead." Abby waved a hand dismissively as she peered into cages, tutting at the overcrowded conditions. *The poor things.*

Lou sat in the van with the window open. The heat had increased steadily even though they'd only been here a few days. Leaning her head back and closing her eyes, she thought about the previous evening. She'd been surprised at her reaction to Juan. Yes, she liked a good-looking fella as much as the next girl did, but ever since Simon she'd been the one to use and abuse, the one who attracted the attention.

Thinking of Simon made her heart flutter and her eyes fill with tears, even after all these years. She remembered his chiselled face softened by kind hazel eyes, the straight, perfect nose, full, generous mouth that knew how to please, and mid-brown hair Simon kept cut to his scalp in line with army requirements. His body was strong, muscular, well defined ... and the scent of him. Oh, God, how she'd adored him.

They had met at school. Fumbling behind the bike sheds had developed into a real, grown-up relationship. She went to uni, he carried out his army training at Catterick Garrison. They made plans for their future. Marriage, two children – a girl and boy – a stone cottage in the country, a Springer spaniel. Then came the news that shattered her life. Private Simon Kavanagh. Killed in action.

Lou still kept his medal for bravery – awarded posthumously after saving the lives of two comrades, and dying in the process – in a drawer next to her bed. The ensuing months after his death were dark to the point of black. Her brothers had been as much use as a chocolate teapot, apart from Rick, but he'd thought the world of Simon and found it difficult to deal with the man's death himself.

Lou shrunk into herself, at times even keeping Rick at arm's length. Abby had insisted on being there for her, but it had taken a long time before Lou could face a world without the love of her life. Of course, there had been men since, a woman has needs, but she never dated any one of them for longer than a few weeks and she was always in charge.

Juan and Simon were poles apart in looks, physique, and personality, so why was it, when Juan had walked toward her last night, with his Andy Garcia looks, slim, lithe hips, and smile that would charm the knickers off a nun, she'd felt her heart flutter for the first time in what seemed forever. Admittedly, the shirt open to the waist was a bit overkill, and his hair looked as if he'd fallen head first into a chip pan, but that charm offensive was something else, leaving her breathless and confused.

The sex, back at his luxurious, if minimalistic villa had been amazing too. Plying her with champagne and compliments, he'd spent hours concentrating on *her* pleasure, something she hadn't been used to in ages. The attention had made her tingle in places she forgot existed. Just thinking about the things he'd done ... and the positions she'd gotten into ... well, you couldn't bend wire that shape.

She must have dozed off, because the next thing she saw was Abby and the smelly man mountain crazily gesticulating like two drunken air hostesses performing the safety drill nobody took a blind bit of notice of before a flight. *Seriously, what good were those flimsy Easyjet life jackets if you were falling 40,000 ft?*

An alarming pile of cages and two sacks of feed sat on the floor between Abby and stinko as eventually, deal struck, cages were heaved into the rear of the van. Abby clambered into the passenger seat, beaming from ear to ear.

"You OK?" She sputtered.

Lou's eyes were red, and Abby could've sworn she'd been crying.

"Yeah, fine. D'you get everything you wanted?"

"Hmm." Abby suddenly appeared distracted.

"Abby?"

Lou noticed two things. Abby's beam had turned into a rather shifty look as she stared out the window, and there was a strange bleating sound coming from somewhere behind her as they headed home.

❧ 26 ❧

"What the—"

The words were barely out of Lou's mouth before Abby quickly cut in. "Aw, Lou, I can't take them back now. They were all squashed in a little pen and look at them, they're just babies."

Eduardo, who'd arrived minutes before to help with the new livestock, stood trying to keep a poker face as Abby pouted and pleaded with Lou not to return the two kid goats that watched them with strange golden eyes.

The larger of the two, whom Abby had already named Atticus, was the colour of cocoa with white patches and long floppy white ears. Scout, the smaller one was delicate, her colouring various shades of cream. If she'd been sitting down, she could've easily been mistaken for a large rabbit. Lou couldn't deny they were cute, but for God's sake they'd only been here a week and had two bloody goats, a dog, two cats, and likely a dozen scrawny looking chickens.

At least Abby had resisted the pigs. Lou quickly poked her head into the van just to make sure there were no more surprises and the rest of the cast of *To Kill a Mockingbird* weren't lurking in the old Citroën.

"They're Nubian goats, good milkers," Eduardo remarked, taking his eyes off Lou's butt for a second.

"I can make goat's cheese," Abby babbled, pushing Chester out of the way, as his presence was freaking out the poultry and they were all manically squawking.

"Oh, for God's sake!" Lou stomped away, declaring her intention to go for a swim.

Abby and Eduardo settled in the new arrivals. Ensuring they were happy in their abode, and leaving plenty of food and water, Abby set about naming the flock. Eduardo proposed naming them after chickeny type foods such as Nugget, Kiev, Stew, and Burrito. Giggling, Abby punched him playfully on the arm. She couldn't bear the thought of her new children being eaten, so decided to name them after film characters.

Consequently, the large red matriarch, flashy, yet incredibly stubborn, became Scarlett O'Hara. Abby immediately christened the rather flighty, smoky grey speckled bantam Holly Golightly. Two plump red girls, who were obviously best friends, became Thelma and Louise. Ripley was a tough looking, shimmering black. With a few feathers missing, she looked capable of taking care of herself. Finally, Abby named the last chicken Annie Wilkes. A smart, sly loner, she seemed the sort who would bully any bird separated from the flock if she thought she could get away with it.

After ten minutes of exploring, the goats had curled up together and were peacefully sleeping. Feeling a mixture of pride and amusement, Abby and Eduardo spent the next hour watching the feathered girls establish some sort of pecking order. Literally.

Walking back toward the pool, they spotted a mischievous Sylvester perched on an upturned bucket, cunningly watching while fastidiously licking his paws.

Abby scooped him up in her arms, holding fast. "Don't you dare go near those chooks," she warned, stroking his warm, fluffy body as he softly purred, the beady, green eyes never leaving the nearby coop.

27

On the third Sunday morning since they'd arrived in Spain, Abby rushed downstairs declaring she was going to church, dressed in a red and white polka wiggle dress that Lou felt inappropriate as it displayed a fair amount of cleavage.

"Have we stepped back in time to the fifties?" she smirked.

Abby looked crestfallen. "Don't you like it? It's the only smart thing I have to wear. I didn't think maxi dresses and hot pants would cut it." She brandished a lace shawl. "Look. I even have a mantilla."

Thinking of the village women in the small chapel, black lace mantillas covering their hair and dressed in their Sunday finest, which if she had to guess would be various shades of black,

Lou couldn't help thinking Abby would stick out like a nun in a brothel.

"Why you going to Church?" Lou probed. "You haven't been in years."

"It's a good way to meet the locals, get involved with the community, and a proper Catholic Mass is so beautiful, don't you think?"

No! Lou didn't think and would not be cajoled into attending.

"You go. I'll knock up some food for when you get back." She smiled, having every intention of sitting by the pool with a large vodka and tonic and the new Dan Brown novel.

"Would you feed the chickens?" Abby called, grabbing her purse.

She needed to hurry as she was calling for Eduardo on the way.

"Sure ... and Abby?"

"Gotta go, Lou."

"Don't go in the confessional, I may not see you 'til next year. You might even get ex-communicated."

"Ha ha, funny. I'm off ... see you later."

28

Lou made her way to the chicken run and poured grain into the feeder. She knew Abby wasn't allowing the birds to roam free until they were used to their new surroundings. As she poured, the birds swarmed round her ankles. She felt as if she were in Alfred Hitchcock's *The Birds*, as hungry beaks viciously pecked at the wellingtons she'd put on by mistake. They were Abby's, and too big for her bloody feet.

Hearing the shriek of tyres at the front of the house, she opened the door of the chicken run and made to leave. The next thing she knew; Sylvester had dashed past her. Surprised, she jumped back as eight pairs of chicken feet thundered into the garden en masse, feathers flying everywhere. Between her screaming at the darn cat, and the squawking of terrified hens, she didn't hear Juan coming round the corner.

Oh, Jesus! He had one.

Sylvester – crafty little sausage – had Annie Wilkes in his hungry chops. In a flap, Lou lurched towards him, trying desperately to make him drop his prey. Not a chance! Mr Mischief was having the time of his life.

"Vester. Stop that, now!" she hollered, tripping over her own feet in the oversized wellies and crashing painfully to the floor. As she grabbed his black bushy tail and wrestled him into her arms, he spitefully growled, still managing to hold onto his spoils. He wasn't letting anyone ruin his fun. Expanding his sharp claws, he dug deeply into Lou's left forearm.

"*Ouch!* That's my arm you little sod!" she yelped at the top of her voice.

The deafening tone of Lou's griping caused the spooked cat to writhe and squirm. In the struggle, his clamped tight jaws opened wide. A distressed Annie seized her chance and scarpered back to the coop, while a stunned Lou covered in dust, scratches, blood, and feathers, salty tears streaming down her face, clung onto her rascally moggy.

Black shiny shoes appeared in front of Lou's downcast eyes. She placed the sulky puss onto the ground, watched him skedaddle to his favourite upturned bucket, and scrambled to her feet trying to impress the visitor with her limited knowledge of Spanish. She was an intelligent woman, after all, how hard could it be? Many of the words sounded similar to English.

"Estoy embarazada," she gushed. "I'm embarrassed," she added in fine English, just in case.

She couldn't understand why at first Juan looked shocked, then fell about laughing. It wasn't until he explained later, after she'd made peace with Sylvester, corralled the chickens, cleaned herself up, and finally poured a large V & T, that in fact she'd informed her new lover she was pregnant. *Oh, no. He must think her a right idiot.*

Taking a large gulp of the ice cold drink, she could feel her face getting hotter. As he gazed at her, other places began to heat up.

"I think the lady would like some private Spanish lessons, sí?"

He reached for her hand and she followed him into the house, chickens, cat, scratches, and vodka completely forgotten.

✿ 29 ✿

The church, as Abby suspected was beautiful, the high beamed ceiling producing superb acoustics as a soothing hymn played softly through discreetly placed speakers. The heavy smell of incense tinctured the air, and rows of highly polished pews led up to an ornately decorated altar. *Blimey, were the proceeds of the Hatton Garden diamond heist stashed up there?*

There was enough gold to warrant sunglasses and the sun, shining through the stained glass window behind drenched everything in hues of ruby, emerald, and sapphire. Small alcoves along the walls contained elaborate statues of saints with a bank of tea lights in front. A large statue of the Virgin Mary stood on the right-hand side of the communion table, enveloped by larger candles and two humongous flower arrangements, replicated on the other side with one of her son.

Abby had taken a seat at the rear of the church and now she knelt, sending up a small prayer of thanks to the man upstairs for bringing her to this country. She watched as the congregation filed in.

Sophia, the lady from the general store, half-carrying half-dragging Alberto, her ancient father-in law whose suit looked as old as he did. Abby guessed his age could be anywhere between eighty and a hundred and fifty. She decided that combing what little hair he had was obviously a chore as it stubbornly stuck to its own idea how to arrange itself, while defiant tufts were desperate to escape from his nose and ears.

Wearing a fitted navy dress, Sophia had made an effort. Unfortunately, her figure seemed to have outgrown the outfit and with all her lumps and bumps, her appearance wasn't unlike a sack of gigantic ferrets cavorting in a windsock.

Eduardo arrived. Abby had knocked for him on her way down but not getting an answer, had gone on without him. Seeing Abby sitting alone, he slid along the pew raising an eyebrow at her dress. *Oh, dear. She really needed to buy something more conservative for next week.* She pulled the lace shawl around her as he smiled and kissed her cheek.

Swooping towards the front pew as one, their saturnine other halves in tow, the three crows appeared, each one a carbon copy of Maleficent attending Sleeping Beauty's christening.

The little chapel filled up quickly and Abby recognised other faces she'd seen in the village.

Once everyone had taken their seats, Father Tomás took his place centre stage, voice clear as he delivered the Eucharist. Old women adorned in mantillas loudly prayed the rosary throughout and Abby felt their faith radiating around her. She hadn't been to chapel for a long time, finding the atmosphere, and experience soothing.

Afterwards, as the congregation left to have a leisurely bite to eat with their families, Abby and Eduardo sat on a shaded terrace, each quaffing a glass of sherry.

Abby looked at Eduardo. "You must come for lunch."

She felt for him on his own. From their conversations, she knew he adored his son Felipe, yet the boy called him intermittently and visited only once a year. *He must be lonely.* She so wished Lou would reciprocate the man's obvious interest.

"Thank you, my dear." A smile radiated across his face. "I would love to."

"Good. That's settled then. Time to go, I think."

Draining their glasses, the couple rose from their seats and made the trek up the hill.

Spanish Sunday evenings reverted to UK Sunday evenings. No matter how hot the temperature outside, Lou insisted on a variation of a Sunday roast so Abby adapted, usually serving up meat, roasted and sliced with a mixture of tasty veg, or mini Yorkshire puds filled with meat on a bed of cabbage mash, either option served with lashings of steaming 'proper' gravy.

On this particular evening, the weather was humid as the women dined on a succulent roast beef dinner, then carried out their usual shared cleaning up duties before retiring to their rooms, each with a healthy glass of wine, to converse with respective families and friends via Skype.

Abby dreaded these conversations. More often than not, she ended up chatting to Paisley who, with every sentence, set her teeth on edge. Clicking on the laptop, she was pleased to see Daniel for a change. She smiled warmly as her youngest launched into a rapid exchange.

"Can't stop, Mum, I'm going over to Chrissie's. Just thought I'd say hi and ask how you're gettin' along. Oh, and can you transfer a hundred quid into my account. The council tax's due, Andrew's skint, and I can't pay everything. I'll email the account details. Gotta go. Bye."

And that was that. Off he went, without waiting to see how Abby was faring, without her even uttering one word, and leaving her feeling more than peeved at becoming a walking cash machine. Again! So much for the pleasurable vibes experienced earlier. *Kids!*

"Hello, Mrs Sinclair ... you're lookin' a bit tired. Mind you, all that sun at your age can't be good."

Paisley's dark face came into view as Abby's eyes rolled skyward. She hadn't escaped the pink-haired one after all, nor her oafish comments. The girl either had been getting ready to go out or was having a night in experimenting with her make-up. Abby stared at the eyebrows plucked to a sliver, enormous false black lashes giving the impression of tarantulas frantically trying to crawl out of her eyeballs.

"Hello, Paisley, how are things?"

Not that Abby was interested about Andrew leaving his dirty pants on the bathroom floor, or Mrs Wilson's complaints about the randy absentee father snoring by her side.

"She says *you'll* need to pay if Ethel needs a G-section." Paisley paused, inspecting her freshly painted talons. "Did you get that?"

Abby would have sniggered at yet another of Paisley's brainless gaffes, had the comment from her ex-neighbour not ruffled her feathers. Her reply was salty. "I think you mean C-section, Paisley, and *I'm* not paying anything. It's not my fault Chester had his way with her bloody yappy Poodle. He's male ... what does she expect? She should have had Ethel spayed, or pulled her finger out her arse and fixed her bloody fence. Cheeky bloody mare."

Abby had only been speaking with Paisley for a few minutes, but already her blood pressure was rising. Conversations with the girl left her feeling as if she were slowly sinking to the bottom of the Arctic Ocean. Hastily, she took a huge slug of wine then looked directly at the screen as Paisley went off again.

"She wants to know if you want one of the pups. cos she says she's gonna have murders gettin' rid of them if they look like Chester."

Hearing his name, Chester looked up, belched loudly, and proceeded to give his long pink tongue a quick workout, licking his balls in short, sharp strokes. Job done, he snorted, rested his stocky head between two hefty front paws, and closed his eyes.

"She should worry more if they look like that snippy bloody mophead of hers." Abby was offended on her precious doughball's behalf. "Anyway, enough of that. Are you and Andrew going out?"

The top half of Paisley's attire hadn't gone unnoticed. The girl was wearing ... well, not much to be honest. Tiny, sparkly gold boob tube barely prevented indecency. Abby cringed to think what the bottom half revealed, *revealed* being the key word.

"Oh, yeah. There's a new club opened on the high street."

"Daniel says Andrew's skint ... he can't pay the council tax and—"

"Don't know anything about that," Paisley cut Abby dead. "Gotta go, taxi's here."

The screen went black. Abby took another glug of wine, slammed the lid down and stomped downstairs, Chester clumping along behind.

Lou's Skype session with Rick hadn't gone much better. The initial pleasure at seeing her younger brother dissipated before she could get a sentence out, as Amanda's whining voice screeched in the background.

"Rick, I feel sick. Could you bring me a glass of water?"

"Be right back." He apologised to Lou before disappearing off the screen, presumably off to the kitchen to fetch the apparently much-needed water.

For God's sake, couldn't the woman get her own drink? Lou's cup of sympathy was well and truly empty.

Two minutes later, Rick's face loomed as he sat back down with a thump. "I'm back. How's it goin' out there, sis?"

"Yeah, great. I love it. I—"

"Rick, fetch the Rennies ... this heartburn's killing me."

"Hang on a tick, Amanda!" he yelled. "Sorry, sis. Won't be long."

Lou couldn't believe it when he disappeared again. He looked knackered. No wonder, running around like a headless chicken after that bone idle other half of his. She needed a rocket up her tush. She tapped her fingers on the keyboard impatiently while knocking back half the glass of Rioja in one gulp.

"Are you sure you're OK?" she probed when he returned looking extremely fed up.

"She's havin' a hard time," he half-heartedly explained.

"Looks like she's giving you a harder time. She's pregnant, not ill." Lou wished she could reach through the screen and give him an enormous bear hug.

"Rick! Jodie's crying." The high-pitched whining interrupted again.

Getting to his feet, Rick gave a resigned sigh. "Sorry, sis, it's no good. I'm gonna have to go. Look, I'll give you a call durin' the week when I'm at work."

"But we've—"

Too late. The screen turned dark.

Scraping the chair back angrily, and sending her cats scurrying for cover, Lou snatched the wineglass, marched into the living room, and paced the floor. She took a swig and bit her lip.

Abby could tell from the expression on Lou's face that she was annoyed. "Went as well as mine then?" she laughed cracking open a second bottle of Rioja.

"Paisley?" Lou guessed, bad mood evaporating at Abby's pained, yet comical expression.

"Yeah. Amanda?" Abby asked, a wry smile nudging her lips while watching Lou's head nodding up and down. "I know you prefer your wine to breathe, but under the circumstances, don't think you'll mind, OK?"

Lou held out her glass for a refill. "Stuff breathing and pour."

Ah! Refreshing how they knew each other so well.

Settling down on the corner unit, Chester glaring at the cats perched just out of Fatboy's reach as usual, Lou grabbed the remote control. Sunday nights were catch up on UK TV time. The couple hardly watched the box anymore but there were certain programmes that couldn't be missed. Tonight, *Masterchef* reigned.

Making themselves comfortable, they tried to forget their family problems, concentrating instead on watching the contestants up to their elbows in fresh figs and prosciutto, as rather aptly they prepared and cooked stuffed quail for twenty taxidermists.

The days in Estepona developed into a routine.

Abby, always the early riser would see to the animals then begin her cleaning ritual. Afterwards, she would either go down to the village with Chester in tow, or pop to spend an hour or so with Eduardo, before spending the afternoon experimenting with various recipes, or sitting on one of the terraces writing whilst enjoying the wonderful weather. She knew she didn't need to work, Lou told her often enough, but the cash Lou had won wouldn't last forever and Abby was the type of woman who liked having her own money and independence.

Funnily enough, the articles she was writing were selling well, and her editor back in London had suggested she write a book about their escapades, especially Chester who was becoming quite a star in his own right. He even had his own Facebook page.

The goats and chickens now roamed free on the land behind the outbuildings, although the area had been fenced off. Abby spent a lot of time there keeping a watchful eye on proceedings. Annie Wilkes never ventured far after her close shave with Sylvester. Instead, she would sit glowering at her sisters from under a bush keeping a beady eye out for the crazed tuxedo monster.

Their respective indoor pets appeared to have forged an uneasy truce. The feline mafia had worked out that Chester was no Edmund Hilary, taking great pleasure tormenting him from worktops, units, anywhere more than two feet off the ground. Both were beautiful animals, but Abby had the distinct impression that they enjoyed taking the piss and she could have sworn when Sylvester wrapped himself around her legs it wasn't a sign of affection, more an intention to trip her, preferably to send her hurtling down the stairs.

On the surface Chester had given up pursuing them, but Abby suspected he was biding his time. He plodded towards her now and she smiled, remembering the first day she'd brought him home. Having just sold an article about an ancient Amazon cure for athletes foot, his cute, screwed up features had stared beseechingly at her from a *Gumtree* ad. That was it. She was smitten. Driving over fifty miles, she arrived at a run-down council house. A burnt out *Ford Capri* sat in the garden half-buried under five foot weeds, and ripped black binbags overflowed with shitty nappies, empty tins of smart price beans, and not so smart-priced cans of lager.

In a similar state, the surrounding houses had copious boarded-up windows and obscene graffiti sprayed on the walls. Abby could hear barking from inside and was about to turn and leave when the door flew open. A man, who wouldn't have looked out of place grappling at *WrestleMania* peered at her with little piggy eyes, in a face the image of the proverbial smacked arse. Standing at least six feet four, he was all sinew and brawn with close-cropped ginger hair, and a voice and manner showing no warmth or social skills.

"You here about the pups?" he barked taking a swig from the can of *Stella* clutched in his hand. He smacked his lips then yawned revealing uneven, nicotine stained teeth.

"Er ...yes, if I'm not bothering you." Abby clung onto her Gucci handbag. (An anniversary present from Mark years ago. *The only bag she'd ever liked, or was it the only gift she'd ever liked? Likely the latter. Didn't matter now anyway.)*

"Yer best come in then."

Without waiting to see if she was following, he led the way down a dingy hallway the smell of urine nearly flooring her. Entering the living room, Abby couldn't decide where the niff was coming from. The three sad looking Bulldogs, the two obviously overbred bitches with bungee ropes for nipples, or the four children in various stages of development up to around four years old, each wearing a nappy, food stains, and little else. Their equally overbred mother sat in the corner dragging the life out of a roll up, eyes glued to *The Jeremy Kyle Show*.

"Here." The man directed her to an old playpen where four puppies, oblivious to their surroundings, played happily amidst yellow stained copies of *The Sun*.

"The big white one's sold, but you can have your pick of the others." Abby looked at each of the puppies but couldn't see the one she'd spotted in the ad and mentioned this to the guy.

"Oh, we were gonna keep him. Most people want bitches, but if yer like 'im, he's yours."

Disappearing into the kitchen, he returned with a small glum looking pup. Settling him on the floor, the little fella promptly squatted and peed on Abby's shoes. It was love at first sight.

He had been so amusing as a baby. After having him checked over at the vets, Abby had spent a fortune at *Pets at Home* on puppy food, bed, and toys. The bed was a waste of money. He cried so pitifully that first night, she'd had to take him into her bed and that's where he stayed. He proceeded to eat the defunct bed not long after, as well as anything else he could get his generous gums round.

He also had a talent for messing in places where people were most likely to put their feet. Cries of, "For fuck's sake!" or, "I'm gonna kill that dog," and, "Mum, I've just trod in shit again," seemed to reverberate around the house for those first six months after Chester arrived.

Smiling, Abby got up and walked back to the house. *Yep, there was definitely another story to write.*

Initially, on most days ending in y, Lou would emerge from her room around ten in the morning bleary eyed from numerous late nights spent with her boyfriend.

"Too much bed, not enough sleep," Abby was fond of teasing.

Lou and Juan were definitely an item. Not only was the sex amazing, spontaneous, and frequent, but they'd actually been on a few dates as well.

He'd taken her to lunch at some of the most expensive restaurants in town where they were treated as if they were royalty. He could be careless, and had forgotten his wallet a couple of times.

His apologies, usually accompanied by intense stares and gentle caresses sent them both rushing back to his villa for their own take on a 'siesta', what they'd eaten, and who paid completely dismissed.

They had also spent a weekend in Cordoba. When they'd eventually emerged from the hotel, Lou had been entranced by the beautiful city. Ruled by the Moors more than a millennium ago who'd left their mark in the stunning architecture, The Mezquita, one of the largest mosques in the world was breathtaking.

They spent the afternoon strolling hand in hand beneath impressive arches and stunning courtyards dripping with foliage and blooms, before having dinner al fresco overlooking the Guadalquivir River, enjoying one of the most stunning views Lou had ever seen. She couldn't remember feeling this happy in a long time. Juan had forgotten his wallet again, but looking into his deep soulful eyes, she handed over her *MasterCard* without a care in the world.

Lou met Sylvia for lunch regularly and arranged a day at the dog shelter, which both she and Abby were looking forward to immensely. The three crows had surprisingly become regular visitors to the villa. Lou was helping them organise the fiesta. Apparently, just what every village fiesta needed was a computer whizz who loved flowers, dodgy blokes, and could barely speak the lingo.

The work in the bathroom was nearly complete and after the initial avoidance, Abby had actually begun to flirt a little with the gorgeous Paul when she took elevenses for him and his workmate. It still came as a surprise though, when on the final day he slipped his number into her hand, asking her to call so they could arrange a date for the following week.

The dog shelter Sylvia ran took in strays and abandoned dogs from all over the Costa del Sol. There were almost one hundred in residence when Lou and Abby volunteered to spend the day there. Sylvia also wanted the couple to see which dogs would be suitable for fostering until they found a permanent home.

The Podencos and Galgos outnumbered all other breeds. These beautiful, placid hounds were easy to look after and easy to fall in love with. Many found new homes in the UK and Lou was helping to run the associated Facebook page, arrange transport, and wade through paperwork.

Abby was a bit wary about taking hunting dogs on after the incident with Sylvester. The last thing she needed were more predators around her beloved chooks. The kennels were shady enclosures fitted with raised platforms for the dogs, the hospital wing, a small building at the rear where a vet from nearby worked four evenings a week without pay. Presently, it housed two bitches with twelve puppies between them.

After a blissful day of cleaning, feeding, and walking the dogs, Abby and Lou picked four they thought would fit in well at the villa. Flash, a rather ponderous Bassett Hound. Pia, a young Shitzhu cross. Luna, an elderly white German Shepherd who immediately stole Lou's heart and Abby surmised wouldn't require a permanent home anytime soon, and finally, Jackdaw, a black Staffy abandoned by his owners who, having obviously given up on the Spanish dream and their responsibilities, returned to Blighty leaving him tied to a dumpster in Malaga.

❧ 33 ❧

The village had now accepted Abby and Lou. Their neighbours realised they were here to stay and it wasn't just a holiday home for them.

People would stop to talk to them as they waited for the fish van in the ever-increasing heat, sat on one of the terraces with a glass of sangria, or sauntered round the weekly market. Abby planned on renting her own stall and selling their produce in future. She was forever trawling through recipe books looking for unusual combinations for pickles and jams. Lou suspected she was also secretly hoping to increase the goat population.

The two best friends had sampled the food in most of the establishments in the pretty square.

The restaurant with the dishy waiter was out of bounds, since Lou had politely asked for a sandwich replacing the word for chicken *pollo* with *polla*, which unfortunately produced hoots of laughter as polla meant dick or prick.

"You really must learn Spanish," Abby had snorted, eyes watery, and liquid running down her nose courtesy of the mouthful of wine she'd just glugged.

The full-of-himself waiter had doubled up pissing himself at Lou's faux pas. Consequently, Lou had flatly refused to set foot in the place again.

The one place they hadn't tried was the *The Bus Stop*. Eduardo had been less than complimentary when speaking about the owners. Apparently, it was usually full of ex-pats or holidaymakers, which did nothing to enamour Abby. The idea of attempting to enjoy a pleasant meal surrounded by middle-aged British men decked in white socks and sandals, with hairy, stretch-marked bellies bulging over Union Jack shorts, was enough to knock her sick. Even worse were those men who exhibited their life stories in the form of tattoos stretched across steroid enhanced muscles, drank copious amounts of lager, raised their arse cheeks and farted, or bawled obscenities at incompetent football teams playing on the large flat TV screen.

Of course, for every muppet there had to be the obedient little wifey, sporting platinum blonde locks, walnut wrinkled skin, and the obligatory unsubtle boob job, tottering awkwardly on sky-high *Jimmy Choos*, or *Christian Louboutins*, the archetypal *Malboro* dangling from pinched, bitter lips. God only knew why these women desperately clung on to their men, terrified of the many up-and-coming blonde bombshells waiting to take their place. *The dodgy lifestyle. The dodgy money*. Walking into the bar on Lou's insistence one lunchtime, Abby was surprised how spacious it was.

"I'm sick of tapas and paella, Abby, don't you just fancy good old fish and chips?"

Abby, who loved Spanish food, didn't just fancy. Nevertheless, she smiled and agreed.

"Look at this place. It's massive!"

Lou looked around taking in the stereotypical British bar. Mounted on one wall, an imposing flatscreen TV dominated above a small stage where Abby presumed the tribute acts and karaoke took place. Cheaply framed pictures of British institutions adorned the walls: The Queen looking regal in a long white gown and jewelled crown, a young Tom Jones looking hot in black skintight pants and blue ruffled shirt open to his nether regions, and good old Hilda Ogden clutching a broom dressed in floral pinny, her three trademark rollers poking out of a green headscarf. Interspersed among the pictures were three blackboards. The first advertised daily specials all including chips, the second, upcoming football matches, and the third, special offers on drinks; large jugs of innuendo cocktails a steal at eight euros, Jaeger bombs, BOGOF, burger and drink five euros.

"Hmm, classy joint," Abby sneered, eyeing a tall girl with spiky black hair and numerous piercings barrelling through the saloon doors presumably leading to the kitchen.

"Mum, customers!" the girl bellowed, taking her place behind the bar to dry glasses with a grubby tea towel.

The hour was relatively early so Lou and Abby, having their choice of table, slipped into a small booth next to a life-size old-fashioned telephone box. The red leatherette seating immediately clung to Abby's bare skin and she knew she'd be in pain when it was time to stand up.

The two women each picked up a large laminated Union Jack menu as spiky hair shouted over. "D'yous wanna drink?"

Rather than raise her voice, Lou stood, strode to the bar, and ordered a large diet coke each, while Abby rubbed at a stain on the table and checked the cutlery. The place was more than borderline grungy and she had visions of being up all night with food poisoning.

A drab looking middle-aged woman appeared from the kitchen, her body with a best before date circa the millennium hidden in a shapeless brown dress. The beaming smile she bestowed upon them didn't reach her eyes, which were murky and dull, reminiscent of pools of stale mud.

"We thought you might have been in here before now. Us Brits need to stick together," she cackled before doubling over with a twenty-a-day induced coughing fit.

"Ken! Ken, come meet the two ladies who moved into Martin's old place."

The broad northern accent neither Abby nor Lou could place, sounded harsh.

"What, the lezzas?"

Abby buried her face in the menu, while Lou looked indignantly at the stunned woman.

"Kindly tell your husband, we are *not* lesbians." Poker-faced, Lou's tone dripped ice.

Abby was surprised Lou hadn't exploded into one of her sarcastic rants, although she could see she was finding it difficult not to.

"I'm really sorry. He doesn't put his brain in gear before he opens his mouth." The woman apologised, introducing herself. "I'm Elaine and that silly twat in there's Ken. So how you finding the place?"

Before Lou or Abby had a chance to reply, said silly twat appeared, wearing a grimy apron with a large picture of a page three model emblazoned on the front. He lumbered over and stood at the entrance to the booth, his face fixed with an arrogant grin. He was everything Lou had imagined. *Mr Steroid Head.*

Standing no more than 5ft 7, Ken had dark brown, heavily receding hair, greying at the temples. His head looked too small for his body, almost as if someone had superglued it onto the thick, tanned, crinkly bull neck perched on a pair of jumbo shoulders. His arms were enormous. All bulging biceps and lavish sleeve tattoos, shown off as he'd intended against a surprisingly spotless white vest top. Lou knew beneath the togs lurked pumped-up pecs, as she could clearly see from his cocky stance that his chest was colossal. The apron was too long so she couldn't define the shape of his legs, but no doubt they were as puffed up as the rest of him. She could see the bottoms of tracksuit pants and a pair of semi-decent trainers covering smallish feet.

"Alright, ladies," he sneered, flexing his biceps and retaining that ridiculous Cheshire cat grin. It snaked all the way up his face, starting at flared nostrils on a squat, piggy nose, slithering into brown, heavily creased eyes sheltered by coarse, untamed eyebrows, and ending in a brow so furrowed, Abby could use it to plant her veg. He suddenly stopped flexing and began scratching his backside.

Within seconds, Abby was quite happy to let him carry on believing they were gay. Half an hour later, after listening to how the couple hated the country, the people, the food, the music, the customs, Lou piped up.

"So ... remind me why you came to Spain?"

Abby bit her top lip and ducked her head at Lou's cutting remark.

Lou knew the question was caustic, but in her opinion, relevant. In thirty minutes of windbag gibbering, neither Elaine, nor her ego-fuelled husband, had given one good reason why they'd left England. All they'd done was whine.

Ken swung his arm around as if Lou were an idiot as well as a lesbian. "All this, luv and the sun, of course."

"We never see the bleedin' sun," his wife grumbled.

Lou bit her tongue. She particularly disliked the term 'luv' when used in the way Ken had used it. It was overworked, overfamiliar, and unfortunately, over here! In her opinion, one of those sentiments that didn't quite cut it, and irritated the fuck out of her when uttered by a conceited, dense tosspot suffering from short man syndrome.

The girls gave Elaine their food order and eventually, after what seemed an interminable wait, two large platters arrived. As well as serving frozen chips, and fish in soggy batter, Lou's whole plate was greasy. A small, limp lettuce leaf, tomato, which in an attempt to be artistically cut looked as if it had been hacked to death with a chain-saw, and huge wedges of onion instead of thinly cut slices, finished off the not so culinary delight.

In a fit of nostalgia, Abby had ordered shepherd's pie. She was severely disappointed with fatty mince under a tepid blanket of anaemic, lumpy mash, and barely warm frozen peas. The bland creation was crammed next to a pile of frozen chips.

"Excuse me!" she called to Elaine, currently buzzing round a young couple who'd just walked in. "I didn't order chips."

A confused Elaine looked round. "That's OK, duck. Doesn't matter what you order, all our food comes with chips."

"Hmm." Lou snorted, discreetly spitting out a mouthful of fish laced with bones. "They missed a trick here. Definitely chose the wrong name for this gaffe. They should have called it Chips with Everything."

"Hey, snap. My thoughts exactly," Abby agreed. "What a shambles. I've had enough of this muck." She flung her cutlery onto the plate of half-eaten food.

A less than impressed Lou followed suit.

34

Abby had dialled his number and hung up three times before she finally croaked "Hi" down the phone to Paul.

Amazingly, he recognised her voice and seemed genuinely happy to hear from her. They'd arranged a date and he was arriving in an hour. She was in her lovely Moroccan-styled bathroom, razor in hand

Tweetie Pie sat grooming herself outside the slightly open door so Chester must be outside, probably grabbing more than forty winks in a shaded place.

Gazing at the overgrown, chestnut forest between her legs, Abby considered her own grooming. She frowned. It wasn't as bad as it had been back in England. Obviously, she'd had to give it a bit of a trim – spiders' legs peeking out of bikini bottoms was so not cool – but it still looked as if an episode of *Bear Grylls Survivor* could be filmed down there. She wondered what Paul preferred. Not that she was banking on sleeping with the guy but hey, as the famous Scout motto says, *Be Prepared*.

The trouble was there was just so much choice nowadays. When she was young, a bit of conditioner and a weekly trim and comb through were sufficient, just in case you got lucky with the spotty guy from Warrington at the student union disco on Friday night. These days, there was shaving, creams, waxing, Brazilians, Hollywoods, even actual topiary with shaping, dying, and most intriguing of all, Paisley had informed her, in a rare boyfriend's mother/Bitch moment, vajazzles! Apparently, all the celebs had them and if it was good enough for *TOWIE* and *Geordie Shore* Paisley gabbled, she might get one herself.

Abby had shuddered inwardly, but she would have bet money that Sugar Tits Janice had a vajazzle. The process all sounded too itchy and painful, not to mention extremely expensive. It couldn't be a quick process. Surely gluing tiny jewels onto your bare essentials took up so much time, time you would never get back. What woman would want to spend hours having their fanny decked with diamonds? Well, fake ones anyway. Apparently, there was even a *Rate my Vajazzle* Facebook page and she was sure there was likely a celebrity reality show in the planning stages.

Personal grooming had gone by the wayside since Mark, who incidentally had preferred a small landing strip. There had been no need for pussy fussing. Thankfully, her eyebrows didn't need much attention. Nails were attractively short and free from varnish, legs, and underarms mowed when necessary during the summer months. She had never had a spray tan or, God forbid, anal bleaching. Young girls today must be exceptionally high maintenance.

Finally, she decided on a trim and backcomb, and after Vidal Sassooning her lady garden, scuttled off in search of moisturiser. Hearing a commotion downstairs, she stuck her head over the galleried landing.

"What's up?" She yelled.

"Tweetie's caught a mouse," Lou shrieked.

Abby giggled as she witnessed Lou, brandishing a broom, chasing the cat across the hallway. She scurried back into the bathroom noticing the clump of pubes had disappeared from the bathtub.

No, Lou, not a mouse. Tweetie Pie's caught a pussy!

35

Almost an hour later, Abby stood critically in front of a full-length mirror.

Since arriving in Spain, she'd developed a deep golden tan, and all the trips up and down that bloody hill had worked wonders for her legs. The drawn, tired face she remembered looking back at her a few weeks ago had disappeared. Instead, her eyes sparkled, and outdoor living had given her face a glow that only required a flick of blusher to enhance it. She finished smoky eyeshadow off with a couple of coats of mascara, and her hair tumbling around her shoulders in a tousled mass of curls gave her a just-out-of-bed sexy look. *She hoped.*

The dress she'd chosen to wear, she made herself. Of diaphanous material in a dark paisley pattern of swirling teal, purple, and gold, the deep V neckline gathered under the bust, draped around her curves, and sat just above her knees. For the first time in years, she felt good about herself. She knew Paul wasn't going to be 'the one'. In fact, she had her suspicions he might even be married, but she was damn well going to enjoy him while it lasted. Grabbing a shawl, she checked her teeth for spinach, or any other lurking gremlins, sprayed a squirt of Angel, and trotted downstairs to await his arrival.

Lou was in the kitchen doing the nightly pet check for tics when Abby walked in. What a difference a few weeks made. Standing before her, she looked lovely ... and so healthy.

"I've walked the dogs and the chickens are all cooped up." Lou smiled. "You look fabulous. Come on then, Anthea ... give us a twirl."

Abby looked puzzled. "Anthea?"

"Yeah. Anthea Redfern ... years ago ... *The Generation Game*. Mr Forsyth ... Brucie ... you know, one of your faves. When he introduced Anthea to the audience, she floated on stage and he'd ask her to twirl to show off her gown. Remember?"

"Oh, yes. Course I do." Abby grinned, "The old grey matter isn't working, that's the problem. I'm so nervous. It's ages since I've been on a date. Well, here goes." She twirled round, almost keeling over into a large plant pot. "What d'you think?"

"Superb! And your choice of undies is simply divine. Small and sexy, yet not too skimpy, which helps keep their subtlety."

"What?" Abby squealed.

"I'm no Coco Chanel, and I've heard of dare to bare, but that's taking it a knicker elastic too far."

"Stop talking in riddles, Lou. What—"

"Your dress, Abby," Lou interrupted, smirking. "I'm sure it would look *so* much better if it wasn't stuffed down the back of your undies."

"Shit! What an idiot." Flustered, Abby grabbed the dress and pulled it upwards. "Give me a hand, will you?"

Smirking, Lou helped her friend rearrange the dress. "There. Perfect."

"Told you I was nervous. Oh, God, I think that's him," Abby muttered, as she heard a knock.

"Stop panicking, you'll be fine," Lou called, scurrying to answer the door.

Paul certainly did have a body that made you want to get a gym card and actually use it, Lou thought as she let him in. He was dressed in pristine white shirt, slim jeans, and black loafers. She could smell the heady aroma of Joop. She had a 'thing' for bums, and boy, his filled his pants wonderfully. She followed him through to the kitchen, making rude gestures and rolling her eyes behind his back, much to Abby's amusement.

"So where you two lovebirds off to?" Lou asked, wrinkling her nose as she caught a slight whiff of something unpleasant. She spotted Chester under the table and liberally sprayed the room with Febreze before the smell of dog fart ruined the mood.

"There's a little restaurant I know of in the mountains. I thought we'd go there." Paul leaned casually against the worktop eyeing Abby appreciatively.

"Sounds lovely," Abby murmured.

"I'll second that," Lou agreed.

Feeling extremely shy, Abby lowered her eyelashes as Paul took her hand and led her out of the house.

"Enjoy!" yelled Lou as the couple disappeared. And for pity's sake, Abby, keep your dress out of your knickers. Bless her.

Hoping they had a lovely evening, she giggled and shook her head at Abby's bumbling antics while making haste to the kitchen to expel the smell of any fluffs dropped by Chester.

❧ 36 ❧

Lou poured herself a brandy and sank into the sofa. She was curling her legs under her when Eduardo knocked on the door.

"Hola, Lou. I've brought these for Abby." He clutched a stack of gardening books to his chest.

"Come in, come in." She flung the door open wide, thankful she'd eliminated the nasty niff in the kitchen. *No doubt about it, Chester was a champion windbreaker.*

Eduardo stood uncomfortably in the hallway looking down at his feet.

"Abby's out, but do come in and have a drink. I've just poured a brandy."

He followed her into the sitting room and took the proffered drink, swirling the honey liquid round the huge balloon glass.

"I forget. She is on her hot date." He laughed, showing straight white teeth.

For the first time, Lou noticed how handsome he was in an understated way. Very Marcus Wareing. They hadn't talked properly before, and Lou found herself laughing hard and enjoying his company as he recited funny stories about different villagers. The conversation then turned to Abby. They both said they hoped she was having a good time.

"She's probably spilled something down her cleavage or tripped and gone face first into the paella." Lou chuckled.

"Yes, she can be a little clumsy, can't she?" Eduardo laughed, remembering Abby falling over her flip-flops and practically impaling herself on one of his large cacti the previous week.

"A little? You're too kind, Eduardo," Lou grinned. "She can be a walking disaster at times, but I wouldn't have her any other way."

The phone rang and he stood to leave indicating that she should answer and he would see himself out. She thanked him, promised to give the books to Abby, and answered the phone as she heard Eduardo close the door. The caller was Juan asking if she'd thought about their conversation the previous evening. Telling him she would phone him tomorrow, she placed the receiver in its cradle and chewed over his suggestion.

She had started flamenco class purely for flirtatious reasons, but quickly realised she was no good. Her normally icy personality didn't sit well with the passionate music and dance and, after stepping on Juan's toes once too often, and becoming increasingly annoyed as his hands roamed all over Mercedes, a barbie look-a-likey with a wonky eye and heavy make-up, she knew she wouldn't be returning.

Sitting on the terrace of Juan's expensive villa afterwards, they had talked into the early hours. He spoke of investments he'd made that enabled him to have the palatial home and fancy cars, and she told him about her dreams for the future, wanting to help the dog shelter, and her worries that the money she'd won wasn't enough to sustain her forever.

She vaguely remembered him offering to help – something about a tip for a future investment, which was going to make him filthy rich. He asked if she'd like to come on board, but by then she'd sank a bottle of champagne, the long elegant fingers of his left hand were caressing her collarbone as he cajoled her to return the favour, and the temptation to stroke something that had just popped up between them proved too hard to resist. He knew how to satisfy her for sure.

She was falling for him. Hard.

She wondered how Abby's date was going. He was a looker that Paul, but she knew he worked all over Spain and hoped Abby wouldn't get hurt. They were probably sitting gazing into each other's eyes whispering sweet nothings. *Sod that!*

Deciding on an early night, Lou bundled up Tweetie Pie heaving the hefty puss into the crook of her right arm, swept a less weighty Sylvester up with her left hand, and headed for her bedroom.

37

Abby woke with her head throbbing as if Lemmy had taken up residence and was having a domestic with Ozzy Osborne.

Despite the pain, she still managed a happy smile as she felt the pleasant ache between her thighs. Yawning, she stretched languidly remembering their lovemaking. Paul had certainly sorted out her plumbing that's for sure. She hadn't screamed like that since her toe got stuck in a mousetrap last summer. He'd left around six that morning, about an hour after he'd stopped blowing her mind. Kissing her deeply, he told her he was going to Madrid on a job but promised to call later. She'd turned over, closed her eyes, and drifted off again.

Purring like a contented kitten, she stretched again and looked at the clock: 10:04. Lou had said she would walk the dogs this morning as she was rising early to discuss important fiesta arrangements with the crows, which meant Abby had the house to herself.

Daydreaming about last night, her mind fixed on the gorgeous restaurant they'd reached via a network of twisting, winding roads. The magical hideaway surrounded by bright lanterns and built into the caves, had a low roof, which gave an alluring, intimate feel. The food had been amazing, each dish an erotic, sublime experience. Paul fed her scrumptious oysters, followed by asparagus spears wrapped in slivers of salty Ibérico ham dipped in rich, golden duck egg yolks, and finally, she'd floated to paradise feasting on the most delectable lemon mousse she'd ever tasted.

She told him about her life back in the UK, her sweet white wine taking on a bitter taste as she mentioned her cheating ex and his squeeze. He laughed as she described Sugar Tits, her love of all things pink, and ever inflating boobs.

Paul's past wasn't much better. He'd recently left his wife after eighteen years of marriage; they too married young due to an unplanned pregnancy. *Condom sales must have been well down in the nineties.* He obviously adored his daughter, his beautiful eyes brimming with tears as he explained how his wife, a control freak and insanely jealous, had turned his girl against him since the split.

"So you don't see her at all?" Abby covered his hand with hers. She couldn't imagine not seeing her boys.

"No. I've phoned, sent emails and text messages, but she's made it clear, she wants nothing to do with me. God knows what her mother's told her."

"That's awful. I can't stand women who use kids as weapons."

Much as Abby disliked Mark, she had never stopped him seeing Andrew or Daniel.

"Rea was always high maintenance. We met at school ... even then she would fly into a jealous rage if I so much as looked at another girl. Looking back, it was probably why she was so keen to move over here, away from the competition, not that there was any. I only had eyes for her." The smile he gave was sad, rueful.

Abby squeezed his hand. If he'd looked anywhere near as good then as he did now, she would have betted his ex would've had to fight off the competition with a big stick.

The conversation had moved on from their respective exes to lighter subjects, becoming flirtier as the evening wore on. They were standing up to leave when he leaned over, barely brushing her lips with his. The faint taste of lemon and sexy smell of aftershave made her tremble in anticipation.

Reaching over for the bottle of water she kept on the bedside table, she frowned realising it wasn't there. *Damn.* She needed a drink. Sitting up, she noticed Paul had left his shirt. He must have left wearing the T-shirt he'd had on underneath. She could smell him as she pulled on the shirt. A fresh, manly aroma with a hint of Joop.

Jumping out of bed, Abby opened the door and skipped past a seriously disgruntled Chester who banished from the bedroom, had made himself comfortable on the landing. Gloating, she bent down and started singing *I'm Sexy and I Know It,* giggling as she carried on down the stairs, making up her own words, dry humping the bannister, and gyrating her hips as if she were actually in the music video.

"Wiggle, jiggle, giggle, yeah!"

Suggestively dancing down the last few stairs, Abby stumbled over the shoes resting on the second step from the bottom, which she'd hurriedly removed the previous night. Landing with a thump on the cool tiled floor, she was stunned to see Lou and two of the crows sitting eyeing her from the lounge area.

Trying desperately to hold the shirt together — she didn't know why because the women had already had a bird's-eye view of her freshly groomed bush and attempting to conceal her boobs was like closing the stable door after the horse had bolted — she backed away. As she did, she clocked Carmen, the third crow coming from the kitchen with a glass of water. As she spotted Abby, the glass slipped through her fingers and shattered on the floor. The others turned at the sound of the clatter, leaving a reddened, mortified Abby fleeing up the stairs, grabbing the shoes as she ran.

She wouldn't be able to show her face in the village for a while and knew, when the crows resumed their position next to the fountain, the animated conversation would probably be about her.

38

With each passing day, the heat steadily increased.

Lou and Abby spent a lot of time at the dog shelter. Three of the original dogs they'd fostered had found their forever homes. Flash had gone to an elderly couple in Denmark, Pia to a family in Valencia, and a young woman from Suffolk had rescued Jackdaw. Luna, as Abby predicted, spent more time in the house with Lou than in her kennel and Lou didn't promote her on the Facebook page. The German Shepherd had an amiable relationship with the cats and even Chester seemed to like her, well, as much as Chester liked anyone or anything, be it man, beast, or inanimate objects.

The word seemed to have circulated in the area about the girls' rescue efforts and as well as the dogs, Abby had gained two more chickens, which Sylvia had saved from a farm while picking up a neglected Collie. After a week or so of being introduced, and attacked at every opportunity by the established ladies, Erin Brokovich and Maria von Trapp became part of the flock. Good layers, they often sat together in an old suitcase Abby had provided, clucking their egg-laying song.

The mosquitoes and sand flies were a constant nuisance no matter how many citronella candles Abby purchased and burned, so Lou and she were having a rare night in together. Lounging in vests and shorts, the air-conditioning a welcome relief, they drank copious amounts of red wine and enjoyed catching up with *Paul O'Grady: For the Love of Dogs*. The TV was rarely on, but they recorded the odd series on satellite for just such evenings.

Giggling about their various mishaps since moving, especially Abby's debacle on the stairs and making plans for the coming months, Lou suddenly sat up.

"Did you hear that?"

"What?" Abby nervously placed her empty wineglass on the coffee table.

Recently, there had been an increase in crime in southern Spain. Many desperate refugees were coming over from Africa and there had been stories of burglaries nearby.

"Shh! Listen."

Lou turned the volume down and they both strained their ears.

Abby jumped when a loud braying disturbed the silence. "What was that?"

With Lou behind her brandishing an empty wine bottle, Abby edged to the front door opening it an inch or so. Tied to the porch stood a skinny old donkey, head hanging low. Abby could see his ribs clearly, and bare patches of skin poked through dusty, matted silver grey fur where heavy panniers must've dug into his skin.

"It's bleedin' Eyeore," Lou giggled, squinting through wine goggles.

"Oh look, Lou." Tears sprung to Abby's eyes as she rushed outside to examine the sad looking creature.

Running her hands up and down his legs then over his body and head, Abby was relieved to discover that he didn't appear to be injured, just exhausted and badly neglected. He gazed at her through eyelashes Cheryl Cole would be proud of before hanging his head forlornly. A crudely cut square of cardboard hung round his neck displaying a single word. *Santos.*

"Who would tie a bloody donkey up outside someone's house?" Lou was flabbergasted at the audacity of people and went towards the gate looking up and down the road in the hope of sighting the cheeky sod.

"He won't move," Abby wailed.

She was gently trying to cajole Santos around the house towards the kennels and outbuildings but he was having none of it and wouldn't budge. Ears laid flat, he lifted his head and bared large, yellow teeth.

"That'll be right. Even the bloody donkey's laughing at me." She groaned.

Tugging the frayed rope, Abby tried once more to move the stubborn animal. Coming up from behind him, Lou gently slapped the donkey on his rump. Suddenly, grabbing the piece of card showing his name, Santos charged up the steps through the front door and straight into the kitchen. Tweetie, who was curled up on top of the range snoozing, jumped up hissing, spitting, and eventually growling, as the beast charged into the room in full voice.

"Fuck's sake, Abby! We are not leaving that smelly creature in the kitchen all night." Lou was incensed as she staggered into the house.

"Of course we aren't. Stop wittering on, will you. I just need something to persuade him with."

Grabbing a carrot from the vegetable rack, she proceeded to tempt Santos through the back door and around to the kennels. The goats were peering curiously through their fence at the new arrival and the two dogs currently in residence – Hugo, a chocolate Lab with a severe flatulence problem to rival Chester, and Skip, a schizo Jack Russell – started barking to the point of exploding.

Abby envisioned that as per, this could end up with her on her arse so was pleasantly surprised when she felt the little donkey nuzzling her shoulder as she bent to unlock the door to his stable.

"Aw, you're such a sweetie." She led him in and filled the feeding troughs with hay and water. She had a lovely warm feeling inside when she saw him bare his teeth, as this time she was sure he was smiling and thanking her.

After settling the dogs and feeling pleased with herself, she half-walked, half-stumbled back to the house where Lou was clearing up and doing her own version of Salome's *Dance of the Seven Veils*, prancing round the kitchen with a can of air freshener.

"So we have a donkey now, do we?" Lou humphed.

"Looks that way." She knew Lou didn't mean her comment to come across in a bad way.

"Tell you what, I'm half expecting Val Doonican to pop up sometime soon and burst into song. *Paddy McGinty's Goat, Delaney's Donkey.* What next? Don't think he ever croaked a tune about chickens, or dogs, or cats, but don't quote me on that."

Abby giggled, knowing Lou was as soft as she was where animals were concerned. Out of habit, her hand strayed to the locket around her neck containing pictures of the boys when they were kids. Her heart flipped. It wasn't there. She remembered the snuffling outside and puffed out a dramatic sigh. "That bloody donkey's eaten my locket!" She exclaimed.

"Just another night in here then." Lou roared with laughter as she made her way to bed.

"Yeah." Abby whispered, smiling widely.

39

The fiesta plans were coming along nicely and as spring rolled into summer, Lou continued to see Juan.

Although he seemed to disappear on business regularly, she was happy with how the relationship was moving along. She'd given the green light for the joint investment he had talked about, which should start showing profit by September he'd advised. She undertook a bundle of work for the dog rescue admin/fund raising with the ex-pat community in the nearby towns, and consequently, bagged invites to various charity shindigs around the Costa. Overall, she was becoming familiar with the party scene, tennis clubs, and golf resorts.

As her vegetable plot matured, Abby spent a lot of time in the outdoor kitchen experimenting with various recipes for jams and chutneys. Peach with champagne and cinnamon was a current favourite, and her chilli, lime, and garlic chutney was apparently delicious with calamari. Not that Lou would be tasting calamari to find out, she declared, after returning from a women's institute lunch, having raised over £400 for the shelter to find Abby up to her armpits in a vat of lemons for her next concoction – lemon and lavender jelly. Wrinkling her nose, and not in a good way, she plonked down on the sun lounger.

"Eduardo tells me you've enquired about a market stall?"

Abby smiled. Lou and Eduardo seemed to be getting on well lately. He was so much nicer than the slimy Juan-ker and she knew the dapper little gentleman worshipped Lou. Bringing a small spoon to her lips, she grimaced slightly. *God, these recipes took an age to perfect at times.*

"Yeah," Abby said, "We already have too many eggs, and I'm hoping for a big harvest of veggies in the autumn. We won't use all this ourselves, especially the fruit and olives. Next year, I'm going to start selling goat's cheese and Eduardo is having some of his pigs slaughtered in November. We're gonna have a go at chorizo."

She'd said the last words with sadness, but that was the way of life in the countryside and had been for years. The seasons were full of parties and events, from the slaughter of pigs (Matanzas), to the planting of garlic, there was always a celebration at someone's home or in the village square with liberal amounts of food and wine. Abby was actually surprised she hadn't piled on the pounds since she'd arrived.

Lou poured her a glass of wine and sauntered over to stand by her side. "Are you glad we came?"

The pungent aroma of lemons wafted on the breeze as Abby gave her a hug. "Oh, yes!" She enthused. "It's a dream come true. I've never been happier."

40

The screams that stirred Abby were the worst she'd ever heard and that included her giving birth to two nine pound babies. Feeling around frantically in the dark for the lamp, about to jump from the bed and charge downstairs, she froze. *Jeez. Sounded as if someone was slaughtering some poor sod. Oh, fuck. Lou!*

Dragged from slumber Chester started barking, which was a rarity in itself. Abby couldn't move and her brain was struggling desperately to make sense of the situation. Someone was obviously slaying Lou in her bed and if she went downstairs, she would likely get it too. But she couldn't just sit up here doing nothing. When they'd done with Lou, the intruder – or maybe a gang – would come upstairs anyway and probably rape and kill her. And the animals. She needed to protect them.

Pushing Chester off the end of the bed, she grabbed a large vase, seized her phone, and with trembling fingers punched Eduardo's number. *Answer. Oh, please, Eduardo, answer.*

Finally, she heard his calm, groggy voice. "Abby, is that you? It's three-thirty in the morning. What's wrong?"

"I think Lou's being murdered, and I'm too scared to go downstairs," she gabbled, panic in her voice. She began to sob down the phone. "Please help."

"Don't do anything. I'm coming up now ... just stay where you are."

Eduardo slammed the phone down and she imagined him dragging on his clothes and puffing his way up the lane. Oh, she couldn't just stay up here. Lou was her best friend and God knew what was happening. The screams were still coming loud, hysterical. After what seemed an eternity, but was likely only a few minutes, she took stock and ventured down the stairs.

"I'm coming, Lou and I've phoned the police!" she shouted bravely.

Pushing open Lou's bedroom door, Abby was staggered to see her still crouched on the bed clinging to her headboard, screeching like a loon but thankfully alone.

"Lou, what the hell's wrong with you?" Feeling such a plum because she'd suspected sinister goings on and had called Eduardo (thank God, not the police), Abby strode over to Lou wondering what had spooked her friend. "Lou! What's the matter? Have you had a nightmare?"

Lou couldn't breathe, nor talk. Abby noticed Sylvester concentrating on something in the corner in a way that shredded her nerves further. *Oh, no*, though it did enter her head that she, not Lou, was the scaredey cat when it came to bugs so probably not a cockroach or the like then.

She looked in the direction of Lou's pointed finger, to where Sylvester sat entranced in a Mexican standoff with the most terrifying creature Abby had ever seen. Seemingly, a foot in length with vivid yellow and black stripes, the 'thing' looked as if it had just shot straight out of a horror film. Friend or not, Abby rapidly began backing up out of the bedroom.

"Sylvester, here puss!" she bawled.

As much as Chester didn't like the tuxedo terrorist, she didn't want to see him eaten by that horrible creature.

"Sylly, come here. Sylvester!"

Abby's patience with the stubborn feline was wearing thin. Hackles raised, he crouched in ambush position growling incessantly, his long, thick tail indignantly swishing from side to side. Abby's patience was also wearing thin with Lou who carried on shrieking.

"Lou, you're making things worse. Will you stop making that fucking racket and come over here. We'll shut the door 'til Eduardo comes."

"No chance. I'm not leaving Sylly. No way! What if it escapes? It could run anywhere in the house," she blubbered incoherently. "The ugly thing was in the bed. It could end up anywhere if we bugger off and close the door. Anyway, I refuse to leave my boy. If anything happens to him, I'll never forgive myself."

Bursting into tears again, she backed farther up to the headboard, a look of terror on her face. The colour of her skin had changed from glowing tan to sickly pale.

"Why would anything happen to him?" Abby asked, dread creeping in. "Did it bite you?" She had visions of Lou's head swelling up and dropping off.

"Don't be so stupid, Abby. If you can't think of anything intelligent to say, then shut the fuck up! Did it bite me? What kind of question's that?"

"*Well I don't know,*" Abby retorted, wishing she had the guts to pick the thing up and fling it at her hysterical friend. That would give her a reason to squeal. "I think it's kind of a smart question. I don't know what happened, I wasn't here. So what *did* happen?"

Lou proceeded to tell the tale. "Sylvester was on the bed pouncing on something and woke me up. When I switched on the lamp, the *something* was wriggling around in the sheet. I didn't have a clue what it was, went into a blind panic, and flung it over there."

A loud hammering startled Abby. Swiftly, she ran to open the front door. Eduardo stood there, still composed, but genuinely concerned.

"Thank God, you're here!" Abby blasted. "You have to kill it ... you have to ... it's horrible." She stumbled over her words,

"Calm down, Abby. May I come in, please? I won't be able to do anything standing here."

"Oops, sorry," she apologised, quickly stepping aside to allow Eduardo access to the villa.

"Hurry, I don't want the thing escaping."

Realising this was some sort of insect related emergency, of which there had been several since Lou and Abby moved next door, Eduardo strode towards the bedroom. He barged in, pretending not to notice a half-naked Lou still overwrought and shaking like a camel shitting razor blades. Pushing an agitated Sylvester to one side and shooing him away, he opened the French doors and managed to shepherd the giant centipede outside.

"Please, do not worry. It is only an escolopendra. We see these all the time here. They like a warm bedroom." He glanced at Lou thinking he wouldn't say no to Lou's warm bed, never mind her bedroom.

Vowing to carry out a thorough nightly bed check for unwanted intruders from that moment on, Abby left Eduardo to calm down the usually unflappable Lou and scurried off to fetch the brandy.

She liberally poured the golden liquid into three large balloon glasses then traipsed back to Lou's bedroom chuckling to herself as she recalled an unforgettable occasion harking back to their university days. The incident occurred while she and Lou were on a night out. Feeling peckish, the girls decided they needed food and agreed on a *Subway* sandwich. Abby recalled how Lou's choice of words in the joint had the punters in hysterics and resulted in the girls defining the episode as 'one of those never-to-be-repeated moments.'

In her mind's eye, Abby could see her and Lou standing in the crowded deli. After choosing her filling, and when asked if she wanted six inches or a foot long, Lou had proclaimed, in a deep, booming voice that nothing short of twelve inches would do.

Following the centipede fiasco, Abby mischievously wondered if Lou still felt the same.

41

Abby's Spanish was improving. Although she could understand more than she could say, she was still able to hold a basic conversation with relative ease. Lou, however, still carried a phrase-book wherever she went and had palpitations thinking back to the incident in the village restaurant where she had only recently dared to show her face again, mainly because the handsome waiter had moved on to Marbella.

Lou counted her blessings in having made a good friend in Carmen, the youngest of the three crows. She'd been married to Isabella's brother, and widowed the year before when he'd been gored in a bull-fighting incident. He'd been a bully, beating her regularly and, she whispered to Lou when her sister-in-law was out of earshot, she wished the bull had received a medal for a job well done. There would have been no fiesta talk without Carmen.

Abby had acquired an additional three female goats – Maudie, and Misses Tutti, and Frutti, in keeping with the To Kill a Mockingbird theme. The three nannies had had babies recently so could be milked immediately.

She finally started making her goat's cheese, once again her imagination running wild with flavourings. Lemon and walnut, one rolled in heady spices to make a Morrocan style crust, and figs and honey. No great lover of Goats' cheese Lou actually began to fear Abby coming towards her armed with a spoon. To be fair, eventually most of her concoctions became more than edible and there was even talk of a future cookbook. Eduardo was never far away, the two of them trawling through old-fashioned recipe books and peeling piles of peppers and onions engaged in fascinating, thought-provoking food conversation, not!

Milking the goats was an art in itself and one Lou was never going to get the hang of, for sure. The first time she tried, the cantankerous Maudie gave her a sharp kick and she ended up drenched in warm milk and surrounded by flies. In contrast, Abby was a dab hand. Early each morning would find her sitting on a minute stool, carefully, productively pulling on teats, belting out Justin Bieber songs as the sound of milk squirted rhythmically into a metal pail. With his head hanging over the fence, and eyelashes fluttering, the adorable Santos hee-hawed the chorus of each song, a damn sight better than Justin Bieber in Lou's opinion.

42

Arriving back from a day at the dog shelter, Lou plonked a shopping bag on the table. She was expecting Juan shortly and had spent far too long in the village caught up in chatting to Carmen and Sophia.

Abby had left a note saying she was going to Eduardo's and wouldn't be back till late, which was perfect for Lou's planned seduction. The chorizo conversations must be scintillating, either that or she must be checking out another sausage she thought, while enjoying a little snigger to herself.

Abby had lodged the note under a large kilner jar of what appeared to be a new flavour of chutney. Beetroot and horseradish stated a neatly written pile of labels. Next to it, there was a large pink stain on the paper, which confirmed beetroot was definitely in the mix. She couldn't read the rest of the note. Something about Jenny and Clare, how she must've missed a phone call and would call tomorrow and have a good old natter. The pair must be back from their honeymoon by now.

Taking out a large tub of prawns, two bottles of Chablis, and a long crusty baguette from the bag, Lou poured a glass to take with her for a shorter than planned soak in the tub. An hour later, after painting her nails and smothering herself in *The Body Shop's* Indian Night Jasmine body lotion, a Christmas present from Abby, she surveyed her handiwork in the bedroom. Scented candles were dotted around discreetly providing a romantic feel. Fresh linen adorned the bed below the newly purchased delicate net to keep out mosquitoes and hopefully, centipedes.

A wine cooler sat on the bedside table chilling a bottle of the white wine she'd bought. There was also a bottle of massage oil fragranced with jasmine, and a silk tie. Lou intended on getting naughty and had rifled through the contents of the contentious box she and Abby had wrangled over back in the UK before departing.

Dressed for the occasion in a red satin basque, which deliciously hugged her slim figure and enhanced her small breasts, Lou pulled on a pair of black Cuban-heeled seamed silk stockings and fastened them onto suspenders lying taut against her long, tanned legs. Incredibly high black velvet stilettos completed the look. She piled her hair on top of her head and painted her face with the expertise of a make-up artist. The full-length mirror told her she looked incredibly sexy and she felt it.

The doorbell interrupted her reverie and she sashayed across the hall, flinging the door wide open and standing one hand on hip for maximum impact.

"*Ooh la la*. Guess Abby forgot to mention we'd be dropping by." Jenny smirked at Lou's astonished face.

"Or maybe she did." The sound of a demented mule could have competed with Clare's guffaw as she eyed up Lou, winking suggestively.

"Erm, err ... I was expecting a friend," Lou stammered, face burning.

"Is that him?" Jenny pointed at Juan who was walking towards them with a bottle of fine champagne and an enormous bunch of exotic flowers.

Lou nodded. Sassily dressed in the guise of a lady of the night, she made the introductions feeling ridiculous in her get-up. She rushed back indoors to grab a robe while the three of them made their way to the pool area and the promise of wine and food.

As Lou entered the kitchen she spotted Sylvester, head deep in the tub of prawns. Agitated, she snapped at him. Paying no heed, he continued munching his way through one of his favourite nibbles. Lou gave a wry smile. *That's the food cancelled then.*

Plonking herself next to Juan with the chilled bottle of wine and a takeaway menu she laughed, thinking at least her bedroom was going to see some action tonight even if she wasn't getting any.

Scouring the menu, Lou piped up, "Well, girls, something must have told me you were coming as I've made up the honeymoon suite. Enjoy."

43

Jenny and Clare stayed for three days. Apparently, their honeymoon had ended in Morocco and they'd extended it for a few days so they could visit Abby and Lou. There had been a mix-up in the email they'd sent and Abby had thought they were arriving at nine the following morning, so was naturally surprised to see the foursome after returning from Eduardo's, especially Juan-ker on full charm offensive having a jolly old time and tucking into pizza.

It was lovely hearing about Jenny and Clare's adventures travelling round Africa. The girls' arrival also doubled as a little break for Abby and Lou while their friends were in residence. Obviously, the animals still needed looking after, but Abby and Lou took some time out and accompanied Jenny and Clare on a lovely picnic at a little deserted cove nearby.

Jenny showed Abby their wedding photos on her phone while Lou and Clare swam in the calm waters.

"Watch out for jellyfish!" Abby shouted. "Or those giant sea centipedes."

Lou's face took on a look of panic and she immediately swam for shore.

Creasing up laughing and gasping for breath, Abby nudged Jenny.

"Good job there's not a bloody shark."

She gave Jenny a blow-by-blow account of the centipede incident, which made Jenny hoot. By the time Lou stomped up the beach, they were both rolling about clutching their sides.

"You do realise that dog is eating the sandwiches," Lou chided, pushing Chester aside and grabbing a bottle of water from the cooler.

"Bad dog!" Abby scolded, wagging her finger at the felonious mutt gulping down the remainder of a ham roll.

"At least someone likes your chutney." Lou grinned. Her reward was a friendly punch in the arm.

The following morning everyone was up early and piled into the van by ten. Stopping to pick up Eduardo on the way, the hour's drive to Gibraltar was stress-free. Eduardo charmed the women, giving them a potted history of the area and pointing out places of interest along the way.

The queue at the border was horrific due to customs and the police introducing a permanent go-slow so they parked up and, after a frantic scrabble for passports, eventually walked across. Hopping on a bus, they were in the main street in five minutes.

Eduardo treated them all to lunch at a lovely seafood restaurant. Lou, put off by the display, where *Catch of the Day* not only stared but also seemed to be doing the *Hokey Cokey*. "I'll have the oxtail paella," she stated, sitting with her back to the fishy audience perusing the menu.

The rest of the group chose seafood and two bottles of crisp, slightly effervescent, refreshing house wine.

"This is the best meal I've ever tasted," confessed Jenny, as thirty minutes later she tucked into a large platter of marinated grilled mackerel.

"It *is* delicious," agreed Abby, mopping the juices from her fish tagine with a generous chunk of crusty bread.

Eduardo basked in the ladies' compliments while munching on razor clams and planning the rest of the day.

"First, we will go up in the cable car to see the Monos."

"Are they tame?" Lou wasn't keen on getting too close to the famous primates.

"You will be quite safe, my dear." Eduardo puffed out his chest, looking as if he would protect her from a charging rhino, never mind an inquisitive ape.

"I think he fancies her," Clare pointed out loudly to Abby.

Eduardo blushed and Lou pushed back her chair.

"Come on then, let's go be tourists for a day." Not waiting for an answer, Lou strolled outside and lit a cigarette.

The group spent the rest of the day visiting the sights. Eduardo's service as a monkey bouncer wasn't required as most of the animals kept their distance, lazily sunbathing and scratching their balls.

They visited St Michael's Cave, oohing and ahhing at its natural beauty. It was cool inside and the mineral formations were breathtaking. Eduardo, back in his tour guide persona, told the girls of the secret tunnel to Africa through which, according to legend, the apes had arrived. Jenny and Clare took hundreds of photos, and even Lou seemed fascinated.

Drinking a cup of British tea on the terrace of a quaint café, the friends ended the pleasing day looking out to the mountains of North Africa watching the sun go down.

44

The house seemed quiet after Jenny and Clare left, although Lou was pleased to be back in her own bed. Topping and tailing with Abby had not been conducive to getting a good night's kip. Abby fidgeted constantly and Lou woke up more than once with a toe jabbing her nose or a knee in her tit. In addition, she hadn't realised the extent of Chester's flatulence. The aroma of fat bulldog wind lingered in the air.

Abby was going to spend today making jam for her stall and had been clattering around for hours banging pots and pans and singing along to favourite *Kasabian* tracks, a marked improvement from Justin Bieber.

Containers full of various fruits – pears, figs, and cherries – littered the terraced area outside the kitchen door and Lou could see Santos looking longingly over the nearby fence. If there was one thing that donkey loved it was food. Lou smiled watching him fiddle with the catch on the gate. Grabbing her bag and van keys off the table, she sniffed the air appreciatively and smiled at Abby stirring a large pan of bubbling raspberries.

"I'm meeting Sylvia later. Gonna pick up the new dog she's rescued."

Apart from Luna, who had taken up permanent residence in the house, the girls currently had three dogs. Max, an overweight Rottweiler scared of everything juxtaposition with Fifi, a neurotic Chihuahua who would fight to the death and was scared of sweet FA. Chloe, a bouncy Boxer cross, completed the trio.

"Can you get some bread?" Abby looked round from her raspberries and took in Lou's smart attire. "Bit overdressed for the kennels aren't you?"

Nervously, Lou ran her hands over her pale blue shift dress. "I'm meeting Juan for lunch first."

Abby turned back to her boiling fruit. "Have a nice time," she mumbled, pulling a face.

She honestly couldn't fathom what Lou saw in that man. Mind you, Lou hadn't, and still didn't like Mark, so maybe it was she whose taste in men was shit. Maybe she was completely wrong about the swarthy creep, in which case, from now on she vowed to make more of an effort.

Abby preferred to make jam in the mornings as it was a sweaty job. She was trying out a couple of new recipes as well as making a batch of peach and amaretto jam, which was one of the best sellers at the Wednesday market on her recently acquired stall.

She hoped the raspberry daiquiri mixture she was experimenting with was going to prove just as popular, along with carrot cake, and pear and ginger flavour she still had to do. Rows of sterilised jars stood to attention like a glass army on the worktops, along with piles of pretty labels Eduardo had printed for her on his computer. She banished cats and dogs for safety and pilfering reasons. She was happy in her work, humming, mixing, and pouring.

From outside, a loud crash almost caused Abby to scald herself. Quickly turning off the heat, boiling fruit abandoned, she ran outside to see that Santos had somehow opened the gate and now had his head stuck in a tin bucket containing the remainder of her pears.

Thrashing about, he'd destroyed two plant pots – maybe more when she had a chance for a closer inspection – and was standing forlornly not knowing what to do. Abby was having a hard job keeping a straight face as speaking softly she approached him, and with a bit of manoeuvring, removed the bucket from his head. She escorted the braying donkey back to the field where the chickens and goats were all peering through the fence at the mayhem. She could have sworn they were laughing. Abby had spent many hours over the last few weeks making sure the goats and chickens were happy, providing them with various forms of entertainment. She'd placed large tree stumps and rocks for the goats to jump on and Eduardo had built them a climbing frame consisting of ramps and platforms from old wooden pallets. Two large tractor tyres, a scattering of barrels, and a couple of old suitcases completed the adventure playground. Abby threw numerous footballs in every morning. Even the chickens loved a game, and could often be found thundering round the enclosure in their own hilarious version of the *Copa del Rey*.

Santos trotted over to stand under his favourite tree. Glowering, he viciously swatted flies with his tail. Abby checked the catch on the gate, but felt sure Santos had learned his lesson, not guessing he would become the equine version of *The Great Escape's*, Hilts 'The Cooler King'.

Her pear and ginger jam would have to wait until another day.

45

Throughout the summer months, Elaine and Ken's daughter Kylie became a regular visitor to the villa. She loved dogs, and when she found out about Abby and Lou's rescue work was keen to help.

The new dog Lou had collected from Sylvia was named Fleur, a friendly, if decidedly unattractive mongrel. Her dirty looking, wiry coat, and distinct overbite were never going to win any beauty contests, but she was incredibly good-natured and also incredibly pregnant, so instead of an easily cared for three dogs plus Chester and Luna, Abby and Lou's lodgers now included nine odd-looking puppies who Kylie absolutely adored.

Both women became extremely fond of the girl. She didn't have many friends her own age and despite numerous piercings, tattoos, and goth style hair and make-up, she was actually an attractive, intelligent, sensitive young woman. The Higginbottoms had moved to Spain from Leeds when she was six. She'd found the move difficult and been badly bullied at school. Rebelling as a teenager, she'd taken drugs, slept around, and admitted giving her parents many sleepless nights, but she'd turned her life around and was hoping to go to college and study animal care.

Abby was surprised to learn Ken had been a prison warden back in the UK, while Elaine had swapped serving chips in a factory canteen for the same work in a sunnier clime.

"Mum never wanted to live in Spain ... it was always Dad's dream," Kylie told Abby one day while changing the pups' bedding.

Abby, hosing down the kennels decked out in old togs and wellies, listened with interest.

"He used to watch *Place in the Sun*," Kylie continued, "and go on and on about buying a place over here."

"D'you think they'll ever go back to England?" Abby was curious.

Elaine seemed disenchanted with the Mediterranean dream when she and Lou occasionally stopped at the Bus Stop for a chip fix. Andrew wouldn't be disenchanted, he'd love the place Abby thought with a grin, recalling her youngster's love of greasy takeaway grub.

"I know Mum would go back in a flash, but everything they have is tied up in the bar and no one's buying businesses over here at the moment."

"Hmm."

Abby remembered Elaine's tired, drawn face the last time they'd spoken, secretly hoping her and Lou didn't end up feeling, or looking the same. Mind you, neither of them was married to that tosspot Ken!

46

Abby left Kylie playing with the pups and went inside. She needed to Skype Andrew as they hadn't spoken for a few days and, surprise surprise, he and Paisley had apparently fallen out again. Nothing new there then. They'd been on and off more times than Sugar Tits's knickers. She didn't want the house descending into chaos without the pink-haired one in charge though.

Abby had recently decided to put the house on the market. The two boys were constantly complaining about huge bills so she'd promised them each a modern apartment in the city with the proceeds, which should leave her a bit of a nest egg too. To be fair, since she didn't have to hear her nasal Essex twang, or tidy away her omnipresent clutter, she could admit to being quite fond of Paisley. God knows, Andrew would be lucky to find anyone else who put up with his loutish behavior, smelly feet, and love of pizza.

She also needed to contact Clive, her editor, in relation to two manuscripts she'd sent him. The first was a jam/chutney recipe book, the second, an amusing anecdotal memoir seen through the eyes of her beloved Chester, about his life and feline nemeses in Spain.

Another string to her bow was an online business she'd started, selling pickles and preserves, which was doing exceptionally well. The downside was it usually meant a whole day standing in the queue in the Post Office, fanning herself with her legs crossed bursting for the loo. That aside, the success was becoming increasingly worth the faff and strain on her bladder.

Chester and Luna were lying side by side on the cool kitchen tiles glaring at Tweetie Pie leisurely grooming herself on the scrubbed pine table. No doubt, the missing Sylvester would be up to mischief somewhere nearby. *God it was hot.* Grabbing a bottle of water from the large overworked fridge, Abby sat down, opened her laptop, and clicked on emails.

Opening the mail from Clive, she read it twice before scaring Tweetie half to death as she jumped up, slammed the lid down, and rushed back outside, all thoughts of her miserable git of a son and his romantic woes forgotten. Eduardo had insisted on taking her out to celebrate her good news when she'd called him on the phone. Lou hadn't returned from tennis with Sylvia, and for some unknown reason Abby wanted to keep the email to herself for the time being.

Kylie helped her feed and put the animals inside, away from the onslaught of sandflies that plagued the sweltering evenings. Nevertheless, as the cicadas began their dusk chorus, Abby Sinclair couldn't remember being happier.

She waved goodbye to the young girl who was leaving to start her shift behind the bar, mixing cocktails, and fending off spotty drunken louts.

47

The restaurant Eduardo drove to in a neighbouring pueblo was delightful. There wasn't a tourist in sight.

Colourful vintage posters covering the walls featured long forgotten bullfights and dramatic flamenco. The restaurant's candle-light cast shadows onto the wall, giving life to the images. One poster from the 50s advertised Andalucia: a towel, large sunhat, sunglasses, and a pair of flip-flops lying on and around a lone deckchair on the beach. Footsteps in the sand, walking away from the chair brought a warm feeling to Abby's insides, as she imagined a bikini-clad girl strolling out in the sun to take a dip in the sea.

"I thought you would like it here." Eduardo smiled, pulling out a chair for Abby at the red and white checkered covered table.

Dragging her eyes away from the posters, she viewed the rest of her surroundings. She thought the slightly raised area on the opposite side of the room must be for dancing. Apart from herself and Eduardo, the only other diners were a young couple gazing into each other's eyes as their hands entwined across the table, but it was still early and the delicious aromas wafting out from the kitchen indicated the place wouldn't remain quiet for long.

Sitting down, Abby noticed Eduardo looked impeccable, as usual. In smart trousers, Italian leather designer shoes, and a crisply ironed shirt, she was glad she had made the effort ironing the bloody palazzo pants she wore. It had taken forever to iron out numerous creases and folds, but for once, she actually looked quite elegant, the white vest top showing off her tan to perfection.

Eduardo had, as she'd predicted the first night they met, become an invaluable friend. She only wished Lou could see what a perfect match they would be.

"So have you thought what you are going to do?" Eduardo summoned the waiter and ordered drinks before seriously considering the notable menu.

"No. It'll be a couple of months before everything goes through anyway so there's plenty of time." Sipping the delightfully fruity wine he'd ordered, she beamed. "Why hasn't some woman snatched you up? Lou is a fool." She sighed.

Eduardo laughed at her facial expression. "I haven't given up yet, my dear." He tapped his nose, as if telling her he had a few ploys up his sleeve.

The food, when it arrived, was exquisite. They both had the ajo blanco to start. White gazpacho made with grapes and almonds. For mains, Eduardo had partridge in rich tomato sauce while Abby devoured chicken livers in rich paprika and sherry sauce. A plate of polvorones, a simple yet divine dish made from flour, sugar, milk, olive oil, and nuts arrived for dessert.

Sipping on her wine, Abby leaned back in her chair and groaned with pleasure. She loved the leisurely way of life in the Andalusian Mountains. The room was starting to fill and from snippets of conversation she picked up, she gleaned a flamenco show was about to start.

"Bloody hell! Look. It's Juan." Abby nearly choked on her drink and peered at the stage from behind the menu.

Eduardo didn't seem as surprised. "So it is. Well, well, well."

There was no doubt Juan was a good-looking man. Slim fitting trousers clung to his hips doing nothing to hide his manhood and the elaborate open shirt displayed a tempting glimpse of chest hair. His slick, greased back long hair hung in a ponytail. The serious visage, hooded eyelids, and slightly hooked nose gave him a cruel look, Abby thought.

"Did you know he was gonna be here?" she hissed.

Eduardo shrugged. "Sssh. Let us see what a good dancer he is."

The performance was passionate and seductive, the audience caught up in the drama of unrequited love. Juan definitely had the look of a gypsy as he stomped his feet, topaz eyes burning with desire. His partner was young, striking, shiny black hair cascading down her back as she raised her arms and pouted. Her red blouse, knotted under her breasts, revealed a smooth flat stomach. The long, frilled polka dot skirt swirled as she enticed him closer, only to push him away at the last minute.

Abby had to admit he was exceptionally good. She was starting to feel tired and wanted to leave now that the show was over, but Eduardo, his eyes suddenly hard, gripped her hand.

"Watch," he whispered.

An elegant older woman, with glossy black hair whom Abby hadn't noticed, was seated at the side of the raised platform. Dripping in gold and able to afford extensive plastic surgery, if her boobs and lips were anything to go by, she caressed a large *Louis Vuitton* handbag, which sat on the table in front of her. And there he was, that bastard Juan whispering in her ear whilst stroking her shoulders intimately.

"What the fuck's he doing?" Abby muttered irately.

She tried to stand but Eduardo stopped her.

"Calm down, Abby. He hasn't seen us. Just watch."

The woman leaned back against the slimy, dark philanderer and closed her eyes as his lips grazed her bare shoulders.

"Wait 'til I tell Lou."

Abby was fuming and it was all Eduardo could do to stop her marching over and decking the couple. Motioning for the bill, and quickly paying it, he manoeuvred her in front of him out into the balmy night air.

"So you see," Eduardo looked concerned, "this will not end happily for Louise."

Abby shook her head, still simmering. She knew Eduardo didn't want to hurt Lou by telling her, but *she* wasn't Eduardo. Her best friend had to know.

"When Lou finds out, it's not gonna end happily for him, the cheating pig," she vowed, climbing into the car and slamming the door.

❧ 48 ❧

"It was probably just a client." Lou was dismissive of Abby's account of the previous evening, as she enjoyed a healthy bowl of fresh fruit and natural yoghurt.

"He was all over her, Lou." Abby emphasised the point with a dramatic grimace.

Lou licked her spoon clean then rested it in the bowl. "Look, Abby, I know you don't like him. I'm sorry I don't fancy your new BFF Eduardo, but please, just mind your own damn business, will you."

Abby was boiling. "For God's sake, Lou, why can't you see what's right under your nose? He's a bloody tosser."

She slammed out of the kitchen nearly tripping over Sylvester who was parading in the doorway flicking his tail in agitation, seemingly conscious of his mistress's distress.

Lou sat with her head in her hands. Breakfast forgotten, she didn't want to believe Abby. Not so much because she was madly in love with Juan. Yes, he was dangerous and incredibly sexy and he did things to her in the bedroom that made her feel alive for the first time since Simon. She knew he wasn't the settling down type, but he had her money. He'd promised the investment would start to show dividends soon. He'd even guaranteed that should the worst happen, he would cover any losses from his own resources so she couldn't lose. But he kept disappearing, supposedly on business, and she didn't want to push him away by nagging. Somehow, he'd crept under her skin and she didn't want to be proved wrong.

Kylie stood at the kitchen door. Lou hadn't heard her come in.

"Are you OK, Miss Walker?"

Lou brushed away the tears she didn't realise she was shedding, and gave a small smile. "Yes, I'm fine ... and please, call me Lou."

Kylie hesitated at the door as Lou pulled out a chair.

"I think Abby's taken the dogs for a walk, so sit here and have a cuppa with me, then you can go see those pups."

49

Abby was furious as she collected the dogs and stormed off down the bridle path running alongside the villa.

How Lou could be so naïve was beyond her. It wasn't like her at all. Juan-ker had fucking brainwashed her, that's what it was. Well, she would be keeping a close eye on him from now on. The first time he stepped out of line, she'd have him. Client, my arse!

Chester puffed along quite a way behind while the other dogs ran on ahead. She loved this walk. Gentle slopes led down to a small stream, wild flowers grew in abundance and in the distance, forests of Spanish fir and pine towered. Butterflies fluttered around her head as she walked. Cornflower blue, vivid reds and oranges. It was impossible to stay angry. She smiled as a gecko dashed past her feet.

She recalled Eduardo's advice to wear sturdy boots when walking, as encountering the odd scorpion wasn't a rare occurrence. She'd heeded his guidance and always wore her old *Timberland* boots, even on the hottest days. She hated falling out with Lou, but she couldn't understand why her best friend stubbornly stuck up for that sleazy greaseball.

Arriving at the stream, she sat on a large rock, her favourite thinking place. She lit a cigarette, taking deep, calming puffs, and watched the clouds drifting regally by and the dogs playing in the shallows. She glanced back towards the path. *Where was Chester?* He wasn't anywhere to be seen and she was sure he'd have caught up by now. Jumping up, she ran back to the path but there was still no sign of him.

"CHESTER," she bawled. Where the bloody hell was he?

Beginning to panic, Abby ran retracing her steps, bellowing Chester's name. Seeing a flash of reddish brown in a clump of long grass at the side of the path, she started sobbing and sank down next to her beloved boy.

"Oh, baby, what's happened to you?"

The dog had glazed eyes and froth spewed from his mouth as he struggled to raise his massive head and lick her hand. The other dogs had gathered round and she pushed them away in case whatever had bitten or stung him was still nearby. What was happening to him certainly seemed to be a reaction to poison.

"Oh, you silly nosy boy. What have you done?"

God, what should she do? She didn't know whether to move him or not. He wasn't easy to lift, never mind carry for two miles. *C'mon, girl, get a grip* she admonished herself. Time was of the essence. Stroking Chester's head, she instinctively knew he wasn't going to make it as hot tears streamed down her cheeks. Scrabbling around in her pocket, she found her mobile and prayed for a signal. Seeing one bar, she desperately dialled home.

When Lou and Kylie arrived, approximately forty-five minutes later, they spotted Abby draped over Chester's body, sobbing inconsolably.

Lou exchanged looks with Kylie, bending down to pull Abby away. "Come on, darlin', there's nothing more you can do."

Wanting to stay close to her boy, Abby shook her head. She gazed lovingly at Chester, stroking his head and body as she fought a deluge of tears erupting from heartbroken eyes.

Lou was upset herself, as she looked at the immobile bulk that only this morning she'd chased from the utility room, a pair of her best knickers hanging from his chops.

Kylie had thankfully suggested they bring the wheelbarrow lined with a blanket to transport him back to the villa. After finally persuading Abby to stand up and leave Chester's side, they managed to get his body into the barrow and cover him up. Kylie rounded up the other dogs who were subdued as if they knew something terrible had happened, especially a distressed Luna who nuzzled the familiar lump where he lay. Kylie pushed the improvised transport slowly along the path with Lou following behind holding Abby upright, talking to her gently.

The flowers seemed to have faded in colour Abby noticed, and the sky had darkened with heavy clouds promising a storm.

The house seemed empty, albeit sweeter smelling without Chester. Abby had spent most of the week holed up in her bedroom crying inconsolably, only venturing out to see to the chickens and goats. Her grief was still too raw to entertain walking the other dogs.

Her weekly Skype session with Daniel and Andrew was full of reminiscing about all the times Chester had destroyed, peed on, or eaten something they all treasured. Andrew had seemed especially morose. Abby didn't know if it was in deference to Chester's demise, Paisley taking herself back to her mother's, in a sulk over him caring more for his mates and football than he did her, or the fact that due to torrential rain they'd been having the town had flooded again and *Dominoes* had been shut for over a week.

She cut the session short in disgust after hearing Daniel half-whispering to Chrissie in the background that he was only a dog, pleading a headache and preferring to sit alone on her balcony with her memories and a large vodka. He wasn't just a dog, he'd been her best friend and confidante. She would miss him terribly. Throwing vodka down her front as she missed her mouth, she gazed off into the distance, drunkenly raised her glass, and made a toast to the one male who had made her genuinely happy.

Lou became worried about her friend. She was spending too much time alone, even avoiding Eduardo when he'd visited on several occasions bearing small gifts in an attempt to cheer her up.

Surfacing only to take care of the animals and the morning

bleachathon, which if anything had worsened this past week, in fact Lou was sure the pong of Domestos could be smelt by the nearest space station, Abby's *I want to be alone* attitude would give Greta Garbo a run for her money. Whether or not the actress had ever uttered those actual words Lou didn't know, but that was the general consensus so she was sticking with her theory.

When Abby did show her face, shuffling round the house speaking in monosyllables, she would have made a brilliant extra for *The Walking Dead*.

L ou didn't do much cooking. She didn't mind popping a Marks and Sparks gastro pub meal into the microwave, or throwing together a salad, but all the chopping, peeling, mixing, and experimenting Abby did was way out of her league, although the results were usually delish. So the fact that this evening she was cooking them both a meal, was a big deal. Proper British fare.

She'd found a beef wellington in one of the English supermarkets along with some microwave new potatoes in garlic and herb butter. After rummaging in the vegetable garden for half an hour, she'd collected a generous quantity of fine beans and cherry tomatoes. Along with ready-made tiramisu, which was Abby's favourite, and a bottle of gin it should be a decent spread.

Lou hated seeing Abby this way and was determined to snap her out of it. She was surprised when Abby even ignored Paul's phone calls from Madrid. Usually, she would jump around like Tigger on crack the second his name flashed up on her screen. While trimming the beans, she pondered on how long the job he was working on would last, and if he and Abby would become more than friends with benefits when he returned, and nearly took the end of her finger off in the process. With a yelp then a curse, she swiftly stemmed the blood flow, dressed the wound, and cracked on. *Those never forgotten first-aid skills had come in handy.*

The smells coming from the kitchen wafted upstairs. Abby wrinkled her nose appreciatively ... Lou must be entertaining Juan. She remembered the last time they'd spoken about the Latino loser and burst into tears. Scrolling through pictures of Chester on her phone had become a bit of an obsession. She smiled through her tears at one of her favourites, him sitting in the laundry basket with a pair of French knickers on his head; he'd been such a comedian. Oh, look, here was one of him swiping a slice of pizza off the coffee table while Andrew wasn't looking and another one of him in the bath ... a cantankerous Moby Dick.

"Abby I've made some food; you need to eat. C'mon, it'll be ready in ten minutes." Lou's wheedling from the other side of the door brought Abby back to reality.

"I'm really not hungry," Abby lied. In fact, her stomach had been protesting most of the day.

"I've made it special. Kylie has seen to the animals and we can have a lovely quiet evening. It's not good for you being on your own so much." Lou tried desperately to change her mind.

"OK, I'll be down in a minute." Abby found the trusty thong to tie back her hair, pulled on an old robe that had seen better days, and slipped her feet into the omnipresent flip-flops.

✢ 52 ✣

The food was surprisingly excellent. Lou had outdone herself. Abby ate everything placed in front of her, even a second helping of tiramisu. Lou chatted about Sylvia's plan to run a raffle to help with fund raising, Kylie's assistance and what a treasure she'd been, Eduardo's concern for her, and how the plans for the fiesta were going. She studiously avoided any mention of dogs or the dreaded Juan.

Clearing the plates away and pouring two large glasses of *Gordon's*, she ushered Abby into the sitting room before she made her exit upstairs once more. The large measure of gin went straight to Abby's head and after another three, she was – although sobbing – at least talking to Lou, if somewhat incoherently.

"I mish him soooo ... much." She handed Lou the empty glass indicating she was ready for a top up.

"Of course you do. We all do." Lou was a bit tipsy too and almost fell as she reached for the half-empty bottle at the side of her seat. Squinting, she poured them both another hefty measure before the sound of the door knocking shattered the peace.

"Jusht leave it ... they'll go away." Abby, red-eyed, and sniffing reached for her refill.

"I can't. Must be important if someone's knocking at this time."

Secretly hoping it was Juan, who she hadn't seen hide nor hair of all week, Lou went to answer the door.

"Oh, it's you! Abby, look who it is."

Lou stepped back into the living room followed by Paul.

Blinking, Abby stared up at the one-night stand she didn't think she'd see again. *Flamin' hell, she was in a worse state than the last time he turned up unannounced at the door.* With a sense of déjà vu, she snatched at the same thong holding her hair up, trying to wipe her nose on her sleeve at the same time. Her state of inebriation mirrored a demented mime artist.

"Whasht you doin' here?" As she stood up, her dressing gown gaped open revealing more than was decent.

"You weren't answering my calls. I thought something might be wrong and well, I had a couple of days off." He shrugged, obviously at a loss.

She walked toward him slowly, concentrating hard. *Hell, how much had she drunk?*

Paul opened his arms. Sobbing, Abby fell into them, pressing her head against his chest. She felt his shirt becoming soaked with her tears, probably snot too.

"I've mishted you." She hiccupped.

Paul stood stroking her hair, lip-reading Lou's two words.

"Chester's dead."

"C'mon girl, let's get you to bed."

He tightened her robe, retrieved the thong-cum-hairband, and lifted her up. Saying goodnight to Lou, he carried a now passed out Abby up the stairs.

53

Paul and Abby didn't surface until the following afternoon. For once, there had been no smell of bleach when Lou awoke. Instead, the pleasant scent of summer flowers surrounded her as she drank her gallon of morning coffee.

She'd received a text late last night from Juan saying he would be back later today, did she want to go out for dinner? Trying to play it cool, she hadn't replied, but she knew as soon as she saw him he would work his charm offensive and she'd be putty in his hands.

Kylie arrived to help with the animals. Smiling at the girl, Lou thought she really must buy her something to say thank you for all the help she'd given. She spent the rest of the morning in the village hall with the crows, Father Tomás, Eduardo, and three members of the organising committee whom Lou had seen around but hadn't yet met.

She'd learned, over the last few months, that in Spain a fiesta took place almost every day of the year on a local or national level. There were celebrations for almost every harvest of fruit or vegetable: olives, grapes, cherries, to the pig slaughtering in November ... *La Matanza*. Any excuse for a party, although butchering piggies wasn't a cause for celebration in Lou's opinion.

Each village or town took its fiesta seriously, especially its saint's day. There was a great deal of competition between them to provide the best and most elaborate celebration with fireworks, floats, bull running, and general merry-making, which sometimes went on for days.

Father Tomás, buried under a pile of bunting and flags, was

querying whether there were enough funds raised to buy some newer, more colourful examples.

"I have arranged with the local schools to decorate the float and make new bunting for the square." Eduardo looked up from his files.

He looked tired Lou thought.

Usually a jovial man, Father Tomás also looked as if the fiesta plans were taking their toll and was scratching his balding head in consternation.

"It is too much if they are to work on costumes also. We must get some of the women to help."

"Abby's good with a sewing machine," Lou piped up.

"Is she?" Everyone round the table spoke in unison, and eyebrows raised.

"Haven't you seen her clothes?"

Oh, yes! For mismatched, gaudy fancy dress costumes, Abby was the perfect choice.

Strangely, considering their love of black, the crows were in charge of the flowers and produced a list of locals willing to supply a truck-load of blooms for the float. Lou number crunched and tried her best to keep up with the conversation.

She needed to start those Spanish lessons!

54

Abby was in the kitchen making Spanish omelette and fennel bread when Lou returned. The aroma made Lou's mouth water and she hoped there was plenty to go around.

Lou imagined Paul was the type of man who enjoyed his food. As she walked into the kitchen, he was sitting at the table with a cup of coffee, a broad smile on his face. Abby placed a large bowl of salad, a smaller one of roasted peppers, and another of homemade garlic aioli in the centre, shooing a crabby Tweetie Pie off one of the chairs to make room for Lou.

"Just in time. You haven't eaten have you?"

"Nope. Mmm, smells delicious." Lou was pleased to see Abby didn't look quite as stricken as she had of late.

"How are the plans for the fiesta comin' along?" Paul leaned back, pecs straining, making the cloth of his T-shirt taut, which was slightly distracting.

"Slowly. Abby, I volunteered you to make some of the costumes. You've hardly used that bloody ancient sewing machine since we got here, so best put it to some good use before it claps out."

"I don't mind you volunteering me to make some of the costumes. I'll enjoy giving the old machine something. Should be fun."

Lunch was delicious. The three of them heartily tucked in as Paul regaled tales of the country's capital, describing Madrid's largest building, probably the most beautiful palace in Western Europe.

"It sounds wonderful," Lou enthused, "I'd love to see it all."

"Yeah ... and there's a lot more work there."

The women laughed as he told the story of how his dour-faced Geordie assistant had inadvertently walked into the bathroom of a pipe-smoking eighty-something señora straddling the crapper.

"Then there was the blocked pipe of this restaurant we were doing up. Stuck like glue it was, so Stan's underneath it with the wrench when the thing gives way and thousands of cockroaches fall onto his head. You should have seen him. It was like one of those bushtucker trials from *I'm a Celebrity*. Bloody hilarious."

The girls fell about laughing as he waved his arms about impersonating Stan, shouting GET ME OUT OF HERE in a terrible Geordie accent.

"Ugh! I'm glad I didn't see it." Lou shuddered, remembering the centipede incident.

Abby sniggered. "Sounds to me as if you've been having a whale of a time." She laid her hand on his, smiling into his eyes.

"It's not bad, could be a lot worse. Work's been flowing in and it looks as if I'll have to relocate."

Lou glanced at Abby to gauge how her friend had taken this last bit of news, unsurprised when she appeared laid back. Abby knew that what she had with Paul would only ever be a fling, so his moving was neither a shock, nor a reason for tears. Besides, Chester still dominated her heart; Paul had merely been a pleasing distraction.

Not wanting to spoil the pleasant atmosphere yet having no choice, Lou placed a box on the table that she'd picked up earlier from the vets.

"I've brought him home," she said tentatively watching Abby's reaction. "I bought this too."

She produced a small, yet heavy white urn with a photo of the lump himself superimposed on the front.

Abby hiccupped, thanked Lou with a bear hug, and then asked Paul to place the urn on the shelf above the living room door.

As she'd predicted, the atmosphere had altered somewhat so Lou took the opportunity to wish Paul well and said she'd see Abby later. Excusing herself, she headed down to the kennels to say hello to her two-legged and four-legged friends, leaving the lovebirds to say their goodbyes.

E duardo Márquez was born to reasonably well-to-do parents just outside Madrid. He was the youngest of four children and, as such, spoilt and cherished by his older sisters. A happy energetic child, his midnight curls allowed to grow long gave him a feminine look.

He adored music and could play piano by age six. He often recalled big family gatherings; tables creaking under mountains of food, his father playing guitar while people laughed and danced. Children running around until they collapsed exhausted on grandparents' knees.

Maria Sanchez lived on the same street. The same age as Eduardo, with beautiful honey coloured hair, eyes the shade of a rich pine forest, and sweet gentle demeanour, it was natural they would get together at some point. They were married at age twenty-one after three years of courting. Eduardo was starting out in a career as a music teacher and Maria worked as a telephonist for a large insurance firm. She was his best friend.

When a fatal car crash claimed his parents and youngest sister the year after he married, Maria held him close on that fateful night as he cried and raged against God and the world. His elder sister moved to Australia not long after. Theresa, the middle sister, sank into a deep depression, spending her days in a drug and alcohol induced haze.

Two years later, when Maria announced she was pregnant, Eduardo thought it was the beginning of something new. His eyes sparkled again and he treated Maria like a princess. Many evenings he would lie in bed by her side, his hand on her expanding stomach telling his son or daughter how much he loved them and chattering about all the adventures they would have. On December 23, Maria began to experience terrible pains necessitating a rushed trip to hospital.

Eduardo paced outside her room for hours listening to her screams, while nurses and doctors rushed in and out not stopping to let him know what was going on. Eventually he heard the pitiful cry of a newborn, but still more people rushed into the small room. Through the crack in the door, he saw sheets soaked in blood. What seemed like hours later, but in reality was a mere thirty minutes, a tall, stern-faced man informed him that he had a son, but he was truly sorry. Señora Márquez hadn't made it.

Staring blankly into his tiny son's cot, tears coursing down his face, Eduardo felt an overwhelming surge of love that kept him alive in the coming months. Father and son moved from the small apartment in Madrid filled with happy memories, to his parent's holiday home in Andalusia. He had hired a nanny for the boy – Carlota – who still came two days a week to clean his house. Over the years, Eduardo had made many good friends in the village. He even began giving private piano and guitar lessons. He also wrote scores for soundtracks and used the money to renovate the house and send Felipe to the best school.

An attractive man, many women had made themselves available over the past twenty-five years, but he had never felt any urges until he'd met Abby and Lou. Abby was a joy to spend time with and her friendship was a gift he had never expected, but it was Lou who had the biggest effect.

Now, sitting in his old leather recliner, his mind turned to the fair-haired lady. Every time she walked into a room, his heart skipped a beat. Her beauty had inspired all the compositions he'd written since her arrival. He couldn't get her out of his mind and he hated that she seemed infatuated with that shifty looking flamenco dancer. He couldn't do anything about that, but he could help Abby feel better.

Done with musing, he heaved himself from his chair, feeling a tightness in his chest. No doubt brought on by all the reminiscing, probably too much heartache. He shook off the feeling and ambled over to the telephone.

56

Abby had hugged Paul goodbye and promised to visit him in Madrid soon, although she didn't think she would actually go. She wasn't in love with him and imagined he was swamped with attention from ladies in the capital. However, the gorgeous hunk did make her feel good and the couple of days they'd spent together had been just what she needed.

She still cried herself to sleep and had a little snuffle every time she looked up to see Chester's ashes on the shelf, but every day it was getting that little bit easier.

Lou mentioned again how Kylie had been such a star and how the villagers had expressed their sympathies at her beloved pet's passing, which was why she was up to her elbows in flour when Lou arrived from Juan-kers on Thursday morning.

"Could you let people know we're having a party when you go to the village later, oh, and give Sylvia a call too."

"I guess so. What's brought this on?" Smiling, Lou dumped her handbag on the table and scooped Tweetie Pie up for a cuddle.

"We never moved to Spain to be miserable. Chester enjoyed his time here." She bit her lip. "We've yet to have a proper house-warming to say thank you to everyone for making us feel so welcome. Also, I have some tapas recipes I want to try out before the fiesta." She gabbled, waving her arms around the organised chaos that heralded a cooking marathon.

Lou's smile remained. She felt happy to see Abby returning to some sort of normality since Chester's demise, even though the cheerfulness seemed a bit forced. A little more time, that was all. Those windmilling arms were a definite sign she was on the mend. *Oh, yes, the girl was almost back.* "I don't know how you can cook in this heat, but it's a good idea. Have you told Eduardo yet?"

"No he wasn't home when I phoned earlier. Here, try this."

She offered a miniscule goat's cheese and caramelised onion tartlet, which Lou devoured in one bite and gave the thumbs up.

"You really are getting like a Spanish, Mary Berry," she laughed

The sound of a car pulling up outside sent them both to the front door, in time to see Eduardo lifting something from the rear seat.

"What have you got there?"

Lou peered curiously around Abby who had started to walk forward then froze mid-stride.

A stunning young Galgo rested in the blanket Eduardo held carefully. Midnight black, soulful dark eyes peered up at the two women. A large scar ran along the hindquarters where one of her legs should have been.

"Oh, poor baby. She's beautiful. What's her name?" Abby stood entranced, her hand reaching forward to stroke the velvet head.

"She hasn't got a name. She was in some rubble, trapped and terrified. Her leg was stuck and unfortunately had to be amputated. She's not doing so well in kennels and I don't think she's ever been loved. I thought you two could maybe become friends."

Eduardo placed the blanket on the gravel and the skinny dog got to her feet and sniffed a nearby plant pot.

"I'm not sure Abby's ready for a new dog yet," Lou warned.

Abby wasn't listening. She sank to her haunches, holding her hand out to the timid hound. "Mabel ... that's her name," she whispered.

57

The day of the party dawned, as every other day did. Hot!
Lou often missed the damp cool mornings back in the UK, but today she was up early to help with the arrangements and the presence of the sun made her want to sing out loud. She let out the chickens – collecting fourteen eggs – and walked the dogs. Abby had already milked the goats and was busy in the kitchen, the large fan above her head stopping her from spontaneously combusting.

Twenty-five guests were attending the get together. As well as numerous tapas dishes, Abby was making bread, marinating meats, and preparing a large paella that she would cook outside when the guests arrived. Abby had delegated Lou decorating duties. With this in mind, Lou had spent much of the morning hanging lanterns from bushes and setting up trestle tables around the pool area. She was also making sure there was enough to drink. Bags of ice filled the freezer in the garage ready for tipping into buckets, to ensure bottles of lager and sparkling wine stayed cold.

Abby had done herself proud with the food. Piled high, next to miniature portions of Spanish omelette, were bite-sized wild boar, chorizo, and pine nut sausage rolls. Small skewers stood proudly in colourful cups next to dishes of roasted peppers. There was a lavish supply of mini lamb burgers with mint mayonnaise, chunks of marinated chicken, and goat's cheese tarts. Jars of chilli jam and various accompaniments interspersed the gastronomic feast.

The fish man had kindly delivered a box of fresh sardines ready for the grill along with mussels, prawns, and squid. Not a great lover of seafood, Lou, a bit green at the gills at that point, had legged it from the kitchen. She had to admit however, the spread was a banquet fit for a king. After ensuring the food was covered, protected from the inevitable onslaught of insects at dusk, thieving cats, and escapee donkeys, Lou went inside to get ready.

Abby was sitting on the floor with Mabel's head in her lap.

"You've done a fabulous job with the food, Abby," Lou enthused. "C'mon, girl, let's knock 'em dead!"

Smiling, Abby patted Mabel, lifted the dog's head from her lap, and got to her feet. The Galgo gave a contented sigh, curled up on the floor, and drifted off to sleep.

Abby shot off to take a quick shower before the guests arrived. She emerged thirty minutes later wearing a gorgeous silver crocheted dress, which showed off her legs to perfection. As past events and singed eyebrows had proved; her hair was a fire hazard so she'd pinned it up leaving loose curls to frame her face, which apart from a slash of lipstick and a coat of mascara, was make-up free. Simple jewellery completed the look.

Lou, dressed in a burnt orange sleeveless blouse with cream tailored linen shorts, ditched the customary heels, and swapped them for a pair of cream toe-post sandals. Applying a dusting of make-up and snapping on a couple of pieces of amber costume jewellery, she was set.

"Ready?" She beamed at Abby.

"Yep ... have been for half an hour." Abby returned the smile, noticing Lou had lost weight.

"Then let's go throw a party."

❧ 58 ❧

Sylvia was the first to arrive. After visiting her friends' current canine lodgers – Stan, a loopy Cockerpoo, Sally, an overweight Beagle, Terence, a Westie who had the temperament of a rabid Rottweiler, and Pedro, a nervous mongrel complete with twitch and Nigel Lawson eyebrows – she settled with a glass of wine.

She was delighted with how Lou was running the admin side of things for the charity and the two of them made plans for forthcoming fund-raising activities. She mentioned a cat in desperate need of rehoming and asked would Lou foster it for a while.

Sylvester will love that Abby thought as she bustled around preparing last minute nibbles and lighting the barbeque.

Within an hour, the terrace was full of people. Kylie had arrived with her parents (who had taken a rare evening off from serving greasy chips and lager), a few of their ex-pat mates, whom Lou had invited, in tow.

Elaine had really tried to make an effort. A large cerise pink trouser suit vainly attempted to hold in the numerous bumps and bulges. Her limp, mousy hair scraped into a bun, pitifully fought to attempt elegance, but the grubby dated atmosphere of the Bus Stop seemed to have impregnated her soul as she stood clinging to her husband's arm. Ken dressed in a knockoff Hugo Boss top, three-quarter length trousers, and the obligatory white socks and Jesus sandals stood, as usual, with that arrogant air.

Abby noticed how the villagers gathered in separate groups to the ex-pats, and was grateful her and Lou were more involved with the locals than the over-tanned, overfed, over the top Brits. Mabel, having perfectly developed the soulful eyed, 'Look at me, I'm a cripple, please feed me' gaze', hopped excitedly between visitors, while the feline mafia perched unobtrusively waiting for their moment to pounce on unattended goodies.

Abby noticed Juan was being extremely attentive to Lou, despite the exaggerated attentions of Mildew Mildred from Scunthorpe, a fifty something hairdresser with a penchant for Botox, gin, and toy boys.

The food seemed to go down well, although she heard Ken complaining a few times, his mumbles turning into raised griping.

"What's with all this foreign shite? Where's the butties? This int a fucking sausage roll. Where's all the chips?"

"Philistine," Lou whispered, grinning as she brushed past with a glass of *Tinto de Verano* for herself and a bottle of *Sol* for Juan.

"You can't eat chips all the time, Ken." Lou patted her flat stomach emphatically.

"Ah, that's where yer wrong, luv," Ken argued, all riled up. "Me dad ate chips every day of his life and was as thin as a bloody rake."

"Oh, I beg your pardon. I stand corrected. Does he live over here, your dad?"

"No." Elaine piped up. "He died. Only fifty-six he was. Heart attack, wasn't it love."

Lou sucked in her gums to strangle a giggle. As Ken had used the past tense when referring to his dad, she guessed he must have croaked it and seized her chance to wind him up. That numpty's arrogant, cocksure air, and him using the 'luv' word in that manner had pissed her off again, only this time in an impish way where teasing the numbskull would be far better than losing her rag.

"Anyway, lovely to see you, *luvs*," Lou lied, giggling to herself at the baffled expression on both Elaine and Ken's faces. "Must dash. Things to do, people to see. Enjoy yourselves."

Catching the tail end of Lou's sharper than a surgeon's scalpel sarky wit, Abby stood behind her and snorted. Turning round, she took Abby's arm and chuckling, the pair moved away from insufferable Ken and his dimwit wife.

"Oh, Lou, you're such a card. I almost felt sorry for him."

"Hmm," Lou retorted, licking her lips. "That man bugs me. He's such an ignoramus. It's bags of fun pulling his leg. He just doesn't get me, nor me him, I guess. And she's just as dense. Never mind. How you doin'?"

"I'm all hot and bothered," Abby gasped, face all flushed. "Feel as if I've run a marathon."

"I'm not surprised, woman. You've been bustling around serving everybody food and drink, and haven't had a minute to yourself. What you tryin' to do? Win the hostess with the mostess award? Sit yourself down. Have a drink ... let people serve themselves."

"Yeah, good idea."

The sun was low in the sky; a golden dumpling sinking into a soup of purple and orange as Abby poured herself a large vodka and tonic, dropped in a thick slice of lemon cut from a plump fruit nurtured by her own fair hands, and plonked herself next to Eduardo and Sylvia.

"You've done yourself proud with this food. It's delicious, Abby." Sylvia brushed crumbs from her linen trousers with a flourish.

"Si," agreed Eduardo. "Just the right combination between British and Spanish flavours."

"Hmm." Abby glanced distractedly at Elaine and Ken.

"I've got quite a few ideas that I'd like to try, none of them including chips," she whispered conspiratorially, bending forward.

Eduardo patted his stomach. "Feel free to try them out on me, dear girl. Those wild boar sausage rolls were sublime."

Lou thought the party was going exceptionally well. Everybody seemed to be having a good time, and Abby's gargantuan spread had gone down a treat. It didn't matter that the locals were hovered mosquito like nearer the house, while the ex-pats congregated similarly around the pool, the obnoxious Ken centre of attention, as usual. Poor Kylie, having a dad like that. She noticed the girl having a cigarette, talking to one of Bernadette's daughters close to the donkey. Two giant ears, a James Brown fringe, and enormous teeth. The equine equivalent of Alan Carr was building bridges years of secondary school had failed to do.

"Where are you, my beautiful lady?"

Juan's liquid velvet voice caressed Lou as he bent towards her ear, his lips brushing her neck and sending shivers to her nether regions.

"Sorry, I was miles away thinking about us making our escape later." She brushed his hand from her derrière ineffectually, while he tantalised her with all the things he would do when they were alone.

Ken's booming voice to her left made her raise her head, all sexy thoughts vanishing.

"Fuck off, yer barmy cow!"

Lou looked to see which guest was the recipient of his ire and was

surprised to see Sylvia squaring up to the burly oaf while Elaine helplessly looked on.

"I think there's been a mistake," Elaine muttered, appearing flustered and embarrassed.

"Mistake? There's no mistake. He slapped my arse." Sylvia was
fuming. Despite her size, she stood defiant.

Then, all hell broke loose.

Donkeys are extremely social animals, therefore Santos, missing
the young girls who'd been keeping him company, decided to join the
party. How in the hell he managed to open that bloody gate again, Lou
didn't know. He was like sodding Houdini and tomorrow, she was
going to buy the biggest bloody padlock she could find.

Guests were trying to dodge the inquisitive mule. Lou couldn't see
Abby anywhere – she was likely playing hostess again – and God knew
she hadn't been able to shift the stubborn animal in the past.

Sylvester and Tweetie Pie seeing the opportunity they'd been
waiting for all evening launched a raid on the garlic prawns. Meanwhile, Jeff, one of the volunteers from the shelter, bravely and drunkenly leapt to Sylvia's defence. It resembled a scene from a *Carry
On* film.

The clamorous, braying donkey trotted through the party, an
unwanted smelly gatecrasher.

Stopping at one of the tables, he buried his face in a large bowl of
figs. Unfortunately, they'd been marinated in rose infused honey and
instead of devouring the forbidden fruits, most ended up stuck round
his muzzle or dangling from his long fringe. The sight of his long
tongue contorting about his face in desperation to reach the sticky
figs had everyone in stitches.

Santos however didn't see the joke and careered towards the swimming pool, plates of food crashing, as the cats, grabbing their
moment, landed clumsily on the buffet table. The great prawn
robbery was underway. Remnants of garlic aioli flew into the air and
splattered onto Elaine's fluorescent suit as if a giant seagull had just
crapped on her from up above. While ham croquettes dive-bombed,
giant green bogies dressed up as olives rained down in buckets. Jeff,
the indignant knight in shining armour was still arguing with Ken who
seemed oblivious to the ensuing havoc and was still bellowing at
Sylvia.

"Don't flatter yourself, luv!" he snarled. "*And you,*" he prodded Jeff
in the chest as Santos came up behind, "why don't *you* mind your own
fuckin' business?"

It all became too much for Tweetie Pie. Spooked, she sprang from the table onto Santos's back, digging her claws into his fur and causing him to buck. Sylvia dragged Jeff to one side just as the donkey charged into Ken, knocking him head first into the swimming pool still clutching his bottle of *San Miguel*. A stunned silence – broken only by a couple of muffled sniggers – descended on the partygoers as they looked on.

Abby came around the corner just in time to see a bedraggled, infuriated Ken clambering out of the pool, every obscenity she'd ever heard – plus a few she hadn't – spewing from his mouth.

Elaine hovered ineffectually nearby like a giant pink balloon, still wearing streaks of garlic dip. Ken kept pushing her away, his temper swelling as she tried to dry him down with a napkin.

"For fuck's sake woman, what's that gonna do?" he spat. "Use yer eyes, will yer. I'm bleedin' drenched. I could have fuckin' drowned there."

He turned his attention to Lou who had Santos cornered before he could cause any more damage. *Shame you didn't*, Lou thought privately, ignoring the loathsome man's remonstrations and planting a gentle kiss on Santos's right ear in way of thanks as Russ Abbot's *Atmosphere* jingled in her head. *Oh, yeah. This party definitely had an atmosphere, although she guessed for some, a happy one wouldn't be how they'd describe it.*

Surprisingly, Juan rescued the sticky situation, smoothly swooping in and calming both the two-legged ass and the four-legged donkey before dragging a stunned Kylie up for an impromptu flamenco performance.

Making a mental note to phone a pool cleaner the following day, Abby apologised profusely to the Higginbottoms sending them home with a jar of her best chutney and a dozen sausage rolls that Lou, face deadpan, chirped in would go down a treat with chips.

❧ 59 ❧

Sylvia arrived the following morning and after a good giggle about the previous evening, produced a large cat carrier.

"Erm, this is Salem. I mentioned him last night."

Lou thought Sylvia looked incredibly shifty, and it was odd she didn't stop for her normal chat and cuppa. Muttering good luck under her breath, she plonked the carrier on the kitchen table, made her excuses, and bounded out the door with a hurried goodbye.

Exchanging curious glances, Lou and Abby peered into the plastic container. Dressed as if due to attend a sophisticated winter masquerade ball, with pale mink fur coat, black mask, and piercing sapphire blue eyes, the sleek predator glared back at the inquisitive pair. Arching his back, he flicked his tail slowly, assessing them both.

"Aww, he looks like the cat in *The Incredible Journey,*" Lou cooed, poking her forefinger through the bars as a paw with fully extended claws flashed towards it. "*Ouch!* You bad-tempered little git," she yelped, swiftly jerking back her finger. "Yikes. That hurt."

"*Bloody hell.*" Abby stood and withdrew a few inches. "He's about as cuddly as a dominatrix armed with a cheese grater and cat o' nine tails ... 'scuse the pun. Sylvester's just gonna love him," she added sarcastically. "Perhaps we should leave him in there until he calms down a little."

Nodding in agreement, Lou went over to the sink to clean her bleeding wound. "No wonder Sylvia's having a hard time rehoming him," she observed, cursing as she wrapped a medicated plaster round her throbbing finger.

The following week would be testament as to how Salem had achieved his name and why it had been impossible to find him a home. Abby and Lou were actually considering asking Father Tomás for exorcism advice. Sylvia had gone AWOL, avoiding all contact, even though both women had sent her what seemed like hundreds of text messages with no response. The only two things the savage puss had in his favour were his looks and the fact he was house-trained. A bit like Juan, Abby thought.

Initially, Abby and Lou set up a bed for Salem in the utility room, but his incessant wailing was too much and, with caution, they released him. Once liberated, he took over the house. Sylvester and Tweetie Pie were both big cats and could take care of themselves as the screaming fights at three in the morning with neighbours' moggies proved, but both were terrified of the newcomer, often retreating to Lou's bedroom to lick their wounds and nurse their injured pride, minus a few clumps of fur.

"Jeez, he's a mini tiger," Lou rasped, entering the kitchen and picking up a tuft of black and white fluff following yet another feline fracas. "You haven't seen that fifty Euro note I left on the table for the shopping, have you?"

"Nope, haven't seen it," Abby replied, tentatively reaching for a slice of toast as Salem's piercing, wild eyes glared at her from his position beside the toaster. "Nice little kitty."

Too late. He attacked, leaving Abby nursing an injured hand, toast on the floor.

"I'm sure he'll settle down and they'll all learn to get along." Lou picked up the van keys and jangled them in her hand.

"Yeah?" Abby grimaced, remembering the same words used about Chester and the feline mafia, which she was quick to point out to Lou. "That worked out *really* well."

"Oh, come on. They learned to live with each other, even if they never became friends," Lou said worriedly, glancing at Mabel and Luna who were slinking past ... well one slinking, one hopping, in an attempt to make the kitchen door without being seen.

Fail. A ball of cream fur flew through the air landing on the table hissing menacingly. Paws skittered across the tiles as both dogs hastily retreated the way they'd come.

"Bleedin' hell, Lou, this is getting ridiculous."

But Abby was talking to thin air. Lou had wisely followed the dogs and made her exit.

Shooing the demon possessed cat out of the kitchen with a mop,

Abby took down her pots and pans. Her lemon, sugar, and olive oil cookies, and fig, red wine, and balsamic jam weren't going to make themselves.

Later, jam making finished, baking done, and dogs walked, Abby was cleaning the fridge when she heard a noise from the utility room. Salem didn't hear her enter. He was too busy vomiting onto a pile of clean washing.

Oh, for God's sake! That bloody cat ... he really had to go.

Cleaning up the gungy mess, she noticed a small piece of paper with the distinctive EU flag. *Ha! She could report to Lou that she'd solved the mystery of the missing fifty Euro note.*

❧ 60 ❧

Lou wasn't as much of a sun worshipper as Abby. While Abby spent as much time as possible under the hot, golden disc's relentless glare slathered in Factor 30, Lou preferred to spend her time in the shade checking for melanomas and wishing for the odd shower or two. Since they'd arrived in Spain, she'd gotten used to some sun, usually an hour spent by the pool late afternoon with a vodka and tonic before getting ready for whatever the evening had to offer.

She'd spend days sat behind her *Sony VAIO* under the grapevine canopy that shaded the patio outside the kitchen. With Luna at her feet, she'd work her way through the adequate amount of proofing and editing work she'd undertaken, or run various charity rescue pages, while waiting for Juan's and her own 'make them both super rich investment' to return heaps of dividends.

The rescue website was easy to manage. The *Dogs for Adoption* page required updating on a regular basis, and a new blog posted once a week. The bulk of the work came via the social media pages, which were manic. Constant queries from people interested in the dogs' welfare, people asking about the work they did with the Galgos, especially questions about the dogs, would they be suitable etc, and dealing with transport arrangements to whatever country. That in itself was nearly a full time job, but Lou loved the work and felt as if she was definitely making a valid contribution.

When her investment paid off, she had dreams of building several more kennels and becoming a partner with Sylvia. Today's update featured Tiny, the massive Newfoundland who surprisingly had grown too big for his idiot owners' bedsit, Parsley, a Boston Terrier, with a harelip and chronic bad breath and finally, Willow, a gorgeous brindle Galgo who, starved and severely malnourished was found down a well where she'd been cruelly thrown. Within six months of rehabilitation, Willow was ready for rehoming. Apart from a slight issue with cats, she would make a lovely pet.

After dealing with several queries, and deleting one, which asked if they could hang on to a young Chihuahua called Geoffrey and post in time for Christmas, Lou leaned back, stretching her arms above her head. She smiled to herself as she looked in appreciation around the small terrace. Her eyes drank in the terracotta tiles shaped hexagonally to create a feeling of separation from the stairs leading down to the pool area, and various potted plants standing against the trellis, which was a foil for cascading bougainvillea and gnarled ancient vines surrounding her; purple clouds in a sky of heavy green pendulous globes of sweetness.

Closing her eyes, Lou drifted into daydreams about the new kennels she would build next year when her keen ears picked up a soft thump. Opening her eyes, she was horrified to see a large scorpion on her keyboard. Shuffling her chair backwards, whimpering in fear and shock, she stared in petrified fascination. The creature momentarily paused, sting curled over its smooth exoskeleton, pincers hovering mimicking a boxer's defence stance. What must have only been seconds seemed interminable.

Suddenly, a blur of mink and black fur flashed past her, deftly landing on the table. The scorpion had vanished, leaving Salem crunching merrily on his unexpected lunch. At that precise moment, Lou fell in love with the devilish feline and decided, after days of umming and ahing to keep him. She also made a mental note to make a new purchase as soon as.

Parasol – protection from falling arachnids.

61

Abby loved Wednesdays and would get up earlier than she usually did. After her OCD bleaching, she would attend to the animals before loading boxes of homemade goodies into the old Citroën and making her way to the village square, the venue for the weekly market.

The stall was Abby's pride and joy. Gorgeous colourful Spanish pottery that she'd picked up in second-hand stores complimented the various sized jars and bottles containing all manner of jams, preserves, chutneys, pickles, infused oils, and homemade liqueurs perched on wooden blocks and covered in a pristine white tablecloth. Small wine crates contained tubes of flavoured goat's cheese wrapped lovingly in greaseproof paper, while large covered platters sold slices of freshly baked goods made the previous evening all from home-grown vegetables and local produce.

Today's specials were goat's cheese, pear, and walnut tart, sun-dried tomato, olive, and basil quiche, and Polish style sweet apple dumplings.

"The stall looks good today," Sophia complimented, reaching for a small sliver of bread and a spoonful from one of the sample jars at the front of the display.

She had recently started stocking some of Abby's chutneys and preserves in her shop, and was curious to taste the new bacon jam concoction.

"Thank you, Sophia. What do you think of this one?"

As Sophia hadn't choked and sprayed the front of Abby's apron with goo, like she had when she tried the super-hot raspberry and jalapeño jam last week, Abby reckoned it must be a success.

"Si, it is very good indeed. I will order six jars, and more of the peach and amaretto. Also the cactus jelly is selling well."

Plonking herself down next to the stall, on a seat Abby provided for chatty customers whilst keeping a sharp eye on the door to her shop, she proceeded to regale Abby with a long list of complaints about her life, the biggest one being Alberto. Carlos, her husband, had been a good man but she would never forgive him for dying of the cancer and leaving her to care for his cantankerous, bossy Papa. "Sophia, where is my breakfast. Sophia, I need the bathroom. Sophia, fetch my cane."

Abby laughed as Sophia, face all screwed up impersonated the old man.

"When I hear his stick tapping, I want to stick it up his backside."

Abby moved jars for fear of them being broken, as the large woman's arms flung around wildly.

"Is there no one else who can care for him?" Abby asked laughing innocently.

Sophia looked at her as if she'd completely lost her mind. "Of course not. He is my family. Who else cares about him like me!"

As Sophia stomped off muttering something under her breath, Abby smiled wryly, shook her head, and concentrated on the coachload of potential customers arriving in the square. Elaine, who'd been sweeping the Bus Stop's large terrace, rushed inside probably to put the chip pan on and Christine, the tall heavy Dutch woman who ran the small art gallery, flung open her door and placed a few paintings outside in the sun to entice tourists. Eduardo was always singing her praises. She and Lou had struck up quite a friendship, but Abby hadn't had the chance to get to know her beyond a wave and a smile.

"Sur ... prise!"

Abby dropped the large jar of preserved lemons she was holding, which landed squarely on her big toe and made her scream out in pain. Gritting her teeth, she hopped about like an Easter bunny on a pogo stick. "What the hell!" she screeched.

A large hand reached out to steady her. Raising her head while looking through tears of pain, she glimpsed her youngest son. A flash of pink hair indicated that could only be one person.

"Oh, God! Sorry, Mrs Sinclair, I didn't mean to startle you. Are you OK?"

As if roaring surprise Cilla Black style in a fucking crowded market square wasn't going to startle her. Abby bit her lip and smiled.

"I'm fine, really. Now, what are you both doing here apart from scaring me half to death and maiming me for life?" She glanced at her big toe turning fifty shades of purple that seemed to have doubled in size.

"We got a brilliant deal and I said to Andrew let's go see how your mum's doing didn't I babe?" Paisley gabbled without drawing breath.

Andrew nodded, looking round the square. Dressed in typical British fashion, his legs resembled two hairy *Walls* bangers poking out of Bermuda shorts and stuffed into white socks. His trainers must have been new as they were a pair Abby didn't recognise. A trip to *Sports Direct* had obviously preceded this trip.

As usual, Paisley was displaying her assets to great effect in a sleeveless white blouse tied under her 36Fs, and the tiniest pair of denim hot pants Abby had ever seen. She may as well have been poured into them they were so tight. Like a second skin, they looked as if they'd been purchased at *Mothercare* for a five-year-old. Had she poked her finger in an electric socket? It certainly appeared that way as wiry flamingo curls framed her pretty, if permanently bewildered face.

Knowing Andrew would turn his nose up at her goat's cheese offerings, Abby sent the couple to the Bus Stop for something to eat with instructions to bring her a large vodka for medicinal purposes. She turned to serve the people who'd come over to surreptitiously watch the freak show, and now felt obliged to buy something from the mad woman. Abby sold out of stock before two. Eduardo had arrived to help her pack the Citroën, showing concern about her swollen toe. He helped her limp towards the crowded British bar where Andrew sat glowering at him presuming that he was obviously one of the many Spanish waiters she'd moved over here to shag. Paisley was deep in conversation with Kylie who, bored to tears at Paisley's not so scintil-lating conversation, was desperately trying to sidle her way back to the kitchen.

Lou pressed send and placed her phone on the table absently stroking Luna's head. She had sent three messages; the first to Abby saying no she wouldn't be in later, especially if she was returning with her obnoxious son and his thick as a canteen mug girlfriend, the others to her friends.

Feeling a headache coming on, she leaned back rubbing at her eyes, waiting for the ping of returned messages from Sylvia and Chris-tine confirming they were up for a night out.

62

Estepona was in full party swing when the trio walked along the busy promenade later that evening. High season was usually to be avoided Sylvia explained as they made their way through the throngs of tourists, but since Lou needed rescuing she knew just the place.

Dressed in white Capri pants and a green silk vest top, which complemented her vivid red hair, incredibly high heels tip tapping on the pavement, Sylvia was a tiny force of nature as the others followed in her wake.

Lou wore a loose crimson gypsy style top, long black skirt, and a pair of black stilettos she'd recently bought but never worn, hoping she wouldn't develop blisters while working them in. She'd swept her hair back into an elegant chignon, and tucked a bright red flower behind her ear, her lover not only taking over her life, but seemingly her fashion sense too.

Christine, the tallest of the group, was an array of mismatched colours and styles Lou concluded would give Abby's dress sense a run for its money, and then some. At over six-feet tall, with long, steel grey hair, the build of a prop forward, and a voice reminiscent of a sonic boom, she was difficult to ignore. Although her English was sublime, her Dutch accent was as diverse as her choice of duds, sometimes strong, sometimes with little or no hint, depending on her mood or the circumstances of a particular situation.

All three women attracted attention and a few wolf whistles as they sashayed past the crowded bars and restaurants.

Lou had struck up a solid friendship with Christine since the art gallery owner returned from the Netherlands where she'd been caring for her elderly mother. She'd lived in the village for six years, moving there after a failed romance. Lou didn't pry, but the overall impression suggested she'd been hurt pretty badly and wasn't keen to take the plunge again anytime soon.

Christine had a mountain of funny stories to tell about the locals. Accompanied by excellent impersonations, she'd relate them loudly and often, much to Lou's amusement. She was also a fine artist, and Lou, who was fairly knowledgeable herself, having on occasion dabbled with the odd landscape, spent many happy hours debating the virtues of contemporary artists over a choice bottle of red with the larger-than-life Dutch woman. Sylvia had only met Christine twice but thought she was a hoot. Lou felt sure they were in for a fun-packed evening.

Sylvia led them to a bar owned by an old friend she advised, introducing them to Phil, who'd ran a pub in Bolton for years until his wife did a flit with the gasman. Fed up with the grey Lancashire weather, he'd sold up and was living La Vida Loca serving pints and paella. With a look of half-man, half-Bullmastiff, his exaggerated muscles strained against a faded *Iron Maiden* T-shirt. The way he fawned over Sylvia, Lou was sure they'd been more than friends, although just the thought of the tiny redhead cavorting with steroid Phil was eye-watering.

The bar itself was not Lou's usual cup of tea. Most of the clientele were half-cut already, including a group of fat, hairy blokes tarted up in French maids' outfits slaughtering *Who Let the Dogs Out* on the karaoke. *Pricks*.

"What can I get you ladies to drink," Phil boomed, steering them to a slightly quieter corner.

"White wine spritzer for me, please." Lou smiled.

Phil doubled over laughing. "Seriously, luv, do I look the sort of bloke who does spritzers?"

There's that word again, though funnily enough Lou's hackles didn't rise in the same way they did with Ken.

"Three lagers then." Christine thumped him on the back.

He looked up, shocked to have met his match in female form. "Well well well, who do we have here?" His eyes lit up appreciatively taking in her curves, and finally resting on her open friendly face.

Sylvia was smirking and Lou had the impression that this might have been a not so subtle matchmaking attempt.

"Dare I ask him for some lime in mine?" she whispered, sitting on a grubby chair around a large barrel, wondering why her heels seemed to be disappearing before realising, with dismay, they were sinking into the sticky goo that was the floor.

Two pretty waitresses in *Hooters* T-shirts moved between tables with large trays of lager and paella.

Sylvia laughed at Lou's serious face. "Oh, loosen up, Lou. It'll be great fun after a few drinks ... wait and see. Makes a change from all the Costa del Crime lot trying to outdo each other. What's your karaoke song?"

"I don't have one ... can't sing for toffee." Lou shook her head. "I'll sit it out, thanks. No way am I getting' up there."

An hour later, thanks to a small pitcher of lager and numerous shots of Sambuca, Lou was swaying around on stage screeching out *Wuthering Heights*. Christine had already done her stint murdering Christina Aguilera's *Dirty*, a performance involving way too much twerking that would haunt Lou's dreams for a long time. Christine even hauled the stag do up, cheering, dancing, and crotch rubbing, which had the few women in the place sputtering into their drinks

Sylvia was up next. Her song choice, *Like a Virgin*, was far from the truth, if the tales she'd regaled were anything to go by.

As Sylvia promised, it turned out to be an extremely fun night. Phil had kept the drinks flowing. There had been some definite flirting between him and Christine. Seeing the large woman batting her eyelashes as she downed copious amounts of cheap lager, the object of her affection flexing his muscles trying not to stare at her impressive cleavage, was more than entertaining to say the least. The bar became crowded as Sylvia, flushed and not in the least bit virginal looking, made her way back from the stage.

"Hey, isn't that your fella?" she shouted at Lou, pointing to the window.

Outside, Juan casually strolled arm in arm with an elderly, elegant woman. Frantically waving, trying to attract his attention, Lou lost her balance, staggering backwards into the French maids and knocking pints of lager flying in all directions. She felt numerous, greedy hands groping at her body, as lecherous faces stupidly grinned.

"Get your paws off of me," she spat drunkenly, turning round, and bringing her fist back to clobber the main offender – a tall, blonde Hooray Henry type with flushed face and lips reminiscent of The Joker – with a wild left hook.

The tanked up, grizzly bear of a bloke to her left grabbed her arm to stop her following up with a nifty jab as her victim, at first standing stunned, proceeded to collapse in a heap on the floor. This seemed to be the signal for all-out war.

God only knew where everybody came from, but fists were flying. Christine rugby tackled a large coloured chap who was shouting garbled obscenities, sending him crashing into a table of drinks. Landing face first in a large dish of paella, he raised his head, yellow rice clogging his nostrils, a large prawn sticking to his forehead. Phil, who unwittingly came to her rescue, received a bottle over his shiny bald bonce from the main Frenchie for his trouble, which sent him into a blind rage. Sitting astride the guy's ample chest, he began pummelling hard before Christine wrenched him off.

Lou clocked someone's false teeth whizzing through the air. Chuckling, she thought of Alberto and had a crazy notion to pick them up for him. She did a double take at Sylvia who, while pleading with everyone to calm down, wound her way through the scuffle, grinding her stiletto heels on unsuspecting feet. Since many wore sandals, she was managing to do a fair bit of damage.

Bedlam was the only way to describe the free-for-all. The air thick with curses, eighteen stone French maids hopping about like demented frogs at a Tourette's convention, the floor, walls, and tables painted with booze, paella and broken glass.

"Told you it would be fun!" Sylvia yelled at Lou.

"Too right." Lou agreed. "You didn't tell me the cabaret was in town."

Next time, she would change her choice of karaoke song. *I Predict a Riot* would surely be more appropriate.

On reflection, Lou had to admit that it actually had been an enjoyable night, even though her knuckles were bloody from having bashed that gormless plank who couldn't keep his mitts to himself, her heels were blistered, and an out-of-tune, blaring brass band stomped savagely in her head.

Looking around at the shambles, Lou remembered what had started it all, the thought quickly sobering her up.

What the bloody hell was Juan up to?

63

Juan's brow furrowed. He was sure he had glimpsed Lou in the uncouth bar he'd just passed.

"Is something the matter, darling?"

His attention snapped back to the woman at his side. She gazed adoringly at him, her voice a soft purr.

He flashed a smile revealing perfect pearly whites. "No, my lovely Diane. I just remembered I left my wallet at home and was so looking forward to taking you to Madre Tierra."

The popular restaurant Juan referred to had only recently opened and was extremely expensive.

"Oh, don't worry. I have my American Express. It can be my treat."

"Definitely not! It wouldn't be right," Juan protested.

Diane waved away his remonstrations. "Rubbish. You can pay for dinner next time. I'm famished, and interested as well as curious to hear about the proposition you mentioned." She bestowed on him a sexy little smile.

Cringing, Juan raised her hand to his lips, the paper-thin skin dry against his kiss. "You really are such a special lady."

He looked into her pale blue eyes as she stifled a coy giggle.

"And you, my darling, are a dreadful flatterer."

Taking his arm, they strolled towards the upmarket marina where the restaurant was located. Inside the eatery was simple and understated, which Juan knew from experience meant old money. He glanced round the room flashing his teeth at a few of the ladies like a shark in a school of minnows. Placing the cash he did have into the waiter's hand, he managed to secure an intimate table and whisked out Diane's chair in a show of chivalry.

"You're such a gentleman, Juan," she giggled, "I'm sure I don't know what you see in an old bird like me."

Juan rested his hands on her shoulders making circular motions on her frail collarbone with his thumbs. "You are very beautiful, Diane, both inside and out."

His lips brushed her ear before he sat down, perusing the exorbitant menu. How he loved this life. Yes, there were sacrifices. He inwardly shuddered thinking of what was to come with the seventy-year-old woman later, but oh, the benefits! This meal alone would cost what he earned in a month as a flamenco dancer.

"I never thought I would find anyone after my Colin died." Diane's eyes filled with tears as her thoughts drifted back to her dead husband, ten years gone. Juan zoned out, as she droned on. Surely, she couldn't imagine that he really felt something for her. He checked in his pocket for the little blue pill that would help him out later. He never needed them with Lou, she was hot and a wild cat in bed. Unfortunately, she wasn't quite as wealthy as Diane here, whose long gone hubby had been CEO of a large hotel group.

"I'll have the lobster to start," he smiled, making a mental note which of the female customers he could slip his number when Diane went to powder her extremely large nose. Ah well. Needs must.

64

Abby had spent the previous evening listening to Andrew's complaints. His job, Daniel, the constant rain at home, Paisley, the flight over, Spanish food. The list was endless.

His wittering wore her down. She could feel him rapidly sucking the life out of her and he'd been here less than a day. She was starting to feel sympathetic towards Paisley. God knew how the poor girl put up with her son's constant whining. The pink-haired one had oohed and ahhed as she explored the villa.

"It's absolutely gorgeous, Mrs Sinclair," she gushed, sitting at the small bistro table located on the terrace as Abby poured a generous gin and tonic. Andrew was splashing around in the pool doing a superb impersonation of the orca in *Free Willy*.

"Mrs Sinclair is so formal, Paisley. I think you've known me long enough—"

"Ooh, shall I call you Mum instead?" the girl quickly cut in.

"Please don't." Abby emptied the tall glass in one. "Abby will do just fine."

"All you need is a fella. I can set you a profile up on MSD if you want."

Paisley began ticking off Abby's attributes. Own teeth. Curvy. Likes a drink.

"God, you make me sound like a fat alki, Paisley. What's MSD when it's out?" Abby interrupted before the girl started listing her not so good features and she needed to employ a suicide watch. "What's your hotel like?" she asked, veering the conversation away from her lack of a love life.

"What? Oh, yeah, it's OK for a two star. It's just a shame there aren't more bedrooms here or we could have stayed with you."

Abby nodded and smiled, failing to mention one of the massive corner units converted to a double bed, while silently thanking Lou, the previous owners, the builders, the architect, anyone and everyone who had chosen or designed this two-bedroom villa.

"You two seem to be getting along better."

Abby sipped at the drink she'd poured. She needed to pace herself. Andrew and Paisley had mentioned going clubbing later, but there were still a few hours in their company to get through. She heard faint sniffles and looked up just as the girl burst into tears.

"Whatever's the matter?" Abby jumped up to put her arms around Paisley's shaking shoulders.

"I'm sorry" the young girl snuffled. "It's just so lovely here and you seem so happy."

"And that's made you cry because?" Abby sat back in her seat, clutching the young girl's hands.

"It's Andrew. I think he's cheating on me."

Abby bit down hard on her bottom lip to stop herself from bursting out laughing.

"Oh, love ... why do you think that?"

Paisley fished a tissue from her bag and blew her nose loudly. "He's always out with his mates. We never do anything or go anywhere. I just seem to spend my time picking up his stuff, cleaning and cooking, and then sit watching soaps on my own while he's out doing God knows what. I understand now why you were always moaning. And I forgot to tell you MSD is short for middle-aged, single, and desperate."

Desperate? God, that girl had more neck than a giraffe. She never stopped to think before opening her mouth, that's after she'd yanked on her size fifteen *clodhoppers*. Despite another two of her howlers, and instead of feeling an urge to strangle the girl, Abby actually felt empathy towards her, which showed as she spoke.

"He's just inconsiderate and selfish, Paisley ... I don't think he would cheat on you." Abby smiled. "Anyway, who else would put up with him?"

Right on cue to prove Abby's point, Andrew, having mutated into a whopping walrus lumbered around the corner. He plonked himself down at the table and reached for a bottle of beer.

"Brrr. Bit cold that pool," he panted, opening his mouth and belching from the pit of his gut.

Abby didn't need to say a word. She simply raised an eyebrow and looked directly at the pink-haired princess.

Paisley sniffled then half-smiled at Abby. "Yeah, maybe you're right."

❧ 65 ❧

Lou woke up the next morning with a stinking hangover to find Salem purposefully shredding her mosquito net. She must've left the door open when she came in last night. Sylvester and Tweetie Pie had obviously abandoned ship and skedaddled.

"Piss off," she hissed, throwing an empty plastic water bottle in the cat's direction. No way was she getting out of bed with psycho puss loose in her room.

"Abby, can you come remove the cat please!" she yelled, holding her raging head and grimacing in pain at her own screaming voice. "Abby!"

Sod it. She must be out with the dogs. What time was it anyway?

Glancing over at the clock, Lou was surprised to see it was almost midday.

Destruction complete, Salem casually sauntered out to cause havoc elsewhere. Lou grabbed the chance, reached for her robe, and gingerly made her way to the bathroom. Looking at herself in the mirror, she concluded arriving home at four in the morning might not have been the best idea. Brushing her teeth and splashing her face with cold water, she looked a little less like Frankenstein's bride. She craved a caffeine fix. If that damn cat was anywhere near the coffee pot, she may just have to commit murder.

The kitchen was empty apart from Mabel who was in her usual spot next to the range in the constant hope of scraps. Lou filled the kettle and scooped ground coffee into a large cafetière.

A note on the table explained Abby had gone to the beach with dumb and dumber, which meant she had the day to herself to recover. The large fan overhead kept the kitchen cool even when the temperature outside soared, which it recently had, the August days regularly topping forty degrees.

A knock on the door startled her and set Luna off barking from somewhere outside. *Good job they* weren't relying on Mabel to be a guard dog. Lou chuckled as the dog snored on.

Juan stood on the step, a huge bunch of yellow roses in his hand. *He'd definitely been up to something last night then.* Pulling the robe more tightly around her body, she led the way back into the kitchen and took another mug from the cupboard.

"Black no sugar, right?"

He nodded, setting the bouquet on the table. Coming up behind her, he wrapped his arms around her waist and nuzzled her neck. *Damn, he still made her tremble.*

"I thought I saw you last night in a bar with lots of men dressed as maids."

Lou thought she detected a hint of jealousy in his tone. "Yes, I saw you too ... with a friend." Her tone was neutral as she tried to keep her accusation at bay.

"Ah, yes. Diane. She is a client. She was unwell. Poor woman suffers from the migraine. I escorted her home."

In her fagged out state, what he said sounded reasonable. Lou released the breath she hadn't realised she was holding. Turning, she kissed him, glad she'd brushed her teeth. Coffee forgotten, she took his hand and led him toward the bedroom, oblivious to Salem ripping up the roses, scattering petals around the kitchen.

66

Only a few tourists were enjoying their time on the small beach where Abby had taken Andrew and Paisley.

Andrew was nursing a hangover, having apparently entered a shot drinking competition when he and his girl had eventually gone clubbing last night. His face had a grey, unhealthy tinge as he shook out a large Union Jack beach towel, demanding they kept the noise down as he was going to crash out.

Paisley stuck her tongue out behind his back. She had outdone herself today. Two teeny leopard print triangles barely covered her nipples while a matching triangle with attached cheese wire got into the groove, helplessly disappearing between the cheeks of her ample backside. Abby felt overdressed in her simple black Marks & Sparks one-piece with extra tummy control.

The two of them settled under a colourful umbrella. Abby had carted along a couple of beach bags, chock full for every situation or emergency. Along with mountains of food, she'd also stuffed in plasters, bandages, extra towels, insect repellent, sun lotion, mobile phone, money, and a bottle of vinegar. It was just as well they had the van or Santos would've been commandeered to transport everything. Abby pulled out a book about vampires she'd been dying to read, while Paisley threw a pile of celebrity gossip magazines onto her thick towel adjusting her *Ray-Bans* as she lowered her plentiful posterior onto a lucky *Teletubbies* face.

"*Primark*. Two for six quid," Paisley piped up, catching Abby's raised eyebrows at the unlucky Tinky Winky.

The golden sand was hot as Abby buried her feet and looked around. The last time she'd been here was with Jenny and Clare. She wondered how the two were getting on with married life and made a mental note to call them when she got home. They had the knack of being able to push her giggle button.

Gazing at her lardarse of a son, she sighed, opened her book, and lost herself in a dark world of sexy blood guzzlers, leaving Paisley prattling on in the background and the sun blazing a scorching trail across the azure blue sky.

She must have dozed off because some time later she awoke, to see the towel Andrew had draped over himself to stop his body burning had fallen off. One of his legs and half of his body was tomato red. Paisley was down by the water talking to some young men who seemed enamoured by her substantial assets.

It was noon; the heat was immense and the sand burnt Abby's feet as she ran down to the sea for a dip. Shaking Andrew awake on the way, and not stopping to hear his diatribe when he discovered he was half-man, half-giant lobster, she was almost at the water's edge when she stood on something.

A sharp pain shot up her leg and she collapsed to the ground trying not to cry. She obviously passed out for a few minutes as when she opened her eyes, what looked like two humongous jellies scantily clad in weeny scraps of animal print, madly wobbled. Rubbing at her eyes, Abby realised she hadn't been having a mare as the 'jellies' were actually Paisley's monster mammories jiggling in front of her face. How she hadn't eclipsed the sun was anybody's guess.

"Are you alright, Mrs Sin— Abby?"

Concern showed in Paisley's eyes as she reached out to help. The older women clocked the gang of goggling young men who couldn't take their eyes off the girl's butt, as bending over, she assisted Abby to her feet. Andrew had obviously seen the guys too and came striding down the beach looking slightly ridiculous and extremely pissed off.

Struggling, and doing her best to ignore the pain, Abby started to limp up the beach before Andrew arrived on the scene and caused chaos, most likely resulting in the much fitter looking young men giving him a severe walloping.

"I'm OK. C'mon, Paisley," she puffed, dragging the bemused girl in her wake. "I always bring vinegar just in case there's a lot of jellyfish around the coast here."

"Jellyfish? Oh, I thought you were havin' a heart attack or something. I mean you never know at your age."

Abby bit her lip and rolled her eyes.

"What the fuck were you doing with those blokes?" Andrew's voice directed at Paisley was harsh, accusing.

"Andrew! Don't talk to her like that."

Abby just wanted to go home. It was hot, her leg hurt, and she really couldn't be arsed with the two of them having a domestic on the beach.

"They were just telling me the best clubs to go to."

Paisley placated her man's dented ego by kissing him on the cheek and whispering something Abby didn't want to think about.

67

L ou took a leisurely stroll up Eduardo's path.
       She and Abby hadn't seen much of their neighbour the last few days and she wanted to talk to him about the fiesta plans. The event was only a few weeks away and finally, things were coming together.

She'd persuaded Sophia to provide free churros and chocolate for breakfast in the square. A brass band would wake everyone, marching through the streets on the first day of the celebrations. There were numerous sporting competitions organised, football, of course, various races, and a treasure hunt for the children. The Bus Stop would be the venue for kids entertainment, which included a magic show, face-painting, a clever fella (whose name escaped her) who crafted animals out of balloons, and Oswaldo the clown, who was really quite creepy. Abby had done the negotiating on that one.

The Higginbottoms were definitely not Lou's biggest fans after the swimming pool incident, even though Kylie still turned up nearly every day to help with the dogs. Santos absolutely loved her and his loud, off-tune braying could be heard the second he spied her. Eduardo was donating a vast amount of wine to the fiesta, as were a few local winemakers, and the more affluent neighbours.

Lou had decided to pay Eduardo a visit so she could finalise the arrangements for picking up his generous wine donation. After knocking at his door, then knocking again with no response, she wandered around the side of the house to the courtyard in which she invariably felt she'd flown back in time. She recalled Eduardo's tale of how his inspiration had been peeked by *The Courtyard of the Lions* at the *Alhambra* in Granada.

A large fountain dominated the centre of Eduardo's courtyard. A rearing stallion surrounded by smaller frolicking horses, the trickle of water calming in the silence. The walls rose high, arches and canopies providing much needed shade from the merciless Andalusian sun. Placed strategically in enormous urns for maximum impact was a beautiful array of palms and tropical plants. Smaller urns overflowed with bright coloured flowers interspersed with statues of one-armed Greek, or Roman goddesses and lovers locked in passionate embrace.

Lou had expected to see Eduardo as she so often did, at the table situated on the patio outside his living room, but the glass doors were unusually firm. Puzzled she tried to remember if he'd mentioned going on a trip. Deciding to come back later, she was about to leave when she glanced through the doors and swore she could see a foot sticking out from behind the large Chesterfield sofa. Shielding her eyes so she could see better, she peered through the windows. *Shit! That definitely looked like a foot.* Frantically, Lou banged on the glass. *Pointless.* Even the birds were silent. The only sound she could hear was the water from the fountain, which now seemed to be a cascade rather than a trickle, or was that her mind playing tricks?

"Eduardo!" Lou screeched.

She wasn't good in these situations and found herself wishing Abby was with her. Crying now, she tried desperately to open the doors but the heavy glass wouldn't budge. *She had to get* inside.

Lou knew there was a smaller kitchen window in the courtyard. Grabbing one of the medium sized statues, she launched it at the glass. Cringing at the sound, she jumped back to avoid being slashed by flying shards. Standing on an upturned plant pot, she pulled herself up, knocking away as many of the jagged edges as she could. Squeezing through the small opening was difficult. She winced as she felt something tear at her arm as she landed practically upside down on the thankfully empty draining board. Grabbing a tea towel to stem the blood flowing from her arm, Lou scrabbled down.

The kitchen was much smaller than the one at home, more of a galley style. Comprising yellow walls with white units, it was neat and compact just like its owner.

"Eduardo!" Lou bawled, venturing into the spacious hallway.

She noticed the antique grandfather clock, the beautiful Turkish – or maybe Persian – rug on the stone floor, and huge paintings depicting bullfights adorning the walls. A window halfway up the wide staircase flooded the room with light. Even with the sun's glare, Lou shivered as she tentatively approached the door of the living room, which was slightly ajar.

"Eduardo?" She whispered without knowing the reason why, pushing the door fully open and immediately clocking the object of her concern lying behind the sofa.

An elegant decanter of what she presumed was brandy stood uncorked on the desk, an empty glass lying beside the man on the floor. He wouldn't have been drinking this early in the morning, which meant he'd been lying here all night. She dropped to her knees and reached for his wrist, feeling for a pulse. Touching his face gently, she tried to bring him round, *He was still breathing, thank God.* She had left her mobile outside with the folder of plans for the fiesta. Picking up the old-fashioned receiver on the desk, Lou's trembling hand dialled 112. She was quickly connected.

"Una ambulancia por favor," she stuttered.

The operator babbled something Lou couldn't understand. She wanted to cry. Never had she wished she had taken those Spanish lessons more than she did in those crippling minutes.

"Habla usted inglés? Do you speak English?" *Please please,* she silently begged.

The operator didn't, but passed her to someone who did. Quickly, Lou relayed the address pleading with them to hurry up. It seemed an eternity later before she heard a loud siren. Rushing to the front door, Lou allowed the paramedics access to the property, standing numbly, tears streaming unnoticed down her cheeks, while they efficiently and quietly assessed the patient. She took the opportunity to scoot outside to retrieve her handbag while the paramedics loaded Eduardo onto a stretcher. Fishing for her phone, she eventually located it, punched Abby's number, and left a frantic message.

The paramedics checked her arm when she returned. Blood was seeping through the cloth so they ushered her into the rear of the ambulance along with an unconscious, sickly pale Eduardo.

✿ 68 ✿

Exiting the Bus Stop, Abby checked the messages on her phone. Andrew and Paisley had gone on a day trip to a nearby waterpark and she was enjoying a little bit of me time.

Bloody hell. What was going on? She rang Lou's number and cursed loudly when the call diverted to answerphone. Hailing one of two taxis permanently stationed in the square, she jumped in, her heart almost pumping out of her chest. Bernadette's husband was the driver, nodding cordially as he turned the ignition.

"Señor Márquez está en el hospital." Her voice broke and she rummaged in her bag for a tissue, puffing out an impatient sigh when her fumbling fingers couldn't find what she sought.

The driver's face registered concern as he delved into the glove compartment and handed Abby a small box. She nodded her head in thanks, pulled out a handful of tissues, dabbed at her eyes, and blew her nose.

Eduardo was well liked and respected in the village, and she knew many would be genuinely upset at the news.

"No te preocupes." He turned back to face the road and set off at speed.

Don't Worry! Easier said than done.

The hospital was an unmissable sleek building, metres from the highway just west of San Pedro. Abby knew it was one of the most modern, state-of-the-art private hospitals in Europe. Paco, as he'd introduced himself, had refused payment for the journey. Expressing thanks, with a promise to let him know what was happening as soon as she could, Abby tore from the cab and raced up the steps to the entrance.

Breathless, she gave Eduardo's name to the receptionist who directed her to one of several intensive care units. She found Lou, left arm heavily bandaged, sitting on a chair outside a private room.

"How is he?" Abby gasped. "I would hug you but I can't ... well you know ... Hell, Lou, what happened to you?" She perched on the chair next to her friend noticing how pale and drawn she looked.

"They're preparing him for an emergency bypass." Lou burst into tears. "He was just lying there. I thought he was dead. I had to do something quick."

Abby clutched Lou's hand. "You probably saved his life. Is that how you did this?" She touched the bandage gently and Lou nodded.

"I broke the window."

The sobs slowed to a snivel as a pretty, young nurse exited the room.

"You can go in for a couple of minutes." She smiled sympathetically at the women who rose as one.

Eduardo was awake, his face grey against the pillow. He tried to smile, but only managed a grimace.

"Don't let Abby near all those wires," he joked, the feeble voice almost breaking.

Surrounding the bed, there were numerous machines monitoring him. Lines and lights flashed in greens and yellows, the rhythmic beeps quietly playing the monotonous tune of life.

Abby carefully walked forward towards the bed. She gave a small smile. "How are you feeling? You gave us quite a scare." She took his hand – cold, yet clammy, the grip, weak.

"Much better for seeing you two ladies." His breath was short as he looked past Abby mouthing thank you to Lou who hovered at the foot of his bed.

"Could you telephone Felipe?" He pressed a slip of paper with the number into Abby's palm before closing his eyes.

"Of course," Abby whispered.

His chest rose and fell, but it seemed too much like hard work as the women retreated to allow the medical staff to get on with trying to save his life.

~

Paco was waiting outside when Abby and Lou eventually came out of the hospital. Lounging against the battered taxi smoking a cigarette, he offered one to each of the women before they climbed into the back of the cab to make their way home to attend to the animals.

Back at the villa, each with their own thoughts after making the call to Felipe who said he'd be on the next available flight, Abby sat Lou down with a large brandy while she went to walk the dogs and put the chickens to bed. An hour later, she sat opposite her friend holding her hands, which were still icy cold. Mabel and Luna both lay at her feet as if knowing she was hurting.

"He'll be fine, Lou. Please try not to stress too much." Abby hoped she sounded more confident then she felt.

She made them both a ham and tomato sandwich, opened a bottle of red wine, and poured two large glasses. Lou took hers with thanks, tears still in her eyes.

"I was so scared Abby ... I thought he was dead."

Abby sat down, sliding her arm around Lou's shaking shoulders. "Well he isn't, thanks to you."

Suddenly a lightning bolt named Sylvester shot through the living room, Salem in hot pursuit. Both Luna and Mabel jumped up in fright knocking wine, ham, and bread out of the hands of Abby and Lou and scattering it everywhere.

"I'll be next for a bloomin' heart attack," Abby muttered under her breath, praying the stain resistant corner unit actually was, whilst admiring Mabel's ability to swallow a ham baguette practically whole.

She looked up to see Lou smiling. "I told you they'd learn to get along."

Both women let go of the emotions of the day, rolling about the floor crying and laughing.

❧ 69 ❦

Felipe had arrived the previous evening as Lou, Abby, and Kylie were trying to round up Santos after yet another escape. This time he'd managed to roam amongst some of Abby's vegetables. Trailing raspberry canes, a carrot dangling from his mouth, he led them a merry dance before leading them to the front drive where an impressive looking 4x4 idled.

"Wow!" Abby came around the corner spotting Kylie who, Santos forgotten, smoothed her hair as she blushed, ogling the spitting image of Enrique Iglesias clambering out of the vehicle.

"Nice hair doesn't compensate for a mouth hanging open as if you're catching flies, Kylie." Abby's voice broke into a teasing giggle.

Snickering, Lou nudged Abby, her mind bouncing back to her days of online dating and her run-in with Mr Bean lookalike Neville, who'd posted a photo of the Latino heart-throb in an attempt to hook a woman. *Ah, memories.* She could definitely appreciate this guy's stunning features. Tall, slim, and muscular he looked as if he were of African heritage, his latte coloured skin stretched over a perfect bone structure.

Abby scowled at them both before moving forward to introduce herself, trying to ignore the entangled donkey who decided to impress the visitor by lifting his tail and pooping all over the drive. The stranger's piercing green eyes flicked between defecating donkey and gawping females.

"Hi, you must be Felipe?" She held out her hand then remembering she'd been the one to push Santos out of her raspberries from behind, quickly withdrew it.

"Yes, and you must be Abby. I have heard a lot about you and your friend."

"Oh? All good I hope." Feeling ridiculous standing there filthy, in shorts, wellingtons, and Yogi Bear T-Shirt, she turned around sensing someone behind her.

"I'm Kylie, pleased to meet you." The girl held out her hand.

Felipe smiled warmly. "Sorry for interrupting." He glanced at the errant donkey who now stood placidly munching the carrot. "I have just come from the airport and wanted to let you know I am going to the hospital to see my father, but I can see you are busy. I shall come back another time."

"Oh, no, it's fine," Lou took charge, "please come in and have a drink before you go. I was the one who found your father and went to hospital with him."

Without giving him a chance to accept or refuse the invite, she ushered him into the house, leaving Abby and Kylie to retrieve Santos and clear up the mess.

70

I t was Andrew and Paisley's final day. In a fit of benevolence, they decided to spend it with Abby because, as Paisley had so politely put it, 'although boring, she and Andrew wouldn't have to spend any money on food and drink and Abby's pool was as good as the hotel's'.

Abby had bitten her tongue as she so often did after Paisley had opened her trap. She also noticed she had a fair few marks from having to nip herself while the pink-haired one had been here. For sure, that girl had a severe case of foot in mouth.

Eduardo had come through surgery fine, the hospital had informed this morning when Abby phoned. Recovering well, he'd asked to see Lou so she and Felipe had left early, much to Kylie's disappointment.

Abby was in the kitchen making lime and ginger marmalade while her offspring and his girlfriend lounged by the pool. Playing hostess again, she'd taken out a bucket of cold beers for Andrew, and a large pitcher of homemade sangria for Paisley who was sporting another compulsory gnats bikini. Today, a vivid tangerine frilly number on oil drenched skin resembling melting chocolate, covered where it touched. Abby had seen bigger plasters for her pimples and felt sure the girl could have brought over her whole week's luggage in a tiny clutch bag.

Peering at the jam thermometer, as it crept up to the temperature required to set the green fruit concoction, she was humming softly to herself when she heard a bloodcurdling scream from outside. Bloody Hell, what was the matter now? There was never a dull moment here.

Rushing outside she was surprised to see Andrew creased up laughing, while Paisley danced a funny jig making gagging noises. Her massive bosom, having escaped the confines of the itsy-bitsy bikini top, bounced like buoys in a violent storm.

"Er ... what's the matter Paisley?" Abby was almost scared to ask.

"That fucking cat, that's what's the matter!" She screamed, still jumping about, knockers madly swinging from side to side.

Abby looked around for Salem guessing he was the culprit. *Jesus, what had he done now?* She had an overwhelming urge to bring Paisley out of her histrionics with a sharp slap around the chops. The girl certainly needed one.

Instead, keeping Paisley's arms firmly pinned to her side, Abby asked purposefully, "What's he done?" It was becoming increasingly difficult to keep a straight face

"He dropped a dead lizard on my face." She began the gagging noises again, milking the drama for all she was worth.

She wrestled her arms free from Abby's grip and brought her hands up to her face and throat. "OMG! It was disgusting."

A choirboy with his nuts caught in a vice couldn't have sounded worse than she did.

"D'you think I'll have to go to hospital? The ugly thing could've bitten me. *OMG, I could* die."

"Not just on her face," Andrew piped up, ignoring Paisley's overblown comments, his face purple as tears streamed down his face. "It was right in her mouth ... you should have seen it, Mum. It was fucking Lethal"

In a late attempt at modesty, Paisley grabbed at her bikini top. Snatching up the half-empty pitcher of sangria, she flung the liquid in Andrew's direction.

"Not fuckin' laughin' now are you, dickhead!" she snarled before stomping off into the house.

Andrew stood dripping wet covered in the remains of fruit punch. A slice of lemon slid down his chest, and a large chunk of apple sat atop his head. "You reckon she wasn't amused?" he huffed.

"Think that's safe to say. Best get yourself cleaned up son."

Abby followed Paisley into the house making a mental note to treat Salem to one of the fresh mackerel chilling out in the fridge.

The Pink-haired One – o

The Siamese Devil – 1

71

August rolled on hot and humid, the heat a heavy blanket, resting on the dry, dusty earth.

Eduardo returned home from hospital with a large scar and instructions to rest. Felipe was taking a hiatus from work in the UK, much to the delight of a love-struck Kylie. Who had taken out her piercings and was letting her spiky hair fall in a softer style. The couple had been out a couple of times, she confided to Abby.

Juan had disappeared on business again, with a kiss and a promise to Lou that everything was in order ... the investment should start bringing in a return during September when they were planning a holiday to the Caribbean. Personally, Abby thought the proposed trip was a waste of money; they had everything the Caribbean offered and more right on their doorstep.

Lou was trying to arrange transport for the remaining pup – the runt of the litter – Abby's old neighbour, Mrs Wilson couldn't get rid of. She was hoping the pup would find himself in Spain in a few weeks. The company who took the rescue dogs to the UK had said they would bring him back on their latest trip. Andrew and Paisley had been taking care of him, and if the irate emails and texts were anything to go by, he was a chip off the old block. Abby was deliriously excited about meeting Chester's offspring, a boy who she'd named Floyd.

"It'll be like having my Chester back again," she gushed.

Although Lou privately grimaced at the thought of perpetual farting, and no doubt a wild hullabaloo when the new arrival met the feline devil incarnate, she was pleased for her best buddy.

Final prep for the fiesta was underway. A shitload of boxes of fireworks had arrived and placed in the church, piled precariously high. The crows spent more time than ever chattering and waving their arms round the fountain, and local schoolchildren made colourful decorations and costumes. Abby had also made a few costumes, but didn't have time to do many, which in Lou's opinion wasn't a bad thing as they were reminiscent of an explosion in a paint factory.

Abby was inundated with sales, not only from her market stall but also online. Cactus jam was one of her bestsellers and the kitchen was often reminiscent of an eighties pop video, neon pink cactus juice splattered everywhere. A regular sight was Abby sitting at the kitchen table pulling cactus spikes from various parts of her body. Even with gloves and tweezers, it was still a difficult process to remove the spines from the fruit. In his curiosity, Sylvester, on more than one occasion, had ended up resembling a poor relation of a porcupine. Oddly, Salem hadn't come anywhere near, and Tweetie Pie's curiosity had never been as sharp as Vester's.

Paisley had phoned a couple of days after they'd returned home informing Abby that Janice had given birth to a 9lb baby girl named Fuchsia Mae Bunny. *OMG.*

Abby could see it now. A world full of pink frills, ribbons, bows, and candyfloss. Blimey. And what a name to lumber the poor mite with. Who did Sugar Tits Janice think she was? Gwyneth Paltrow? Mark didn't even like the colour pink. Laughing, she fired up her laptop and ordered a cute hand-knitted lemon cardigan for delivery with a congratulations note.

Life was so funny. Before she'd moved to Spain, Janice had been a major thorn in her side. Now Abby couldn't give two hoots.

The day of the fiesta dawned beautiful, as did most days on the mountains, the pale morning light mushrooming into a radiant display. Reds and pinks chased wisps of cloud from the sky as birdsong punctured the air celebrating another golden sunrise.

Standing on her balcony, Abby's eyes devoured the beautiful scenery as she felt that wonderfully familiar feeling of catching her breath. Surely, this vista had no comparison in the world. To the left, the ocean glistened, as if every star in the universe had fallen during the night to rest until dusk the same day. To the right, the mountains' jagged outline was a tear in the blotting paper sky.

Dragging on combat pants and a vest top, Abby scrunched her wild tresses into an untidy bun. She needed to walk the dogs and feed the ever-increasing menagerie before doing anything else. Hastily, she ran downstairs, grabbed a bottle of fresh orange juice, and bolted out the door.

Over the past few weeks when walking the dogs, Abby had also been exercising Santos. She'd made a necessary decision in an effort to curb his attempts to escape.

Also trotting merrily along, Pork Pie, and Sausage Roll, a couple of piglets recently acquired from the smelly man who ran the gaff where she and Lou had purchased the chickens. On her visits to pick up feed and other 'farmy' items, Abby had noticed the piglets in a filthy pen. Determined to rescue them, she'd nagged Lou to death until she finally gave in. Within minutes, Abby had jumped into the old Citroën and sped off at speed to release the two little porkers from a life of miserable squalor. Proper characters, the two new additions to the tribe fitted in beautifully with the growing number of waifs and strays.

Abby and her brood were a comical sight as they mooched along on their morning strolls.

A donkey, two pigs, five dogs and, bringing up the rear, the Siamese devil who usually slunk along for the first half mile before dashing off elsewhere to cause merry mayhem.

The celebrations had already started by the time Abby and Lou arrived in the square, although the band, despite practicing for months, was making a terrible racket. Abby was glad to see them making their way up the winding streets. There was definitely no chance of anyone sleeping through that din. Children scampered madly, screeching at the top of their voices. Both women decided there and then that they would need a shitload of sangria to get through the next few days.

Sophia was frying churros outside her shop whilst Alberto, glued to her side, sported the grouchy look of a bulldog chewing a thistle. The smell of warm dough, sugar, and vanilla drifted on the breeze along with the not so pleasant whiff of three donkeys, borrowed to provide rides for the children. Scheduled for later that afternoon was a parade with horses and decorated floats, along with various competitions for both adults and children.

Christine came toward them with cups of strong coffee and a plate of steaming, sweet pastries. "Looks as if you could do with these." She smiled warmly, handing over the goodies.

"You're a life saver. I didn't realise there were so many children in the village." Lou grimaced.

"It's the Spanish way ... to let them run wild." Christine laughed. "You're lucky. I get to spend most of the day painting the little gits' faces."

Abby grinned and sipped her coffee. She wasn't staying long as she had to return home to collect produce to enter into the relevant competitions and was also preparing some of the food to eat after the bullfight, which she definitely would not be attending. Eduardo was meeting up with them later for an evening of live music, dancing, and fireworks. Felipe and a handful of men from the village were setting up a gigantic pan so they could take turns supervising the cooking of an enormous paella.

Spotting Elaine and Ken across the square, Abby made her excuses, leaving Christine and Lou gossiping. She wanted to see if the

Higginbottoms had had a chance to consider the conversation she'd had with them last week.

"They've been awful chatty lately," Lou remarked, taking a delicate bite of the sweet confection.

Christine shuddered. "Ugh! Can't stand that man. I wish he were fighting the bull this afternoon. I know who I'd be cheering for."

Christine's comment made Lou snort into her coffee. While licking the drops off her top lip, she felt a hand on her shoulder. Swinging round, she was startled to find herself face to face with Juan. "Oh!" she gasped. "You're back. I wasn't expecting you 'til the weekend."

"I return for flamenco." Bowing slightly at Christine, he smiled and ran hungry, possessive eyes over Lou's body. "You look very beautiful. We will dance together this evening, si?"

Before she'd had a chance to respond he leant over, whispering something in Lou's ear that made her blush. Then he was gone, disappearing into the crowd like a fart in a fan factory.

Abby had brought preserves, vegetables, and lemons to enter into a few of the many food competitions. The olives hadn't yet been harvested – wouldn't be until winter – and she was hoping to be one of the main contenders in the olive oil challenge next year. As well as food competitions this year, she had also entered the flower-arranging contest the following day, along with Lou, Sylvia, and Christine.

After dropping off her produce at the relevant tables – making sure her name was visible to highlight her contribution – Abby weaved through numerous tables where men of the village arm-wrestled or tried to beat each other in various tests of strength, both physical and mental. She smiled at people she knew, stopping to chat along the way. This was what she dreamed of when she was younger. The sun, blue sky, laughter, good friends ... it had all come true. Almost hugging herself with pleasure, she began walking home.

The animals still needed looking after, fiesta or not.

73

After making a large tray of Spanish omelette, another of tomatoes stuffed with goat's cheese, olives, and capers, and two *Tupperware* containers full of almond cupcakes, Abby walked round to the kennels.

She smiled warmly as she looked at the chickens either sitting in the shade or pecking in the dust. She and Lou had been lucky this summer with only two animal fatalities, both chooks. Mr Fox had unfortunately eaten Erin Brockovich, and Maria von Trapp had succumbed to a particular strain of chicken disease, which after a week's quarantine proved fatal and the hills had no longer been alive with the sound of clucking. Fortunately, it hadn't spread, and the remainder of the flock looked well cared for and content. The goats were happy and she could hear the rattle of tiny hooves on the play equipment in their paddock.

As Abby unlocked the first dog run, Presley, a scruffy Wolfhound cross, who apart from the obvious sneer looked as different from his namesake as shit from clay, nearly bowled her over.

"Come on now, we aren't going far today."

She unclasped leashes from the pegs, rounding up the rest of the motley crew while singing happily, if slightly out of tune. A loud hee-hawing bellowed from the donkey enclosure. Furious that Abby was intending to leave him behind; Santos was making his voice heard. She threw him a couple of carrots to shut him up and took the dogs for a shorter walk than usual, although she had a Frisbee, tug toys, and balls so they were still worn out when they returned, and looked relieved to be back in their cool kennels.

"Dinner is served."

Abby placed bowls of kibble and fresh water down for the dogs before feeding and bedding down the pigs for the evening.

After a short siesta, and refreshing thirty-minute shower, she was ready for the evening festivities. Dressed in a short, pleated Grecian style dress, diamante flip-flops adorning her feet, Abby happily sauntered back down to the square.

Thankfully, the bullfight – held in an ancient arena on the outskirts of the village – was long over. The men, chock-full of testosterone sounded raucous, laughter and shouts filled the air, groups sat drinking around dancers, and live bands clapped and stamped their feet in time to the music. Roars of olé rang out as the sun said goodbye, a melting orange ice lolly sliding down the mountains, the sky turning a vivid crimson and purple before fading to navy blue lit up with a million fireflies.

The tempting smell of food permeated the air as Abby placed her offerings on the trestle tables surrounding the giant paella, which had obviously been popular if the lack of leftovers were anything to go by. Sardines grilled over open fires and women in traditional costumes passed round bread and drinks.

Abby found Eduardo sitting with Christine, Sylvia, and Felipe. Paco sang in his rich baritone while Bernadette gazed at her husband adoringly, her many children chasing each other like hyperactive whippets, except Juliana, the newly-crowned carnival queen perched on a makeshift throne decorated with flowers in the centre of the square surrounded by her new subjects.

Teenage boys desperate for her attention placed gifts at her feet. Face flushed, her eyes shone with excitement. She'd probably remember this night forever, Abby thought.

Stray cats mooched around the fringes of the family gatherings hoping for the odd titbit. Abby stepped on a particularly scrawny specimen's tail as she ambled over to sit down on an overturned crate, narrowly missing the fire as she tripped. Red scratches ran parallel down her calf.

"Bleedin' hell!" Steadying herself, Abby examined the wounds as she sat down and accepted a drink from Bernadette, hearing Eduardo mutter something about *everywhere she goes.*

"You OK?" Sylvia's voice sounded a little slurred, making Abby sip the offered mystery drink gingerly.

"I've had worse," Abby murmured, ignoring Eduardo's snigger. "No Kylie tonight?" She turned towards Felipe.

"No. There's some sort of family crisis ... she's over there with her parents."

Felipe pointed to the terrace outside the British pub where Kylie sat with her parents, the three of them in animated conversation. Elaine, frequently dabbing at her eyes appeared upset, while Ken chain-smoked, glancing over at Abby every few minutes, and shaking his head.

"Who put the fireworks next to that prat?" Sylvia observed.

As the church had become a temporary nursery, someone had removed several boxes of fireworks and piled them perilously high between the church and the Bus Stop, a makeshift fence offering scant protection.

Abby shook her head at Spanish Health and Safety. "Does anyone have a match?" she laughed.

74

L ou had spent an extremely pleasant afternoon in Juan's bed. Stretching catlike, she looked around the room wondering when he would start to make the place look more like home. A scattering of cushions, paintings, or ornaments wouldn't hurt. They would definitely add that welcome feeling.

As she reflected, the sound of running water stopped from the adjoining en suite. The door opened and her lover appeared, a towel draped low on his hips, drops of water glistening on his dark skin. Lou licked her lips, feeling her insides turn to slush. *God, man, you're sexy.*

"I have to get ready for the show," he advised, bending to kiss her on the lips.

"Mmm. I'm looking forward to it," she purred.

He smiled, eyes twinkling. "You are a distraction, lady," he teased, playfully slapping her backside as she scrabbled around looking for her knickers whipped off earlier in lustful passion.

Ten minutes later, Lou was walking the short distance home, a large, dark cloud hovering ominously on the horizon. Remembering Eduardo's warning that morning, that storms had been reported farther north, she hoped bad weather wouldn't spoil the celebrations. She was so grateful Eduardo seemed to be doing well. She hadn't realised how much she cared for him until the day of his heart attack. Feeling a small shiver in the clammy heat, she rushed the last few metres home.

Luna lay curled up in her basket with Mabel when she walked into the living room. She was surprised and unnerved to see Salem roosting on the coffee table, his posture not unlike Bastet the Egyptian goddess.

"Hey, puss," she grinned, as the cat eyed her suspiciously.

Hastily retreating, Lou took a quick shower before completing her 'going out' routine. Dressed in black bodycon maxidress and compulsory high stilettos, she brushed her hair to a gleaming shine, grabbed a shawl, and strolled down the hill, eagerly anticipating the joy of watching her lover dance.

75

This is the life. Delicious food, good drink, spending time with friends.

Seated next to Lou, a smiling Abby basked in the rousing atmosphere. The friends sat side by side soaking up the revelry. A loud cheer interrupted Abby's tipsy musings. Turning her head, she noticed someone had cleared a space. A small, wrinkled man she didn't know sat on a rickety old chair, a roll-up dangling from his mouth. In his hands, he held a beautifully decorated guitar.

Lou nudged her sharply. "I can't wait. Juan's show's about to start." She gabbled excitedly.

"*Oh, joy*. And there was me thinking something good was about to happen."

Abby reached for the large pitcher of sangria resting on a table specially reserved for drinks.

Christine let out a loud guffaw. "Come on, Abby ... you must admeet he is a veery attractive man." The Dutch twang was apparent.

"Yeah! So was Ted Bundy," Abby quipped, looking at Christine with a poker face then, on seeing Lou's face darken, quickly lifting her hands in defeat and apologising.

"Shut up and watch will ya!" Lou barked. "You can be a right cow at times, Abby."

Another man the girls hadn't noticed started thrumming a heartbeat on a set of small drums.

The guitarist joined in, and as if in pain started wailing.

Juan strutted into the centre with his partner.

"Blimey! Do my eyes deceive me, or is that Isabella?" Abby was taken aback to see one of the crows.

'Your eyes don't deceive you and yes, indeed it is. I have never mentioned it, but she is the best dancer in the village," Eduardo explained.

Dressed in traditional costume, Isabella was almost unrecognis-able. An oversized blue peony rose, and intricately carved comb adorned the severe bun fashioned from long, dark hair on the right side of her head. Dramatic, dark make-up transformed the woman's face, making her look mysterious and beautiful.

Her incredible flamenco outfit – *traje de flamenca* – drew gasps. Sapphire blue, the dress clung like a second skin, flaring out from high on her hips to allow freedom of movement. Trimmed with layers of ruffles and black lace, the skirt swished from side to side. Tiers of ruffles embellished the sleeves of the gown, while black embroidered flowers cascaded from her shoulder across her body, a black lace shawl covering the skin revealed by the low cut V both front and back. In her hand, she clasped an enormous black lace ornate fan. Hiding shyly, her eyes lowered.

"Bloody hell! Why does she keep that figure hidden?" Abby was stunned.

"Don't ask me." Sylvia gawped, as amazed as the others. "That dress must have taken some work. You think she made it herself?"

Only Eduardo seemed composed.

"Shh ..." Lou hissed.

Losing herself to the music, her feet encased in cubano heeled black flamenco shoes Isabella raised her arms above her head, rhyth-mically stamping in time to the hypnotic drumbeat.

This was the cue for Juan's grand performance. Lou had seen him dance before, of course, but always as a teacher, never in a show. Slim black trousers left little to the imagination, the satin shirt a perfect colour match with Isabella's dress. Clenched between his teeth, lay a deep red rose, the normally hooded expression even more brooding as he sidled toward his partner.

The enthralled crowd clapped and cheered as the duo swirled and stomped in passionate, seductive flow, telling a story as well as any ballet could. Surprisingly, Abby found herself caught up in the moment. She had to admit Juan was bloody good – both were – but surely it was the drink making her feel this way because his erotic movements were making her knickers a bit damp. Mind you, it was hot, and she'd had a few sangrias and she *did* have a weak bladder, so maybe not.

It seemed most people in the village had gathered to watch the flamenco, except for the Higginbottoms still ensconced on their empty terrace, so nobody heard the clip clop of tiny hooves on the cobbles. In fact, nobody noticed at all as Santos seeing Kylie, his favourite person in the world, trotted over to the Bus Stop. Standing behind Ken, he hee-hawed his pleasure at finding his friend.

"What the devil!" Ken jumped up. Flinging his arms up in terror, his cigarette catapulted into the air and landed in one of the boxes behind him.

"It's that soddin' donkey again," he growled, raising his fist before Kylie grabbed at it.

"No, Dad, don't. He doesn't know any better."

She went to put her arms around Santos who seemed quite pleased with himself.

Panicking, as usual, Elaine fussed over her husband. "Are you alright, duck?"

"Course I am. Stop flappin', woman." He pushed her away and was about to go inside to nurse his wounded pride when there was a hissing sound from the side of the terrace.

"What was that?" Elaine raised her eyebrows, cocking her head to one side.

Abby could hear shouting but presumed it was the crowd caught up in the dancing. It wasn't until the sky lit up and exploded in a waterfall of sparks that she frowned.

"I thought the fireworks were later."

"They were supposed to be." Eduardo stood up, looking puzzled.

Following Eduardo, Lou also rose to her feet. She spied the crowd thinning out, moving to see what was happening over by the British bar.

"Oh, for fuck's sake, not again." Lou dropped her head into her hands as she spied Santos.

"Abby!"

The onslaught of several explosions, fireworks of all colours and sizes shooting into the sky and across the square drowned out Lou's booming voice. The men of the village, although running to try to move the rest of the boxes, laughed as they did so finding the whole scene hilarious. Shrieking in panic, women gathered their children to their breasts, while the older kids watched enthralled at the impromptu show.

"It's that bloody donkey again!" Ken hollered.

While her father barked and cursed, Kylie desperately tried to calm the terrified animal, steadfastly clinging to his neck as he repeatedly bucked. It was too much – the noise, the flashes of light. Santos lost control. Charging around the square, he smashed into the paella pan sending it crashing to the ground.

"Abby, do something!" Lou squawked. Santos's shenanigans at their own party had been bad enough, but this was mortifying. Feeling helpless, she started to cry.

"Come, come, it's not that bad." Eduardo, serene as ever took her arm. "Its' a bit much for my old ticker though. Shall we go home and have a cup of tea? Leave them to it?"

Lou looked round for Juan but couldn't see him anywhere. "Yeah, that sounds good." Smiling weakly, and feeling a little foolish for what she now saw as overreacting, she linked her arm through Eduardo's.

The noise was unbelievable. Abby quickly snaked through the crowd towards Santos. She couldn't understand how this could be his fault, but she needed to get to him and calm him down. Kylie arrived at her side.

"Sorry, Abby, I couldn't hold him." The girl was genuinely upset.

Abby squeezed her arm. "Don't worry, love. It's not your fault."

One of the fireworks had caught in the wheel of Alberto's wheelchair. As he came hurtling across the square, the old git resembled a giant human Catherine wheel. Wailing, Sophia stood nearby wringing her hands and shaking her head.

Felipe joined Abby and Kylie, helping to corral the now knackered and woebegone Santos.

"You two go enjoy yourselves." Abby, staggering slightly nodded towards Felipe and Kylie. "I'm gonna take him home."

Lou must have gone with Juan, she couldn't see either of them. The fireworks had begun to slow down, so snatching a bit of bunting from the railing outside the restaurant Abby tied it round the donkey's neck and began a slow zigzag walk up the hill.

The racket in the village had calmed down by the time Abby reached their open gate.

"You're a right bugger." Smiling to herself, she scratched Santos on the neck and led him to his paddock. For once, he seemed quite relieved to be home and trotted over to his favourite tree.

"Yes, you think about what you've done," she laughed.

Deciding on a nightcap before bed, Abby had just reached the kitchen door when she heard a noise.

"Lou, is that you?" she called out, searching in the dark for a weapon and hoping she didn't come across a spider or God forbid, a snake in the process. Turning the corner, she bumped into Juan.

"Oh! It's you," she said. "Where's Lou?"

"I do not know. I have left my watch inside. That is such a shame. I was hoping she would be in."

"You better come in then."

Turning the key, Abby could feel Juan's hot breath on the back of her neck. The sensation was slightly disconcerting.

"Would you like a drink?" she shouted through to Lou's bedroom where she could hear him rummaging around. "Have you found it?"

He emerged from the room brandishing the missing timepiece. "Si." He grinned broadly.

"Did you enjoy the flamenco, Abby?"

Jeez! This guy had no comprehension of personal space. Holding two glasses in front of her as a flimsy shield, she backed up against the kitchen table.

"Er ... yes ... very entertaining," she stuttered.

The next thing she knew his lips were on hers, his hand moving swiftly from her waist to her left breast. Turning her head sharply to the side, she bashed his nose.

"Ow!"

"What the hell are you doing?" Swiftly, Abby moved away from him. "I think you better leave." Abby turned her back, instantly regretting the action as he came up behind her.

"You do not mean that." Obviously, he wasn't used to being rejected. His fingers stroked her arm.

"Yes, I do! Now fuck off!"

As if to emphasise the point Salem arrived, jumped onto the table, and began hissing menacingly. Juan, who didn't like cats at the best of times stood back.

"If that is what you want, I shall go. I don't think there is any reason for Lou to hear about this, do you?"

"Just get out!" Abby screamed.

She hadn't realised she was trembling.

T he first thing Lou noticed when she awoke the next morning was the absence of eau de Domestos. Going through to the kitchen for a couple of paracetamol, she was surprised to see Abby sitting at the table, head in hands.

"Heavy night, eh?" Lou mumbled, opening the massive fridge to grab a bottle of water. She unscrewed the top and glugged almost half of the cold, refreshing liquid. Her mouth felt dry as old bones. "I'll have to get a padlock for that gate today. That animal's becoming a liability. What a carry on with him last night. Talk about embarrassing. What's he—"

"Lou, would you mind sitting down. I have something to tell you," Abby quietly cut in.

"Whoa! That sounds serious." Running her fingers through tousled hair, Lou sat down opposite Abby. "I have something to tell you too. You first. What's up?"

Lou reached over for her hand as Abby burst into tears.

"When I left the fiesta and brought Santos home I made sure he was OK for the night and came back to the house and Juan turned up and made a pass at me. I know you won't believe me but it's true I pushed him away honestly I did but he'll tell you it was my fault I know he will and I don't want us to fall out." The words came out rushed and garbled through her sobs.

"Shh, Shh. It's OK. Of course, I believe you. D'you know where I was last night?"

Abby shook her head.

"I went back to Eduardo's." Lou watched Abby carefully for a reaction, but she didn't seem to be catching on.

"Eduardo's? Why?" Abby appeared puzzled, furrowing her brow.

Lou stifled a yawn, the effects of a late night catching up. She smiled at her friend. "We talked. I've decided to finish things with Juan ... but there are some complications. Eduardo and I like each other ... I mean, really like each other."

Comprehension finally dawned on Abby's face. "You ... and Eduardo?"

"Yes, silly, you don't mind do you?"

"Of course, I don't mind. Not at all. Some good news. Brilliant news, actually. What's the matter?"

The pleasure on Abby's face froze when she clocked the frown on Lou's.

"Why was Juan here last night? Did he come home with you?"

"No. He was already here. Gave me a bit of a fright as I heard a noise and didn't know what it was. He said he'd left his watch in your bedroom."

Lou's face took on a look of panic. "No he didn't! He had it when we were at his place yesterday afternoon."

Pushing back the chair, Lou jumped up and sprinted to her room almost tripping over Sylvester lounging in a pool of sunlight in the hall.

"What's wrong?" Abby bolted after her friend, wondering what had spooked her so.

Lou stood shaking her head in disbelief, gazing into the drawer of her bedside cabinet. "Oh, Jesus! He's taken them," she spluttered, legs feeling intensely weak. Eventually, she sank to the tiles, weeping like a child.

"Taken what? Lou, will you please tell me what's going on." Worried now, Abby slowly approached a distraught Lou.

"Simon's medal ... and my engagement ring," Lou stammered. "He's taken them." A deluge of hot, salty tears streamed down her stricken face.

Knowing how important the two items were to her best friend, Abby felt the rage rise within. *That fucking slimeball.* She knew her gut had been right about him from the start, but Lou's present distress meant Abby couldn't make too much noise and cause more anguish. Oh, how she wanted to make a right fucking racket. An explosion louder than all the fiesta fireworks. A rumpus that would cause more damage than Santos, Salem, or the feline mafia combined. She had to hold back and bite her tongue, which was gagging to say, "I told you so". This was neither the time nor the place for smug, tactless comments. Her friend needed comfort not puffed-up, senseless wittering.

Going over to hug her, Abby spoke in gentle, reassuring tones. "We'll get them back, hun. We'll go up there now ... he's probably still in bed. Come on."

Pulling Lou to her feet, Abby had visions of kneeing the bastard in the nuts.

"He won't get away with this. Lou, what is it?"

Her friend's face had turned sickly pale.

"Lou?"

Lou sat down on the edge of the bed, shaking her head. "Abby, I've done something really stupid."

Abby couldn't imagine what the 'really stupid' thing could be. Lou wasn't the stupid type. "Oh, God ... you're not pregnant are you?"

Lou almost laughed through her sobs. "At my age? If only it were that simple. No. I gave him some money to invest ... he said it was a sure thing, we were both going to be rich. I trusted him." Another wave of crying ensued.

"Oh, is that all?" Abby waved her hand dismissing Lou's words. It wasn't as if Lou couldn't afford to lose a couple of grand. She had a fair whack of her winnings left. Then, seeing Lou's wide, frightened eyes, she froze. "How much, Lou? *How much did you give him?*"

Lou raised her eyes to Abby's. "The lot." The reply was barely a whisper as her head dropped to the floor in shame.

"*Fucking hell.* Right ... well, that's it. Come on." Abby grasped Lou's hands and hauled her to her feet. "We're gonna pay that thieving twat a little visit."

A bby and Lou marched up the hill each with their own thoughts, although their own thoughts were identical. How the fuck could Lou have been so gullible?

On arrival at Juan's, they were surprised to see a tall, smartly dressed man at his front door. Dressed in dark linen trousers, light grey shirt, and highly polished black loafers, a shock of light brown hair fell over his forehead and caressed the small designer shades perched on his nose.

"Out the way, buster!" Pushing past him, an incensed Abby started hammering on the door. "We know you're in there, you thieving bastard. Get out here. Now!"

Giving the door a kick, she turned to the astonished man who stood mouth agape. Lou stood shuffling her feet in the gravel, eyes downcast.

"Who are you?" Abby shot at the stranger, her tone implying she was not in the mood for any more shit this morning.

The man removed his sunglasses revealing soft, hazel eyes, reached in his shirt pocket and pulled out an official looking badge. He flashed it in front of the irate woman's face.

"You are policia?"

The man nodded. "Now can I ask, what is going on here, ladies?"

Abby gave him a garbled version of events while he scribbled in his notebook.

When Abby finally managed to draw breath, the man spoke once more.

"You should both come to the station with me where you can make official statements," he advised. "Come, I will take you there."

He drove them into town where they spent most of the day repeating the story, waiting around to sign paperwork, and sitting in waiting areas on uncomfortably hot plastic seats.

"I always knew there was something shifty about him," Abby snorted, as she and Lou stood outside the police station stretching their bodies and puffing on a much-needed cigarette.

The friendly detective had informed them that the villa didn't belong to Juan, but was the property of one Pablo Álvarez, a surgeon who worked in America. Juan had rented the place, but the rent hadn't been paid for the past three months. Señor Álvarez had contacted the Spanish police fearing items he'd left in the villa may have also been stolen.

"No shit, Einstein," Abby had muttered under her breath.

There had also been reports coming in from a few wealthy ladies confirming they had been victims of the con man. One, named Diane, had lost her life savings – over £100,000 – in some bogus investment. Lou had been tight-lipped throughout the ordeal. She was standing now gazing out towards the sea.

"I don't understand how I could've been such an idiot," she said, shaking her head again. She was more distraught over the medal and ring than the money.

Abby had wondered the same thing but kept schtum. To be fair, it was she who was responsible for Lou's precious mementos going awol.

"I've got an idea. C'mon." She strode away with Lou bringing up the rear.

79

The celebrations were in full swing again by the time the best friends arrived back in the village, scorched bunting, and a few burnt boxes of fireworks the only remaining evidence of last night's shenanigans.

In the square, a children's fancy dress parade was underway, with a rather disorderly game of football off to one side. The Bus Stop was open for business but there was no sign of the Higginbottoms. Abby left a shell-shocked Lou in the care of Christine who was sitting alone outside the gallery, a large pitcher of lager, small bowl of olives, and a massive slice of tortilla cluttered on an undersized table at her side.

While Christine fussed over Lou, Abby went down a side street to make the call. He answered on the third ring.

"Si ... who is this?" Just the sound of his smarmy voice raised Abby's blood to boiling point, but fighting her anger she smiled sweetly.

"Juan, hi, it's Abby" She had expected him to hang up but he waited in silence.

"Look, I'm so sorry about last night. You took me by surprise that's all. I don't want to betray Lou, but I can't stop thinking about that kiss." She paused imagining his smarmy grin on the other end of the line.

"Unfortunately, something has come up and I have to go away on business."

Damn. It wasn't going to work. Thinking on her feet, she carried on. "Ah, that's a shame. Lou mentioned that you'd invested some money for her and well ... I have a little nest egg. I was hoping you could give me some advice over dinner tomorrow, everyone will be attending the final night of the fiesta so we would have privacy to talk or ..." She left the sentence hanging in mid-air.

"Of course ... of course ... I have a few things to pick up from the villa so I will be able to drop by around ten in the evening. Is that good for you?"

Yes, yes, yes. Abby punched the air victoriously. Trying to maintain her poise, she replied, "That would be wonderful. I'm looking forward to it. Bye for now."

She disconnected and slowly breathed in and out in an attempt to stop her heart beating madly. *She had him.* Oh, how she'd known he wouldn't be able to resist the thought of more money, though God knows how much he'd conned off those poor saps. A bloody fortune she would wager.

"What are you up to?" Abby jumped as Eduardo came up behind her.

Trying not to look shifty, Abby smiled. "Shouldn't I be asking you that?" she laughed, punching him gently on the arm. "Sly old fox."

He raised his eyebrows. "She told you?"

"Yes ... and I am delighted for you both."

Linking Eduardo, the two of them walked arm in arm back to the square.

Eduardo went over to sit with Christine and Lou, while Abby sauntered over to the Bus Stop to put her second plan of the day into action.

80

Juan couldn't believe his luck.

He was finished for the season and boy, what a season it had been. Having made a fortune this time round, next year he would go to another tourist area and begin again, but for now, he was ready to go home to Seville where his wife and four children waited.

The money he had transferred to his wife's bank account would enable them to buy a house, leaving enough for rent in advance on another luxury villa next year. He'd been surprised to receive Abby's phone call. He thought she had made her feelings perfectly clear last night.

She'd reacted to his kiss, of that he was in no doubt, feeling her shudder, her nipple hardening as his thumb brushed against it. She was a passionate woman, he was aware of these things, and he'd yet to find a woman who could resist his charms. Even better, she was practically offering him her money on a plate.

Feeling himself harden, Juan went in search of the pretty landlady of the small hotel. He had stayed here earlier in the year while waiting for the rental of the villa to be finalised. The widow who ran the place was attractive. Juan discovered she had expensive silver and jewellery, which he intended on getting rid of when he returned home, along with the medal and ring courtesy of Lou. In addition, there was a healthy selection of trinkets from the lovely Diane.

The air was humid, heavy clouds gathering as he made his way outside to the elegant courtyard. It might be worth staying an extra day or two. As the petite vibrant woman walked towards him, he made up his mind to go see Abby the following evening, but first things first. He took the woman's hand and led her back inside.

❧ 81 ❧

The final day of the fiesta wasn't for the faint-hearted.

The band seemed to be expanding by the day as well as becoming louder. Similar to a weird brass alien in a horror B-movie, it spread out from the square in various directions drowning out all conversation, punishing eardrums. On more than one occasion, an ear-splitting burst of trumpet too close for comfort had startled Lou.

The square was not only filled with villagers but also hundreds of tourists, who'd descended to watch the final days parade followed by an elaborate mass in chapel then drinking, eating and dancing until dawn. Abby had other plans for this evening but was keeping them to herself, doing her best to act normal. Nobody bar Lou thought tripping over, nearly falling into the fountain, and sloshing an apple juice down the front of her best blouse was anything out of the ordinary for clumsy clogs.

"Blimey, Abby, what's up with you today?" Lou probed. "You remind me of a female Norman Wisdom."

Abby had just walked into the door of the Bus Stop after dropping by to see Kylie. Eyes watering, clutching her nose, she plopped down on a small wall taking one long gulp of bottled water.

"And why aren't you drinking? Ha! I knew it. Come on, spill ... what you up to?"

The arrival of Eduardo rescued Abby from answering. The colour still hadn't fully returned to his cheeks after his heart attack, but his eyes shone when they rested on Lou. He slung his arm around her and she lay her head on his shoulder.

"How are my two favourite ladies today?"

"Well I'm fine, but Mabel isn't here." Abby quipped.

"Have you had lunch?" He inclined his head towards the Bus Stop.

"Pfft ... if food poisoning's my desire, I could always try Abby's new chutney recipes," Lou retorted, licking her finger and drawing an imaginary number one in the air.

"OK! Quits," Abby laughed, shuffling in-between Lou and Eduardo, threading her arms through theirs, and dragging them across the square.

"I'm going home when mass finishes," she declared, after the trio had shared a large platter of beef and potato empanadas.

"Going home? You mean to see to the animals? I expected that so I'll come give you a hand."

"No, it's fine. I need to talk to Paisley so I won't be back down."

"You're missing the biggest party of the year. Bigger even than when Jenny and Clare's freezer accidentally defrosted." Lou sounded baffled as to why Abby wasn't returning.

Abby's face broke into an enormous smile and she started laughing remembering the party. Two days of drinking, eating everything from vol-eu-vents, prawn rings and Viennetta, to large foil containers of Jenny's batch cooked meals that really could have been anything. They had listened to eighties music, had food fights, and invented the strongest punch in the world. Jenny had fallen asleep with a slice of Hawaiian pizza stuck to the side of her face after chasing Clare around the living room a pair of Elmo knickers on her head, Abby had vomited in the tumble dryer, and Lou had the shits for a week after eating a dodgy Scotch egg. Yes, that had definitely been some weekend.

"She's going through a bad time, she's not got many friends, I feel sorry for her." Even to

Abby's own ears the excuse for not coming back sounded lame, especially as she and Paisley weren't exactly bosom buddies.

Lou pursed her lips saying nothing, but not believing a word.

A bby was a bag of nerves.

She had phoned the police leaving a message for the detective in charge of the case to say that Juan would arrive at Lou's villa around ten that night. She was worried he wouldn't get the message though, or wouldn't arrive on time.

The dogs had sensed her unrest when she'd walked them earlier and crowded round her legs offering comfort. Consequently, she'd gone arse over tit more than once, ending up with a grazed knee and a twisted elbow. Sitting on the large rock by the nearly dried up riverbed, she smoked at least three ciggies while having a lengthy one-way conversation with Chester. *Oh, how* she missed him. He would have been the perfect partner in crime for this situation. Smiling through her tears, she looked up at the heavy clouds that had been culminating over the last couple of days.

"Your son will be arriving soon, my boy. I wonder if he'll be like you." From all the grumbling received from the UK that eventuality seemed likely.

Glancing at her watch, Abby scrambled to her feet and made her way home. She needed to prepare the dinner she'd promised, even though it wasn't likely to be eaten, as well as feeding the goats and tucking her beloved chickens in safely for the evening. Two hours later, butterflied balsamic chicken with roasted veg in the oven, and a golden saffron broth simmering on the hob ready for last minute addition of seared scallops, Abby flew upstairs to turn herself into a sexy siren. Time was short. Maybe she should have returned earlier.

Mmm not bad, but something's missing. Abby twirled in front of the mirror, not convinced on the look she'd created for herself. Thirty minutes later, she was wearing the same dress she'd worn on the date with Paul; it had certainly done the trick that night. Her hair tumbled over her shoulders in a mass of curls, artfully captured here and there with small elaborate combs. The tan was so deep now that the only make-up she needed was eyeliner, mascara, and a slash of bright red lippy. Spraying herself liberally with *Flowerbomb* she fished out the one and only pair of heels she possessed from the bottom of the wardrobe. Slipping her feet into them resembling Bambi on stilts, she teetered down the stairs.

Juan was early. At nine-twenty, she opened the door to the slimy swindler himself.

"Wow! You look amazing, Abby."

Before she had time to think or speak, the greasy Lothario was all over her, quicker than an outbreak of measles.

Bloody hell. She hadn't had time to prepare herself or make a proper plan. Jeez, his hands were everywhere.

"Hey, hold your horses." Feigning laughter, she playfully pushed his hands away while trying to wriggle out of his grasp. A sodding octopus couldn't have done a better job of touching her up.

"We have plenty of time. Food, and business first, si?"

She did a mental calculation of how long the meal and investment chat would take, praying the police would arrive at ten as requested. Taking his jacket, and leading the way to the terrace outside the kitchen, she handed Juan a beer keeping up the false smiles and coy little giggles. She had to give the best performance of her life, far better than any performance she'd given at those endless dinner parties given while married to Mark.

"Where is your car?"

She'd noticed the absence of the black beast of a machine when she'd let him in.

"In for a service," he replied, wishing he'd kept the rental car a few more days. He hated taxis.

Pouring herself a glass of sangria Abby kept the conversation going, at the same time as attempting to avoid both his gaze and ever-wandering hands.

"So ... Lou said this investment is a sure thing, is that right?"

She guessed correctly that discussing money was the one thing that kept his mind off getting her into bed. Poor Lou. What an arse-hole this man was. Abby was so pleased her friend had finally seen sense and hooked up with their neighbour instead. She seemed much happier already. Now, if she could just get that medal and ring back!

"So how much do you have to invest, Abby?"

Juan-ker's smug voice shouted through to the kitchen where Abby was searing scallops, as well as adding a few ground laxatives to his broth.

"Oh, not much. I've inherited a small amount of cash ... only a quarter of a million pounds."

She snickered as she heard him choking into his Estrella. That should keep the slimy bastard's attention. He was rummaging in a small briefcase when she returned, carrying two steaming dishes.

"I have papers here for you to look through." He flourished a large file of official looking documents. Boy, he was good.

She waved them away dismissively, batting her eyelashes. "Later, Juan. I'm hungry. Let's eat first."

Depositing the first course on the table, she eased herself into one of the dining chairs, rubbing her foot up and down his calf while her eyes gazed doe-eyed into his.

"I have always liked you, Abby. Your beauty is like precious jewel."

Smacking his lips in appreciation, Juan slurped on the golden broth the heavy flavour of saffron masking the bitter taste of *Dulcalax*.

"Really?" She giggled shyly, eyeing him closely from behind lowered lashes.

How had Lou ever fallen for this sickly patter? He really did talk a load of shite. Glancing at the clock, she willed the minute hand to go faster as she bit her lip, while stroking his thigh.

"How's the soup?" She smiled, hoping the laxative would work its magic and produce speedy results.

83

"I'm telling you she's up to something," Lou stressed, trying to convince Eduardo and her friends something was amiss.

"Like what?" Cheeks flushed pink, Sylvia was already a bit tipsy. The others snatched up their endangered drinks as she waved her straw sunhat around to accompany her words.

"I've called her three times, she's not answering," Eduardo muttered placing his phone on the table, willing it to ring. *Perhaps Lou was right.*

"Maybe that Paul bloke's in town," Kylie piped up, immediately regretting her lewd arm gestures as Felipe threw her a scathing glance.

"Mmm ... maybe," Lou mumbled, although she wasn't convinced.

The final night's celebrations were in full swing. Most of the villagers were in the square awaiting the firework finale. The evening sky was heavy with dark storm clouds, which Lou suspected would spoil the show that was supposed to start at midnight. A rare cool breeze made her shudder.

Pushing her chair back, she stood up. "Think I'll go up to the house and check."

"Oh, sit down, Lou. She'll just love you turning up, when she's probably arranged a romantic evening with the plumber," Christine chided.

Lou reluctantly sat trying to join in the animated conversation about the fight that had ensued the previous evening between two drunken tourists. Apparently, it had all kicked off in the Bus Stop but the two blokes ended up rolling about the square until Sophia had stepped in, hitting them both round the head with her best frying pan.

"Look, they're over there." Sylvia pointed out two burly men, each with a bandage wrapped around their head.

"Makes a change from me and Abby being the entertainment," Lou murmured. She just couldn't shake the feeling something was wrong, even when Eduardo squeezed her hand.

"Sorry, it's no good. I'm going home." She stood up and grabbed her shawl.

"We'll come with you." Eduardo got to his feet.

Sylvia didn't seem pleased with the idea but knowing Abby and Lou always had a plentiful supply of booze she staggered to her feet along with Christine. Kylie made to get up, but Lou waved her back down

"You stay here with Felipe. I'll text you later."

Winking at the smitten girl, Lou pulled the shawl around her shoulders. Looking up into the sky, she was sure she felt the first spots of rain.

84

Abby heard the first crack of thunder as she brought out the main course, almost dropping the plates as Sylvester bolted past her scarpering from the torrential rain. There had been one or two brief showers since arriving in Spain, but nothing like this. Fascinated, she stood gazing in awe as if she'd never seen a downpour before.

"Perhaps we should go inside." Juan had picked up their drinks.

The terrace was sheltered from the sun by the vines but rain was starting to drip through.

"Erm ... yes." Abby didn't want to go inside, knowing his attention would be firmly back to getting her knickers off. She frowned as he walked towards her.

"I will be right back." He hurried towards the bathroom.

Abby plonked the plates of chicken on the table and rushed over to Juan's briefcase. She lifted the lid. Damn it was just papers, most written in Spanish. No wonder Lou hadn't cottoned *on*. Shuffling through them, she noticed the lining of the case had come away in one corner. Sliding her hand underneath, she felt what appeared to be a plastic bag. Pulling it out of the case, she was ecstatic to see Simon's medal, Lou's engagement ring, and a few more pieces of seemingly expensive jewellery. She was so engrossed in her find she heard Juan's voice before she heard his footsteps.

"What are you doing?" He stood in the kitchen doorway looking a bit green around the gills.

"Oh ... not much," Abby replied, trying to keep her voice even. "I thought I would have a look at those papers while you were in the bathroom." She slid the plastic bag under the table where Salem sat leisurely licking his front paws, piercing eyes fixed on Juan. She was sure her face must have been scarlet.

Slamming the case shut, she stood up and fluttered her eyelashes.

"Are you OK? Come sit down ... finish your meal. I have figs for desert." She knew she was babbling. Backing up against the table, she wished she'd thought this through more. *What if* he were dangerous?

"My stomach is not good. I have had enough food ... my hunger is for something else. Why don't we sit?" He picked up the case, leading the way to the sitting room.

Reclining snakelike across the leather, he indicated he wanted Abby to sit next to him. Reluctantly, she perched on the edge of the cushion, nerves jangling, the lump in her throat growing. Juan's fingers grazed her bare arm and she shivered involuntary. It was almost quarter past ten. What in hell was keeping the bloody plod?

"Ah, Abby, sweet, sweet Abby. I saw the bag you slipped under the table. Now do you want to tell me what you are up to? There is no money, is there?"

The stroking didn't stop, even as his voice hardened. She was afraid to move or speak while his greedy lips brushed her neck, his tongue lapping at her earlobe.

"No money to invest, I believe you have done something to my food, and now all that is left is the last thing I came here for. *You!*"

He shoved her back against the cushions pushing her dress up to reveal her naked thighs. He gripped the left, squeezing it hard.

"You, bitch! Did you really think you would get away with this?" He was fiddling with his zip, his other hand covering her mouth.

Galvanised into action, Abby sank her teeth into Juan's palm trying to bring her knee up to defend herself. She gasped in pain, tears spilling down her cheeks, as he viciously slapped her face. This wasn't how the night was supposed to go. Where in God's name were the sodding police?

"The police are on their way!" she screamed, in an effort to get him off her.

"Of course they are," he sneered, looking at the teeth marks on his arm, but he looked uncertain. His stomach was making awful gurgling noises and feeling a bit crampy.

"Do not move."

He stood up and went into the kitchen presumably to retrieve the bag of loot. Abby struggled to her feet to straighten her dress, spotting Sylvester watching her from the high shelf above the living room door.

"Fat lot of help you were," she muttered, tasting blood in her mouth.

A loud yowling came from the kitchen accompanied by a barrage of Spanish curses and shouting. Juan appeared in the doorway to the sitting room his face and arms a mass of angry scratches.

"Get in there and move that fucking animal now before I kill it!" The stony, livid face resembled thunder, his words, clipped as if he were finding it hard to control his temper.

"Unless you have an AK-47 or an atom bomb that's not gonna happen." *Good old Salem.*

Without warning, the front door flew open and three drowned rats in the shape of Lou, Eduardo, and Christine tumbled in. Astounded, they stood rooted in the doorway taking in the situation.

"Abby?" After what seemed an endless time, Lou was the first to speak. "What's he doing here? You're bleeding ... are you OK?"

Eduardo made to move forward but Lou held him back.

"No, no. Your heart," she whispered. "He's not worth it."

"I've had enough of this," Juan spat, turning as if to go.

Perched furtively on the shelf above the doorway, twinkle paws Sylvester pushed his way behind the heavy urn holding Chester's ashes. Abby stood hypnotised as in slow motion she watched the vase wobble, right itself, wobble again then fall with a powerful smack on Juan's greasy head. His dark eyes flickered, as he gave a dull, surprised grunt before thumping unconscious to the floor.

You little beauty.

"We all having a drink then?" Oblivious to the goings-on, Sylvia staggered through the front door, short hair stuck to her head as if she'd taken herself off for an impromptu swim. "D'you know the law's outside. *Oh, hello.* Who's this?"

She gazed in confusion through sangria goggles at the immobile form heaped on the floor, and the clapping hands of her friends hailing Mr Mischief. Sylvester now sat on the shelf expertly grooming his long hair, completely unaware that he'd timed his latest antics to perfection.

Juan was just coming round as the police arrived. Snapping on handcuffs, two officers escorted him outside, roughly shoving the thieving toerag into the back of their car. The last night of the festival had caused them to be late ... many streets blocked in the village, they explained.

Abby gave a statement. She was shaking so much Lou found a warm hoodie – that proclaimed she'd been to the University of Paris – and poured her a large brandy. A half-cut Sylvia made short work of the rest of the bottle, as strains of *Like a Virgin* drifted through from the kitchen. Salem had happily given up the bag of jewellery to Abby and, along with his partner in crime, Sylvester who'd finished sprucing himself up, was now tucking into a hastily opened tin of tuna. Tweetie Pie had probably done one when Juan's bawling shook the air. No doubt she'd surface soon.

After the police left, Christine hastily brushed up Chester's remains returning them, along with a few stray cat hairs, into the urn. She placed it back on the shelf and turned round to hear Lou admonishing her best friend.

"You shouldn't have done it, Abby. He could have hurt you, but thank you so much." Hugging her tightly, Lou started to cry.

"I'm just glad you got your things back." Abby smiled weakly. "I was so scared though, when I thought the police weren't coming. I had to play for time."

The rain had stopped so the friends took their drinks outside. For once, the air was fresh and the moonlight glistened on wet leaves and stones, the sound of cicadas singing, soothing.

Only the distant sound of fireworks broke the night's serenity, along with the sound of Sylvia's drunken snores.

85

L ou woke up with a start, forgetting where she was. With wide eyes, she gazed lovingly around Eduardo's bedroom.

Wooden shutters kept all but thin slivers of golden light at bay, while the soft whirring of the overhead fan kept the room cool. Beams overhead, matching the massive mahogany bed and heavy antique furniture, gave the room a cosy feel. The dark wood could have made the room look gloomy, but soft cream plaster walls adorned with colourful artwork offset the furniture. Classic works sat happily side by side with modernistic paintings. The room was luxurious, the beautiful embroidered satin bedspread just one indication, but it was also extremely homely, much better than the sterile operating theatre of Juan-kers.

She smiled wryly. Even she had picked up Abby's nickname for the slimy git.

The police had called the previous day apparently to inform them they'd remanded slimeball in custody, and were conducting a thorough investigation. The money he'd stolen hadn't been found in his bank account so they were now trying to locate it but didn't seem optimistic about the cash being found anytime soon. Lou didn't care. She had what was dear to her back in her bedside drawer, thanks to Abby.

With a contented sigh, she turned over. Eduardo lay on his back gently snoring. She trailed her fingers through the greying curls on his chest, careful not to touch the scar that ran from just below the base of his neck to his stomach. Much to her relief, he was recovering well. That awful day she thought he'd died had made her realise just how much he meant to her. He was everything she had ever wanted in a man; intelligent, kind, loving. As a couple they'd discovered a deep connection and she couldn't have been happier.

The sex wasn't as acrobatic as with Juan, but she'd probably have put her hip out if that had carried on and Eduardo wasn't short of a trick or two. His fervent kisses, gentle caresses, and reverent lovemaking gave her a warm, wonderful feeling of fulfillment. Snuggling into his side as he put his arm round her and pulled her to him, she frowned as a loud ping announced the arrival of a text message.

"Mmm. Ignore it." Eduardo's kisses on the back of her neck were making Lou shiver in all the right places as she read the words.

I need to see you it's really important.... Bus Stop 1pm. Don't be late!

"It's Abby. She needs to see me ... urgently apparently. I'm not going to the bloody Bus Stop though, she can screw that."

"Do you know who I would like to screw?" Eduardo murmured suggestively, burying his face in her golden hair while slowly sliding his hand down to her waist.

"The doctor told you to rest," Lou playfully scolded, pretending to stop his advances as she giggled.

"This is the best medicine I could wish for." Eduardo silenced her half-hearted protests with a kiss.

Not wanting to leave the gigantic bed, nor the man beside her, Lou ardently returned Eduardo's passionate kiss. Mmm. What the hell. Just another ten minutes.

🌿 86 🌿

There had been no changing Abby's mind when Lou had eventually called her back. So insistent, Abby said it was imperative they meet at the dingy bar.

Lou was starting to panic as Ken had waffled on incessantly about making a claim for compensation due to injuries caused by 'that fucking maniac donkey'. Had Lou thought logically about his ramblings, she would have concluded there was no such claim to make and, as usual, the obnoxious clown was talking out of his arse. Mind you, considering the last few days' capers and woes, rational thinking hadn't been hot priority.

On arrival at the bar, she was pleasantly surprised to find neither Ken, nor his downtrodden Mrs in attendance. The windows were all open wide, the odour of chip fat usually impregnating the place, all but gone. A young family were the only customers apart from Abby, who sat by the window smile on her face, gin in hand.

"Where's Ken and Barbie then?" Lou probed, sliding into the chair opposite Abby.

"Shh." Abby inclined her head as Kylie sauntered over with a glass of something Lou didn't recognise

"What's this?" She wrinkled her nose before taking a tiny sip.

"Orange and lavender infused gin," Abby informed. "What d'you think?"

Whilst Lou was essentially a vodka guzzler, she found the concoction pleasing. "Not bad," she concurred, "but I'm sure you didn't drag me here to discuss the merits of orange and lavender infused gin. What's so important we had to meet in this dive?"

"All in good time."

Abby sat back smiling, as Felipe approached the table carrying two large bowls. He placed one containing steaming onion soup in front of Abby then deposited the other in front of Lou.

"Why is Felipe here?" Lou questioned, staring at the bowl of Caesar salad. "What's going on Abby? Spill." She looked baffled, experiencing a severe case of déjà vu.

"As I've said, Lou, all in good time. Did I tell you about the boys?"

Lou began to pick at the salad. She didn't know salad was on the menu here ... well, not a 'proper' salad anyway. She knew limp lettuce, hacked tomatoes, and chunky onion wedges were par for the course in this dump, but the fare in front of her wasn't the usual tripe. There wasn't even a side order of chips.

"As I was saying, the boys ... well ... they've both moved out."

This revelation caught Lou's attention. "*Moved out? Both of them?* What d'you mean?

"Why?" Boy, this salad was good. The lemon juice tasted so fresh, the olive oil was obviously quality, and the crunchy croutons had just the right amount of seasoning.

"Questions questions," Abby grinned. "Because I've sold the house, Lou."

"Oh." Lou tucked into the romaine lettuce oblivious to Abby's excitement.

"Not only have I sold the house, but my books have been in the bestseller chart."

"Oh, Abby I'm sorry, I've been so wrapped up in my own world I haven't even asked how they were doing."

Wracked with guilt, Lou paused and stopped stuffing her face. She hoped Abby wasn't going to say she was going back home, but if she were, why would she sell the house?

The son of the young family ran outside, the energy of the young too much for the bar as Abby looked squarely at Lou.

"I've bought this place!"

Silence hung in the air before Lou began choking on a salty anchovy.

Kylie came running over with a glass of water. Abby jumped up smacking Lou on the back as tears streamed down her face.

After calm had resumed with Lou sitting speechless, Abby continued. "I'd really like it if you came onboard with me as joint owner."

Lou hesitated ... she didn't want sympathy. Yes, that rat had pissed off with her money but she could get by doing some proofing and editing work and said as much.

"It has nothing to do with that, we're a team," Abby proclaimed tears pooling in her eyes.

The young boy suddenly came charging back into the restaurant, squawking at the top of his voice. "Mum, Dad, there's a donkey loose in the square! Come and see!"

Both women watched the couple leave their seats and follow their son, his excited voice squealing with delight as Santos's face loomed through the open window of the bar.

Hearing her phone ping, Lou fished in her pocket and tapped on the screen. A message from Eduardo.

She looked upwards into the expanse of a stunning blue sky beautifully peppered with delicate wisps of angel's breath cloud then lowered her gaze to watch locals and tourists alike basking in the glory of a ripe, golden sun. The same sun that bathed her in a rich, sexy warmth she'd come to love.

Her head was all over the place. She could feel Abby's eyes boring into her, waiting for an answer.

Think, Lou. Think.

But it wasn't Eduardo and his romantic words of adoration, nor a yearning to forget greasy slimeball Juan and the stupid mistakes she'd made, nor even Abby's uncorked excitement that made up her mind. Granted, that little menu was more than enough to make her want to start anew. What sealed it was Santos. As he gazed longingly through the window, lengthy eyelashes fluttering, long, pointed ears twitching, the inquisitive face looking as happy as she felt, Lou felt a tingle ripple through her body. As if willing her to make a decision, Santos let out a short, jubilant hee-haw prompting the best friends to look at one another and burst out laughing.

Reaching for the flavoured gin, Lou raised her glass. The words she whispered to Abby were short and simple.

"Count me in."

To be continued...

Read on for jam recipes.

ABBY'S JAM AND CHUTNEY MAKING TIPS

Making your own jam and chutney is a satisfying, therapeutic way to spend your time. The methods are easy to follow, the combinations infinite, and the finished results make great gifts for any occasion.

Equipment needed

A heavy based jam pan is a good investment. If you simply wish to make a few batches, you can use an ordinary saucepan. Make sure there's enough room in the pan for the jam to increase in volume on the rolling boil.

A jam thermometer is essential for the beginner so you know the jam has reached the right temperature for setting – around 220°F. Once you've become more experienced, you'll be able to judge yourself when it's set.

A funnel makes life a lot easier when transferring the jam from pan to jar.

A long-handled wooden spoon is also essential to keep your hands as far away as possible from potential splashes. When jam is boiling, it becomes extremely hot.

A water bath is handy to sterilise your jars, but this is not essential. I simply wash, dry, and place in the oven on a medium heat for 15 minutes.

Jars, seals, and labels. Always store jam in sterilised glass jars. Cover with either a silicone disc, cellophane, and rubber band, screw top, or use Kilner jars. Leave labelling until glass has cooled to avoid burns. There are programs on your PC to print lovely labels or you can buy them; they are relatively inexpensive.

Getting started

Fruit - The secret of good jam is fresh fruit. Try to make your jam using freshly picked fruit. If this is not possible, freeze the fruit to keep its freshness. Some fruits are high in pectin, which is the setting agent occurring naturally in many fruits, whereas some fruits are low in pectin.

High pectin fruits include lemons, oranges, apples, blackcurrants, plums, redcurrants, and apricots.

Low pectin fruits include strawberries, figs, pears, blueberries, cherries, and blackberries.

A good idea is to combine fruits to achieve the desired consistency, ie apple and blackberry. I prefer to macerate most fruit for a few hours before starting as coating it with sugar allows syrup to develop. This process stops the dry sugar burning when you add it to the pan. The method doesn't work with blackcurrants or gooseberries however, as the sugar hardens the fruit.

Sugar - I always use granulated sugar for jam making and usually brown sugar for chutney or savoury jams.

Pectin - Living in Spain, I have no need for pectin, as lemons, which do the job just as well if not better, are grown in abundance. Pectin is readily available in supermarkets, as well as many smaller shops. Powdered or liquid pectin is suitable, especially for blackberry or strawberry jams, which can be difficult to set. You could also add a tart apple pulp such as Granny Smith, which will help to set the fruit.

Cooking the jam

Once you have your ingredients, you can start making your own batch of heaven although it does take practice. Jam making involves three stages.

Stage 1 – the dissolving stage. Heat up the fruit and sugar. Dry sugar will burn so stir until the juices flow.

Stage 2 – the rolling boil. When the sugar has dissolved, the fruit will begin to bubble and foam. Try not to stir too much at this point; it can bubble up high so please take care not to let it overflow. From previous experience, if this happens the result can cause one hell of a mess.

Stage 3 – once the bubbling has slowed, skim off any foam that has formed on the surface. Add lemon juice, simmer, and stir constantly to prevent sticking. A temperature of 220°F should ensure the jam sets.

NB Savoury jams need to simmer for longer to thicken.

Remember this process can be trial and error. Everyone has their own preferences and tastes so experiment with small batches and remember, if you do make mistakes, sweet or savoury runny jams make delicious sauces and flavourings, while jams that are too thick can be melted down to glaze meats.

Peach and amaretto jam
    1.5kg peaches
    600g sugar
    3 tbsp lemon juice
    2 tbsp amaretto
Method
Before you start, chase any cats from kitchen.

Peel peaches the same way as you would tomatoes. Steep in boiling water for a few minutes; the skin should then be easy to remove with fingers. Slice and stone the fruit. Add to a pan along with the sugar and lemon juice on a medium high heat, using a potato masher to break up the peaches. Bring to the boil then simmer for up to 60 minutes stirring frequently and skimming any scum off the top. Add amaretto 15 minutes before the end of cooking. Meanwhile, in those last 15 minutes, sterilise your jars in oven.

When ready, pour jam into jars leaving around 6cm space from the top. This recipe will make approximately six x 250g jars. Seal immediately. Leave to cool, and enjoy.

Tomato and jalapeño jam
    2.5kg tomatoes
    750g sugar
    2 apples peeled and sliced
    1 onion sliced thinly
    2 cloves of crushed garlic

1 tsp salt

5 jalapeño peppers with seeds

5cm size piece of crushed ginger

1 lime (juice and zest)

1 tsp cinnamon

1 tsp paprika

1 tbsp soy sauce

200ml red wine or cider vinegar

Method

Combine all ingredients in a heavy based pan and bring to boil on a medium high heat. Once sugar has dissolved, simmer (for around 1-2 hours, stirring frequently) until jam reaches required consistency. Remember, the mixture will thicken slightly once cooled. Taste again once cooked, adding extra salt or lime juice if required. Pour into sterilised jars. This recipe makes around six jars and is delicious with cold meats or my delicious goat's cheese tart.

Tuna or cactus jam

(Don't worry, tunas are what prickly pear fruits are also known as)

10-12 prickly pear fruit (take great caution when picking)

600g granulated sugar

1 cup of water

Juice of 1 lemon

Method

Peel prickly pears extremely carefully using tongs or a fork to hold, as you make vertical cuts in the skin peeling away with a knife in sections. Cut fruit into small pieces and place in a pan with the water. Simmer on a low heat until the fruit softens. Remove from heat and pass through a sieve to get rid of the seeds (they can break teeth). Place cactus pulp into pan, add sugar, bring back to boil until sugar dissolves, add lemon juice, and simmer for around 40 minutes until thickened. Leave to cool slightly then pour into sterilised jars. This will make around four small jars.

Bacon jam

450g smoked bacon, cut into 2cm pieces

1 medium red onion, diced

3 garlic cloves, roughly chopped

1 tbsp olive oil

45g dark brown sugar

1 tsp dried red chili flakes or 1 fresh chili finely chopped
125ml strong black coffee
65ml cider vinegar
85g maple syrup

Method

Fry the bacon until it begins to crisp (don't burn) then leave to drain on kitchen paper. Meanwhile fry onion and garlic until soft, add rest of ingredients and 100ml of water. Simmer for one hour stirring occasionally. (I do this as I come inside to top up my glass of sangria.) Add more water if necessary. After leaving to cool for around 20 minutes, pulse in a food processor until the jam reaches the consistency you require. Pour into sterilised jars, refrigerate for up to one week.

Caramelised onion chutney

6 red onions
2 Spanish onions
1 tbsp good quality olive oil
200g brown sugar
150ml balsamic vinegar
150ml red wine vinegar
2 tsp fresh thyme leaves
2 bay leaves
1 red chili finely chopped
Pinch of dried chili flakes
1 tsp mustard seeds

Method

Finely slice onions and chili, cook in oil over a gentle heat for around 30 minutes until soft, but not brown. Stir in a couple of tablespoons of the sugar, increase the heat, and cook for a further 5 minutes until brown, stirring frequently. Add rest of the sugar and all other ingredients then simmer for about an hour until thickened and dark in colour. Spoon into sterilised jars. Seal and label when cool. This makes around six x 300g jars

Pear and ginger jam

1.5 kg pears
225g preserved ginger
1kg sugar
1 tsp cinnamon
2 lemons (juice and zest)

Method
Peel and chop pears. Place all ingredients into pan, bring to the boil to dissolve sugar then simmer until thickened, stirring frequently, Meanwhile, sterilise jars in oven. Pour warm jam into jars sealing immediately. Makes seven x 340g jars.

Chili jam
150g fresh red chilies
150g red peppers
1kg sugar
600ml cider vinegar
Method
Deseed the chilies and peppers and place in food processor to chop finely. Dissolve sugar in the vinegar over a low heat, stirring occasionally. Once dissolved, add peppers and chilies. Bring to the boil then continue cooking for around 10 minutes. Setting point should be around 220°F. Remove from heat and leave to cool. The mixture should thicken and be ready to pour into sterilised jars within an hour.

ABOUT THE AUTHOR

I live in the North East of England with my partner and two beautiful boxer dogs; Floyd and Freya.

From a very young age my head has always been full of stories and I've been wanting to write a book since way back when, well forever really but finances (running my own business,) procrastinating, and self-doubt have conspired to hold me back.

Dithering about what to write was another stumbling block, my reading taste is so eclectic; Vampires, Serial killers, Dystopia, Vikings, Witches, History, Travel, Autobiographies, the only genres I don't really read are Spy Fiction, Westerns or Chick Lit Comedy.

Oh, I know I'll write a Chick Lit Comedy!

Anyway, I digress. After my Eureka moment I decided to scrap all my almost finished, half-finished, ten chapters, first page attempts, concentrating on actually finishing my first novel.

Flip-Flops, Fiestas, and Flamenco is the first in a series of three novels, I am currently writing the second. I'm on a roll!

When I'm not writing I enjoy reading, travel and cooking I'm passionate about animals and consider myself a bit of a Gin connoisseur

ACKNOWLEDGMENTS

I would like to thank everyone associated with Junction Publishing especially Marco and Netta for all their support, hard work and belief in this story. My good friend Wendy who did the first edit (Lou is absolutely not based on this lady) My mum Astrid and sister Dyane who never stopped nagging me and wouldn't let me give up on my dreams, my kids who would never let me live it down if they didn't get a mention and my partner Douglas who has supported me throughout this journey, is the love of my life and strangely still hasn't taken the hint;

"I want to live in Spain!"

10749565R00150

Printed in Germany
by Amazon Distribution
GmbH, Leipzig